D0193097

SISKIYOU COU

3 2871 00363419 9

DATE DUE

Donated to Yreka Library
by________________________________

DARK REVELATIONS

also by anthony e. zuiker

LEVEL 26: Dark Origins

LEVEL 26: Dark Prophecy

DARK REVELATIONS

a level 26 thriller featuring steve dark

anthony e. zuiker

with Duane Swierczynski

DUTTON

SISKIYOU COUNTY PUBLIC LIBRARY
719 FOURTH STREET
YREKA, CALIFORNIA 96097

DUTTON
Published by Penguin Group (USA) Inc.
375 Hudson Street, New York, New York 10014, U.S.A.
Penguin Group (Canada), 90 Eglinton Avenue East, Suite 700, Toronto, Ontario M4P 2Y3, Canada (a division of Pearson Penguin Canada Inc.); Penguin Books Ltd, 80 Strand, London WC2R 0RL, England; Penguin Ireland, 25 St Stephen's Green, Dublin 2, Ireland (a division of Penguin Books Ltd); Penguin Group (Australia), 250 Camberwell Road, Camberwell, Victoria 3124, Australia (a division of Pearson Australia Group Pty Ltd); Penguin Books India Pvt Ltd, 11 Community Centre, Panchsheel Park, New Delhi – 110 017, India; Penguin Group (NZ), 67 Apollo Drive, Rosedale, Auckland 0632, New Zealand (a division of Pearson New Zealand Ltd); Penguin Books (South Africa) (Pty) Ltd, 24 Sturdee Avenue, Rosebank, Johannesburg 2196, South Africa

Penguin Books Ltd, Registered Offices: 80 Strand, London WC2R 0RL, England

Published by Dutton, a member of Penguin Group (USA) Inc.

Copyright © 2012 by Anthony E. Zuiker
All rights reserved

REGISTERED TRADEMARK—MARCA REGISTRADA

ISBN 978-0-525-95197-1

Printed in the United States of America

PUBLISHER'S NOTE
This book is a work of fiction. Names, characters, places, and incidents either are the product of the author's imagination or are used fictitiously, and any resemblance to actual persons, living or dead, business establishments, events, or locales is entirely coincidental.

Without limiting the rights under copyright reserved above, no part of this publication may be reproduced, stored in or introduced into a retrieval system, or transmitted, in any form, or by any means (electronic, mechanical, photocopying, recording, or otherwise), without the prior written permission of both the copyright owner and the above publisher of this book.

The scanning, uploading, and distribution of this book via the Internet or via any other means without the permission of the publisher is illegal and punishable by law. Please purchase only authorized electronic editions, and do not participate in or encourage electronic piracy of copyrighted materials. Your support of the author's rights is appreciated.

To Uncle Denis Scinta, my biggest fan

DARK REVELATIONS

It is well-known among law enforcement personnel that murderers can be categorized as belonging to one of twenty-five levels of evil, from the naïve opportunists starting out at Level 1 to the organized, premeditated torture-murderers who inhabit Level 25.

What almost no one knows is that a new category of killer has emerged. And only one man is capable of stopping them.

His targets:
Level 26 killers.

His methods:
Whatever it takes.

His name:
Steve Dark.

WILL

YOU

STEP

INSIDE

THE

LABYRINTH . . . ?

chapter 1

LABYRINTH

The homeless man sways back and forth, back and forth, on the street corner just across from the big gleaming white phallus of Los Angeles City Hall.

He's either preparing to cross the street or keel over and die.

But he won't die.

Not yet, anyway.

After a few moments he wipes his brow, hoists the box under his arm, then ambles across the street.

Good puppet.

Watch him walk through the neatly designed plaza, enter the front doors of the gleaming new Police Administration Building, and make his way right up to the smooth polished wood partition of the security checkpoint.

The homeless man stands there and waits for a guard to see him, just as instructed.

Guard asks,

Help you?

The security detail is used to men (sometimes women) showing up in this condition, looking for handouts or a smoke or a bathroom, but this homeless man merely smiles, revealing rotted, pulpy gums and meth-ravaged teeth, holding up the box like a moron, wordlessly gesturing for the guard to take it.

Just like I told him to.

The expression on the guard's face practically screams:

BOMB

Everybody scrambles.

The new administration building has state-of-the-art antiterrorism gear—you don't go dropping $437 million on a new police facility without dedicating a fat chunk of that money to security, not in this post-9/11 world where government buildings, and public servants, are prime targets.

Through the plate-glass windows I watch as the homeless man and his box are forcefully and quickly separated.

I sit on the bench and sip a cup of slightly bitter shade-grown coffee.

At long last, it begins.

I can do many things.

Things you couldn't even begin to imagine.

Powers, skills, and abilities beyond the human ken.

However, I cannot see through walls.

Still, I know exactly what is happening inside police HQ right this very second.

By now, the suspected B-O-M-B would have been brought to an outside facility for examination using the latest equipment. X-rays. Chemical tests. Each test costing the residents of Los Angeles a stunning amount of money.

The old protocol used to be simple: Blow it up first, sift the remains later.

But not now, in these heightened times.

If only they would open the box, all would be explained. But I knew they wouldn't open the box, because they feared a bomb might be inside.

And truth be told, they are right. I did send a bomb.

Only it's not in the box.

Now the homeless man would be brought to an interrogation room with two deputy chiefs of the Counter-Terrorism and Special Operations Bureau.

I checked the rosters and knew exactly who would be in that room with the foul-smelling homeless man.

Men with checkered pasts.

And the homeless man wouldn't say a word. He'd be semi-coherent, at best.

Wouldn't ask for a lawyer, nor respond to direct questioning.

Wouldn't dare.

Just like I trained him.

[To enter the Labyrinth, please go to Level26.com and enter the code: boom]

chapter 2

DARK

Downtown Los Angeles, California

When Steve Dark arrived at the chaotic scene at LAPD HQ a burly row of uniforms yelled and tried to push him back—no access, no nothing, *don't care who you're with, don't care what you say.* Dark calmly removed the cell phone from his jeans pocket, pressed a button, then showed the screen to the nearest cop.

"Oh, okay," one of them mumbled, then parted to let him through. "Guys, he's okay. Let him in."

Dark still had his get-into-any-crime-scene-free pass, courtesy of Lisa Graysmith. The digital image on his phone allowed him passage into pretty much any law enforcement perimeter in the world. It was a universal COOPERATE WITH ME OR ELSE badge, with clearances at the highest level. Dark had received it in an instant, but he knew it could just as easily be taken away.

He was led to the interrogation room, which had been rocked by the explosion. The blast, Dark could see, was brutal yet short-range: meant to kill those in close proximity, but not cause structural damage to the building. The rooms were too small, too well insulated. The blast would have nowhere to go but through them all. Dark thought about the flesh ripped from bone, the pulpy fragments of what used to be a human life splattered over the walls of the interrogation room.

"What happened?"

An LAPD crime scene investigator glanced at Dark's badge, then explained that the two detectives were in the same room with the suspect—a homeless man who'd carried in a suspicious package.

"Turns out the package wasn't the worry," the CSI said. "The guy was a living bomb. We're trying to pull enough together to figure out what type."

"Where's the other package?" Dark asked.

"Over in the forensics lab. Ask for Josh—"

"Banner? Yeah, I know him. Thanks."

Dark had heard about the blast while making breakfast for his daughter. He immediately put on his headphones and tuned in to the police band for the details: A homeless man had shown up at LAPD headquarters with a package thought to be a bomb. But instead of the package exploding, the *man* did—killing two seasoned deputy chiefs and injuring six. Within minutes Dark was handing off his daughter to his mother-in-law and climbing into his Mustang, hell-bent for downtown.

This was no ordinary terrorist incident.

Ordinary terrorists don't leave mysterious packages behind.

Steve Dark used to be a cop.

The best of the best, working for the most elite manhunting unit in the FBI—Special Circumstances Division. He'd worked for Agent Tom Riggins, the man who'd carved Special Circs out of the Justice Department's ViCAP—Violent Criminal Apprehension Program—during the mid-1980s. For years, Riggins and Dark and their colleagues hunted the worst monsters to ever scuttle across the face of the earth. And Dark was usually leading the hunt.

Until one of the monsters struck back in the worst way imaginable.

Dark had been raised by a loving foster family here in California. His new parents, Victor and Laura, thought they would never be able to conceive. They adopted Steve. Then soon after, Laura got pregnant. Twin boys. Still, they treated Steve no differently than his younger siblings.

Years later, a forensic-proof killer who came to be known as Sqweegel butchered Dark's foster family in the most brutal way Riggins had ever seen. Dark left Special Circs and crawled into seclusion. He only came out when Riggins forced him to—and together, in a grueling cross-country chase, they caught the maniac responsible.

But at a terrible cost. During their final confrontation, Dark had lost his true love, his bedrock of sanity—his wife, Sibby.

Now Dark was hunting the monsters on his own and trying to raise his five-year-old daughter, Sibby—named for her mother. Dark hunted killers without a badge, without Riggins, without the support of the FBI, without any official sanction whatsoever.

In its place, Dark had the clandestine support of a silent patron with ultradeep pockets and forensic gear that would be the envy of any law enforcement division in the world.

This support allowed Dark to walk into any crime scene and do what he was born to do:

Catch the monster.

One elevator ride and three turns later down a clean, bright antiseptic hallway, Dark found Josh Banner's lab.

"What do you have, Banner?"

"Well, we ran every explosives test and we . . ."

Banner froze midsentence then spun around on his stool, a confused look on his face.

"Huh? Steve? What the heck are you doing here? You're not back with Special Circs are you? Because if you are . . . Wait, don't answer that. I don't want to know, do I?"

Dark and Banner shared a peculiar history. Five years ago, Banner had helped Dark track down Sqweegel. Banner joined Special Circs soon after, and worked with Dark for four years until circumstances put them on opposite sides of a case. Even though Dark had officially cleared his name, he could tell that Banner was still wary. And since that case, Banner had panicked and jumped back to his old job in the forensics unit of the LAPD.

"No, I'm not with Special Circs," Dark said. "So what was in the package?"

"Can I . . . uh . . . I mean, am I *allowed* to speak to you?" Banner asked, glancing around nervously at the other techs in the room.

Dark showed him the badge on his phone. "Yeah, you can."

"All righty then," Banner said, clearly relieved there were no ethical dilemmas to navigate. Dark showed him the badge; Banner would show him the evidence. "Well, there were no explosives in the box. The terrorism guys did every possible test on it, and then I did a few more. Not even a microbe of anything that could go boom. So we cut it open and found something really weird."

Banner led Dark over to the main desk positioned in the middle of the room. On the surface were three objects:

A handwritten note.

An alarm clock.

And a drawing on a piece of paper ripped from an artist's sketch pad.

"Ta-da," Banner said. "And yeah, none of it makes any sense."

"Let's start with the note," Dark said.

"Well, the message was written in allegedly analysis-proof plain block letters," Banner explained. "We've got a handwriting expert working on it. Strangely enough, the note was on LAPD stationery—straight from the chief of police's office. And it was not a threat letter. Not an obvious threat letter, anyway."

Dark leaned over for a closer look. Written on the note was a riddle:

> A WOMAN SHOOTS HER HUSBAND. THEN SHE HOLDS HIM UNDER WATER FOR OVER 5 MINUTES. FINALLY, SHE HANGS HIM. BUT 5 MINUTES LATER THEY BOTH GO OUT AND ENJOY A WONDERFUL DINNER TOGETHER. HOW CAN THIS BE?
>
> LABYRINTH

Dark pondered it for a moment but decided to move on. If this unknown subject—"Labyrinth"—wanted the focus to be the riddle, then he would have sent it alone. Chances were, the riddle would only make sense in context, when examined with the other two objects.

And you don't kill two cops in cold blood without having something important to say.

"What's the deal with the alarm clock?" Dark asked. "Anything unusual?"

"Yeah, that gave the bomb squad guys a nice little jolt when they X-rayed it, let me tell you," Banner said. "But there were no traces of explosives, no hidden wires, no nothing. The clock is harmless, unable to trigger anything except a really annoying ringing sound."

Dark looked it over. The thing looked like it had been plucked from someone's bedside table back in the 1950s. "Maybe it's merely parts for a test run."

Test runs that had been so popular over the past year. Send bomb parts through—timers, wires, circuit boards—then sit back and watch how a particular security detail reacts. Or doesn't react. Homegrown anarchists and international terrorists have tried it plenty of times before. The entire state of California was still reeling after the bombing of the Niantic Tower up in San Francisco a few months back. Security precautions, already tight, were now sphincter tight. The thinking was, you don't waste real explosives until you've exploited the right gaps in security.

"Could be," Banner said, "but then how do you explain this?"

Banner pointed to the sketch.

Which was a pencil rendering of a beautiful—and completely naked—woman. Dark could tell this wasn't just a practice sketch of some anonymous nude model who worked for an art studio. You could tell because of the care and detail given to the woman's face. The high cheekbones, the slow sultry smile, the life in her eyes. Which, in turn, made the woman easier to identify.

"Bethany Millar," Dark said.

"Who?" Banner asked.

chapter 3

LABYRINTH

I drive west on Wilshire toward Santa Monica, stopping to complete a few quick errands along the way, ticking off the items on the long checklist in my mind, making a few untraceable phone calls, buying supplies via anonymous Internet cutouts.

The car I drive is from a long-term lot near LAX and won't be reported missing for another three weeks. The license plate is a forgery with bogus tags, incredibly easy to obtain. Makes me wonder why anyone in the United States would go through the hassle of actually buying and registering a motor vehicle.

Not that I need to take these extra precautions, really—there is no physical evidence whatsoever to link me with the gentleman who had entered LAPD headquarters. We just spent a little time together inside his mind.

I stop for more coffee—check the time.

Were the LAPD starting to put it together now?

Had they opened the package by now?

Of course they've opened the package. They didn't have a choice. Which is why I was forced to destroy those detectives.

I am not sadistic.

I needed the LAPD to open my package, and I knew there was no way they'd risk destroying the only shred of evidence in the now high-profile murders of two highly decorated, highly respected police officers.

Me? I would have rather just dropped off the package and let it be done at that.

Today, though, you really have to go to extremes to get someone's attention.

As I think about what might be happening across town, a woman approaches.

She's pretty in that bland California way.

Probably thinks she's someone's idea of PERFECTION, even though inside she's just another filthy whore, two life-altering experiences away from becoming a moist hole for rent.

She says,

Hi, sorry to bother you. . . .

And then proceeds to ask me directions to some high-end clothing boutique, perhaps I've heard of it.

People are always asking me for directions or help.

I've got that kind of face—someone close to me once told me that.

Approachable.

Ordinary.

Friendly.

And that was the point, originally.

But if they could see through MY own eyes . . .

See the world as it really existed, not the one that had been sold to you by the governments of the world—

They'd run SCREAMING.

Like this woman should be.

I tell her,

No, I'm really sorry. I'm not from around here. I could look it up for you on my phone, if you like?

She smiles, suddenly bashful, and says,

Oh, no worries, that's okay. Where are you from?

I nod and smile. She's not really interested in directions. She wanted an opportunity to meet me.

I COULD introduce myself.

I COULD let her in.

She doesn't realize how easily I could coax her into my labyrinth—she's practically begging for it. Just one step and she'd be stumbling down the first corridor, faster than she realized, making her first sharp turn, confused, the first tremors of terror running through her veins, then thinking that the only way out is to turn around and go back the way she came, but that way would be blocked, and she'd have no choice but to wander deeper and deeper into the maze . . .

. . . to me.

All of this would take a matter of hours—the afternoon really. And her life would never be the same.

(If I allowed her to keep her life.)

But I have things to do, much BIGGER subjects to coax into my maze.

So I tell her,

I'm from Chicago, out scouting property for my wife and kids, they're really excited about moving out to sunny California, you know? All this fresh air and sunshine and friendly people?

And I see the light dim in her eyes when I say the words *wife* and *kids* and she's polite but she's also clearly disappointed.

She doesn't know how lucky she is.

She doesn't know what she's narrowly avoided.

As I cruise down Moomat Ahiko Way toward the PCH, I wonder how far they've gotten with my little message.

Are they still staring at the photo of the nude whore, wondering what I may have done to her?

chapter 4

DARK

LAPD Headquarters / Downtown Los Angeles

Dark stared at the drawing.

It was Bethany Millar—in the flesh, during the prime of her life.

Dark recognized her right away. The blond hair, the upturned nose, the classic alabaster skin and full lips. He'd spent many years sitting up late at night, trying to drink himself into a half-coma, watching old movies on cable TV. Bethany Millar was a late 1960s/early 1970s screen siren who starred in a string of B-movies and exploitation flicks, almost all of them released before Dark was born. To the best of his knowledge, she'd done plenty of cheesecake-type stuff, but never nudes. If any members of the LAPD working inside the administration building today were aware of her, it was because their *New Centurions*–era fathers used to keep a pinup of her in their lockers. Millar was largely forgotten now.

Except, of course, by the *unknown subject* who'd sent this package.

"Uh, Steve?" Banner asked. "Who's Bethany Millar?"

"Hang on," Dark said, pulling the phone from his pocket and aiming it at the sketch. One click and he had a hi-res image saved to his phone.

"Uh, you really shouldn't send that image to anyone outside the department," Banner said.

"I'll be right back."

"At least lie and tell me you're sending it to Riggins."

Dark stopped. Looked at Banner, deadpan.

"Okay. I'm sending it to Riggins."

All of the tension seemed to gush out of Banner for a moment before he sucked it back up again.

"Wait—you're lying, aren't you?"

Dark was already spinning through his contacts. Vincente Valentine had been a film director until he retired in the 1990s, living in his huge, ostentatious Malibu beach house just a few houses away from where Dark and Sibby used to live. Valentine had once bragged about working with Bethany Millar—"yeah, *the* Bethany Millar"—in an early 1970s gangster flick called *Deep Cut*. At the time, Valentine had been astonished that a whippersnapper like Dark even knew who Bethany Millar was.

CALL ME, Dark typed in the subject line, then sent off the image.

Valentine called Dark within sixty seconds, and picked up the conversation as if they'd spoken just last night as opposed to five long years ago. You could always count on retired creative types to call you back right away. Most of their lives had been spent waiting by the phone, and it was a hard habit to break.

"Nice sketch, Stevie," Valentine said. "Where did you find it?"

"Inside a box the LAPD thought contained a bomb."

"Sheesh. Is that what I've been hearing about on CNN? Bombs? The only thing that bombed was *Deep Cut*. Definitely a low point in my career."

Another old-timer trait: Pretend like nothing shocked you. Ever.

"Does the sketch mean anything to you?"

"A man my age, it means a lot," Valentine said. "Bethany's never looked better. I might have to disappear into the bathroom for a while."

Vincente Valentine: always the joker, even after two and a half cardiac arrests and three ex-wives. Every time he saw Dark and Sibby, he made an obvious pass at Sibby—which she thought was cute. Dark knew it was habit for a lifelong lothario like Valentine. Like breathing.

"Anything else about the sketch?" Dark asked.

"What should interest you, *Stevie*, is not the subject, but the artist."

"What do you mean?"

"My retired eyes could be failing me, but I swear that sketch was done by Herbie Loeb. Which would be strange, because . . . holy shit, does this mean Herbie Loeb was boffing Bethany Millar? And how did I not know about it?"

Right there—the connection Dark had needed.

"Thanks, Mr. Valentine. I owe you one."

"Not at all, Stevie. You've given this old man *plenty*. And you kiss that beautiful wife of yours for me. With tongue, if you don't mind."

Dark realized, with a jolt, that he didn't know.

It had been five years, and all over the news, but Valentine didn't know.

Sibby was gone.

"Yeah," Dark said, then pressed END.

Within thirty minutes an art expert from Holmby Hills had been rushed out to LAPD HQ to authenticate the sketch. Yes, it was a previously unknown sketch by the great Herbert Loeb, one of the most widely acclaimed pop artists of the late twentieth century. This sketch *shouldn't* exist, *couldn't* exist . . . yet here it was. The art expert looked like he was going to have a stroke.

"Where did you say you found this? And what will happen to it after it's . . . uh, evidence?"

Dark strolled away, pondering the implications. So they were dealing with someone who could pull off an art theft as well as a terrorist attack and a double homicide. There was the remote possibility that this was some sicko who'd rifled through a dead artist's possessions, and this was some bizarre way of announcing to the world that there were priceless objects now available for purchase.

But that didn't fit in with anything else—not the clock, nor the riddle.

This wasn't over.

The unsub was asking a question. No—it was more than that. He was daring them.

Figure this out before I strike again.

"Did you pull anything from the note?" Dark asked Banner.

"Not a thing. And the in-house handwriting analyst kind of just laughed when she saw it. Pretty much a textbook example of how to write in the most nondistinctive way possible. Right down to the ink, which came from the most common pen in the known universe."

"Hidden messages?" Dark asked. "Any microdots?"

It was unusual but possible. Microdots were secret messages compressed into a minuscule piece of typography—a comma, a period, the dot in the letter *i*. Cold War–era spies were fond of using microdots to smuggle sensitive material out from behind the Iron Curtain.

"Not a thing," Banner said. "We ran it through every test we have."

"So our unsub's being literal," Dark said. "He wants us to answer the riddle."

A WOMAN SHOOTS HER HUSBAND. THEN SHE HOLDS HIM UNDER WATER FOR OVER 5 MINUTES. FINALLY, SHE HANGS HIM. BUT 5 MINUTES LATER THEY BOTH GO OUT AND ENJOY A WONDERFUL DINNER TOGETHER. HOW CAN THIS BE?

"She's a photographer," Banner said; a sheepish look washed over his face. "I, uh, Googled it."

"Right," Dark said. "She *shot* her husband with her camera, then she *drowned* the film in chemicals to develop it for five minutes, then *hung* it—like, in a darkroom. Then they go out and have dinner while it's drying."

"I would have gotten it eventually," Banner said.

"Yeah, but it's too easy to be the real puzzle," Dark said. "Like you said, you can easily look up the answer online. The question is, what's this riddle doing on LAPD stationery, packaged along with the nude sketch and the clock? Why the art? Is he threatening Bethany Millar? Is this some crude way of saying that her time is running out?"

Banner's eyes lit up. "Okay, hang on . . . here's a weird thing for you," he said. "When one of the bomb techs looked it over, he noticed that the alarm clock was set to go off in a little less than five hours." Banner glanced at his rubber digital wristwatch. "Well, uh . . . make that forty-five minutes now."

"Shit, Banner—why didn't you tell me this before?"

"We kind of got sidetracked on the whole nude sketch thing, remember?"

The clock was the most obvious message of all.

Figure this out before I strike again . . .

. . . in forty-five minutes.

There was one person who might be able to tie it all together.

Not Herbert Loeb. The artist had been dead since 1988, having famously overdosed in his Tribeca apartment. Dark needed to find Loeb's secret model.

Before the alarm went off.

chapter 5

DARK

Hollywood Hills, California

Dark parked his Mustang on a downward slope in an illegal, instant tow-away, no-questions-asked, *fuck you have a nice day* zone. You could say this much about people who lived in the Hollywood Hills: When it came to protecting their parking spaces, they meant it.

But nobody would touch Dark's car. That's because Lisa Graysmith had given him a plastic hangtag that would grant him the parking equivalent of diplomatic immunity anywhere in North America. Much as Dark hated to admit it, the thing came in handy, especially in a perpetual traffic nightmare like L.A.

Especially when you might be racing to save an old woman's life.

Dark had quickly dug up Bethany Millar's home address and number and called it as he raced up the 101 toward the Hollywood Hills. There had been no answer; a machine picked up instead, and the voice on the digital recording sounded frail and confused. Still, Dark recognized it. You see someone on a screen and it's as if you know them; your brain learns to recognize the way they look, act, and speak.

Now he hoped Millar was still alive.

Dark darted uphill, hopped a wrought-iron fence, then ran toward the house.

❧

An elderly woman answered the chipped-paint door. Dark recognized her immediately.

Bethany Millar: in the flesh.

Dark was not the type to be starstruck, but even he had a vague feeling of dislocation that he should be looking at her on a black-and-white screen, not in living color.

"Ms. Millar? Can I speak to you for a moment?"

One look at Dark and the former starlet assumed he was a cop, here to deliver bad news.

"This is about my daughter, isn't it," she said, without preamble. "Oh God, please don't tell me you found my baby girl, please don't."

The decades had been cruel to Millar. Dark could smell the gin on her breath, as well as the mint mouthwash she no doubt swigged right before she answered the door. Her house, too, screamed *faded glory*. The front was overgrown with plant life and was a probable brushfire hazard. No doubt her neighbors hoped a little seismic jolt would wrench the old house from its foundations and wipe the slate clean.

"I'm here for you, actually," Dark said, casting a wary eye behind her, making sure no one was lurking in the shadows.

"Me?" Millar asked. "I'm fine. It's Faye I'm worried about. Is she okay? Please tell me she's okay."

"Do you think Faye is missing?"

"Missing?" Millar said sharply, as if she'd been grossly offended. "I didn't say anything about her being *missing*. I know exactly where she is. With that slimy rat bastard."

Faye Elizabeth was Bethany Millar's daughter, and she'd achieved something her mother never had: A-list status in Hollywood, headlining a series of top-grossing action movies. Elizabeth rarely spoke of her mother, adopting her own middle name as a stage name, and avoiding all questions about her parents. Her father had been an accountant, and had drank himself to death as quickly as you could on six figures a year. Her mother had faded into obscurity.

But it was clear that Bethany Millar still cared a great deal for her daughter.

"I can check on Faye if you like," Dark said, "but I'm here about you."

"Me?"

Dark stepped inside and eyeballed the room. It was spare to the point of absurdity—almost in move-in condition, if Ms. Millar were about to sell the place. Not a personal touch anywhere. No old posters, no memorabilia, no framed photos, no books, not a single piece of entertainment anywhere. She could vanish in an instant and you'd be hard-pressed to tell who lived here. Just someone who clearly didn't keep up this shell of a house, with its faded, chipped paint and deep cracks running up and down the walls.

"Do you remember an artist named Herbert Loeb?" Dark asked.

"Oh God."

"So you *do* know him."

"I didn't say that! Why do you keep putting words in my mouth—I don't even know who you are, and you're making this accusation. . . ."

"Did you know he once drew a sketch of you? Perhaps you modeled in a studio at one point, and Mr. Loeb was in attendance."

"I was never a model and I don't know Herbie and I'd like you to stop talking about me and go look for my daughter and bring her home. She has to be brought home right away so I can talk to her. Will you do that for me? Please!"

Of course Dark knew she was lying, and doing an extremely bad job of it, hobbled by either the gin or some kind of painkiller. Most likely both. Bethany Millar didn't want to be in her own head, let alone her own house. Why?

And why the focus on her daughter?

Never mind the fact that Millar never asked Dark's name, or to see identification of any kind. . . .

"Have you had any strange phone calls? Noticed anyone in the area who shouldn't be around?"

"No, I haven't, and I'd really appreciate if you could go out and find Faye. I can pay you whatever you like. Name your price."

"Who would know where she is, Ms. Millar?" Dark asked.

"David, that prick. I never liked him. I told her that. Did she listen? I told her what they were all like. All of those producers."

"Who's David?"

"Aren't you even listening? That sneaky prick David Loeb!"

Dark made the connection instantly. You don't hear the same surname twice in one day and chalk it up to just another Hollywood coincidence.

"Excuse me, Ms. Millar."

"You bring her back here! I'm begging you!"

Dark was already halfway to his Mustang by the time he reached Josh Banner in his lab and asked if Herbert Loeb had any children. By the time Banner came up with the answer, Dark was behind the wheel and slamming down on the accelerator.

Herbert had one child: a son named David Loeb.

A Hollywood producer.

⁂

Back in Josh Banner's lab at LAPD headquarters, the alarm clock rang.

[To enter the Labyrinth, please go to Level26.com and enter the code: arts]

chapter 6

LABYRINTH

As I leave the Malibu home, I'm almost disappointed to see there are no police vehicles, no flashing lights, no nothing. No one was watching me.

No one responded, no one figured it out, no one came.

And this was the easy one.

Ah, well.

There's always a learning curve with these kinds of things. You can't expect everyone to understand the rules of the game on the first move.

From the driver's seat I glance at the crashing waves on the lovely pristine Malibu beach as the sun continues its languid descent across the sky.

I greedily suck in the fresh ocean air as it blasts across my face, whipping the hair from my forehead, which is still damp from the salty mist, and for just a moment I can understand the appeal, why people worked so hard for temporary little pieces of *this*.

Of course, the beaches should be free and open to all. Any human being should be able to sit down and enjoy this primal spectacle at any time, not because they've jumped through a series of hoops for the mighty and the powerful.

The pimp and his whore—not so powerful now.

I think about how easy it all was.

How the lock on the house was junk.

How surprised they were to see me—the pimp and the whore in swimsuits, dirty feet up on a coffee table that was littered with imported beer bottles, fashion magazines, candy bars, and baggies of cocaine.

How they squinted like maybe they knew me, because on the outside, I look like I could be part of their world—healthy enough, handsome enough, groomed enough, confident enough.

But I am most definitely *not* part of their world.

It was even easy to force them to strip.

I wondered, though, if they understood the significance of that.

I wanted them stark naked so they could truly see each other's bodies. Not in a lustful manner, but a clinical manner

Because if they did, then soon certain anatomical similarities would manifest themselves.

Did they ever consider the matching birthmarks?

Or the idiosyncratic shapes of their hands—the long ring fingers on the left hand?

Or their eye color—which suggested burned gold in the middle of a lush New Guinea jungle?

Did none of this occur to them, even through the narcotic haze, as they were fucking each other?

It is important that they realized why this was happening to them. Because if they could not be made to understand, then the rest of the world wouldn't. They need to really *sell it*.

If we're going to save the world together.

chapter 7

DARK

Malibu, California

Dark glanced at his watch the moment he pulled up to the address Bethany Millar had given him. If the alarm clock in that package had been a countdown to something, then they'd reached zero hour just a few minutes ago.

Fuck.

He hammered the brakes, leaped out of the Mustang, and vaulted over the wrought-iron fence, hoping he wasn't too late.

The door was ajar. Dark pulled his Glock 19 from his jacket and nudged the door open with his boot, then cleared the living room, which was an absolute mess. Baggies of coke, high-end junk food, half-empty beers. From the looks of it, Elizabeth and Loeb had been holed up here for a long time. Days, probably.

Were they out on the beach, or making another drug or booze run?

Deep down, Dark knew that wasn't the case. He could feel the tremor in his own blood the same way an animal can sense a thunderstorm.

The next room was a kitchen, and off to the side, a bedroom. This home wasn't big. Just a multimillion-dollar beachside crash/fuck pad, apparently. Dark moved efficiently and quickly, sweeping the kitchen before moving into the bedroom, checking every corner and square foot of floor space before pushing forward. His muscles were wired and he steeled himself for anything. A fight, or a horror show.

Even the scent that suddenly filled his nostrils—the copperish scent of freshly spilled blood.

Dark moved forward and nudged open the door with his knee. The bodies of the A-list actress and her producer boyfriend were in the bathroom.

Loeb was facedown in a blocked toilet, a bloody exit wound in his back. Faye Elizabeth was now slumped over in the tub, gun in her hand, head twisted at a very unnatural angle.

Time had run out.

At first glance, Dark could see the scenario that was *supposed* to have unfolded:

Producer David Loeb goes crazy, beats and strangles his actress girlfriend—the famous Faye Elizabeth. In a desperate act of self-defense, she shoots him in the chest. Both collapse and die of their injuries.

But Dark knew that wasn't the case. They had been forced. Their bodies had been arranged. Forensics would prove that.

Whoever had done this had taken the time to arrange everything from the beginning. Now he was daring the police to catch him before he killed again.

The FBI arrived a short while later, having strong-armed the Los Angeles County Sheriff's Department out of their own case. The special agent in charge threatened to have Dark thrown into "fucking Gitmo" for contaminating the crime scene. Dark allowed him to vent—he knew the frustrations of the job better than most people—before showing him his digital badge on his cell phone. At which point the SAC shut up and mumbled a promise to keep Dark apprised of any developments. Dark thanked him and waited on the fringes.

The bullet that had blasted through David Loeb's chest and buried itself in the bathroom's tile wall was traced back to the gun in Faye Elizabeth's hand. No other DNA in the bathroom or the rest of the rental property—except for that of a lone cleaning woman. All signs pointed to: They did each other.

Time of death . . . well, the crime scene guys could tell, it had been just a few minutes after the time the alarm clock went off in Banner's office.

Dark stared at the house and thought about something his old director pal Valentine had said. About Bethany Millar "boffing" Herbie Loeb.

He asked the forensic guys for samples of each victim's blood, which they gave after a curt nod from the SAC, and sped away in his Mustang.

chapter 8

DARK

West Hollywood, California

Back home in his basement lab, Dark loaded the blood samples from the crime scene and began the process of DNA testing.

The gear in this secret room beneath Dark's West Hollywood abode was also thanks to Lisa Graysmith. It enabled him to analyze his own forensic samples and check the results against the most sophisticated (and secret) database in the world.

A few hours later, DNA testing on the vics confirmed it: There was an 88 percent likelihood that Faye Elizabeth and David Loeb were half siblings. Their common parent: famous artist Herbert Loeb.

A crude childhood rhyme drifted through Dark's head: *Incest is best, put your sister to the test.*

Somehow, the killer had known their dirty little secret. Was this personal, then?

If so, and the goal was to shame them in the most public way possible, why take out two LAPD detectives along the way?

Dark stared at the ceiling, putting together the narrative of the day from Labyrinth's point of view, trying to tune in to his particular, sick wavelength.

He closed his eyes and began to put it together.

He went into *brooding* mode.

⁂

Back at Special Circs, Dark was known as a brooder, especially when sinking his mind into a new case. Other agents would joke that when Dark was in the zone, he moved *so* slowly he almost went back in time a few days. Riggins, however, would defend him. Dark may be a tortoise, Riggins would say, but you should see the collection of mounted rabbit heads on his living room wall. It was true. When Dark turned his mind to a case, it was as if nothing else existed. His focus bordered on the preternatural.

Only difference now was that Dark had to divide his life into two distinct parts: manhunter and . . .

"DADDY!" shouted Sibby from the living room. "We're HO-OOOME!"

That would be Sibby, freshly sprung from her first grade classroom, escorted by her grandmother. Now it was time for Dark to turn off the quadruple homicides running through his mind and focus on his five-year-old girl, who'd want to tell him all about her day. Dark would have to stop thinking about the DNA testing and nude sketches of B-movie starlets and think about pouring his daughter a cup of juice and asking what kind of homework she had tonight.

The full-time father thing was new. Recently Dark had moved his daughter down from Santa Barbara to live with him here in West Hollywood. His formerly spare living room—nondescript furniture, movie posters—was now overwhelmed with little-girl stuff. Gone were the nightmare-inducing movie posters of boyhood favorites (*The Hitcher, To Live and Die in L.A., Dirty Harry*). In their places:

framed art from little Sibby herself. Sometimes Dark could swear that all she'd learned to do in kindergarten up there in Santa Barbara was generate a ridiculously huge catalog of original art.

So yeah, his life, his house—all in a state of extreme transition. It wasn't just his home anymore. It was Sibby's, too.

In the past he never would have thought that his life as a manhunter and his role as a father could coexist. Seemed an either/or proposition. That's the way it had been with little Sibby's mother. The two of them had *worked* . . . just so long as he could keep the demons at bay. It had taken Dark a long time to reach the place where he could be both a father and a manhunter. And he knew he could do both.

The hard part, though, was flipping the switch.

Snap out of it, he told himself. *Put the monster out of your head. Be here for your daughter.*

"Steve?" his mother-in-law called out from above. "Are you home?"

Dark was ready to reply when his smartphone buzzed—a text message.

From Graysmith:

WATCH THIS RIGHT NOW

Followed by a link to an online video.

The image opens with the actress, holding up the nude sketch her father drew. She smiles, even though it's clear she's been crying. She tells us: "The notion of a painting being worth two million dollars and being owned privately will be no more. Art is for the people; it's free. Everyone must understand it and have access to it. Not for just the rich and privileged—the spoilers of our world . . ."

Then the actress lifts a gun and points it at the camera. Someone off-screen says: "What are you doing?"

Smash cut to black. A scream: "OH GOD NO." A gunshot. A scream—male this time. Then a title card:

I WILL SHOW YOU

THE WAY OUT OF

THE LABYRINTH

chapter 9

DARK

Once the Labyrinth video hit the Net—and minutes later, the mainstream media—there was no way of containing *any* part of the story.

The Elizabeth-Loeb incest/double murders pushed everything else out of the news cycle—foreign revolutions, economic meltdowns, gas spills, political summits, and every other celebrity scandal.

The Labyrinth video attracted over 2.7 million views in the first few hours alone. YouTube had almost instantly yanked it from their site, but mirror sites had popped up everywhere, and every effort to contain it caused the video to spread even faster, like a malignant tumor on steroids.

And the news didn't *leak* to the media so much as spontaneously *manifest* itself, independent of hard facts or reporters making phone calls. Over the past few years Dark had been observing a shift in the way people received their news. Gone were the days of dogged newshound reporters and stentorian anchors filling us in on the events of the day—packaging it, processing it, delivering it. Now media consumers craved news instantly, and they wanted to curate it themselves. When disaster struck, some people still turned on the television. But an increasing number also had their phones in their hands, so they could see what their friends were writing and linking and joking about. In a sense, it was a return to a village mentality, where like people huddled together. Instead of occupying the same piece of turf, people followed one another on social networks.

But something strange had happened with this new "Labyrinth" case.

As Dark had waited for the results of his DNA test, the rumor that Elizabeth and Loeb were half siblings was already trending. Somehow, people out there in social network land knew—and began to spread—*information that nobody else had yet.*

One alleged fact was Tweeted within the hour:

> Dead actress girl? Dead producer boyfriend? They were half siblings!
>
> *1 hour ago*

Followed by endless Retweets and forwards and further comments:

> Grossburgers. RT: Dead actress girl? Dead producer boyfriend? They were half siblings!
>
> *54 minutes ago*
>
> Hollywood types will do anything.
>
> *40 minutes ago*
>
> Impossible. She's hot, he's a dork, no relation.
>
> *32 minutes ago*
>
> You should see my little sister/she can raise quite a blister
>
> *19 minutes ago*

How did the word travel so fast? Dark wondered if this was one of those open Hollywood secrets. He called his insider to ask.

Hell no, claimed Vincente Valentine, who had consulted a host of usual suspects—flacks, agents, producers. The Elizabeth-Loeb relationship itself wasn't a secret; online gossip sites had been reporting that they'd been palling around for at least six months. But the incest thing? Not a hint. "And I would have known," Valentine said. "Believe me. Bethany, you sweet old idiot . . ."

When the story hit the mainstream press, reporters practically fell over themselves racing to Millar's barren Hollywood Hills home. Microphones were jabbed at her face. *Why didn't she tell her daughter the truth? What kind of monster was she?*

Dark knew the answer to that one:

The kind who didn't want to admit the truth. Not even to herself.

But the incest thing didn't bug Dark. This was L.A., a virtual pit of twisted secrets. Lying to your daughter about the true identity of her father was nothing new, especially in a world where lineage could mean everything, and the wrong set of parents could doom you from the moment the doctor slapped you to kick-start your first breath.

What Dark kept coming back to was that this Labyrinth *knew*.

Not only knew, but targeted them and exploited this fact in the most sensational way possible.

Someone who wanted to make a point to whomever would listen.

Which, at this point, was pretty much *everybody*.

All Comments (43,978)

A senseless tragedy . . . cause she was HOTT even if she was banging her bro

Alx9722 55 seconds ago

If celebrity deaths come in threes does this count for two of them? Or only one? Is there a brother/sister discount? HELP ME I AM SO CONFUSED

petme1029 1 minute ago

Who the hell is LABYRINTH??? This what I want to know.

Mesta mysteries 1 minute ago

Wow. This looks fake.

gossoon 2 minutes ago

nipple!!!

zzzzmango 3 minutes ago

Good riddance to all of these hollywood faker types, I say. Overpaid, undertalented hacks. They probably just crossed their drug dealer. Who was most likely their first cousin or something.

Joeno ono 5 minutes ago

Alx9722 is right I woulda tapped that shit before she died and all WHAT A WASTE

discostixxx 5 minutes ago

How happy this vain little tart must have been to have died on camera.

Omnigatherum111 5 minutes ago

What is wrong with you people? These were human beings for gods sake?

CrystalShawATL 6 minutes ago

More coming soon . . .

labyrinth 8 minutes ago

After Dark put Sibby to bed for the night, he returned to his basement lab and wondered if the FBI had finally called in Riggins and Constance and the rest of Special Circs.

Part of Dark wanted to reach out to Riggins and kick the case around with him. Riggins was in many ways his opposite—brash, crude, given to wild hunches, and a shoot-first-ask-later attitude—but their skills complemented each other. They'd put away countless monsters. Put many of them down for good, too.

Ordinarily, this would have had Special Circs written all over it. Back when Dark was still a young and hungry agent, he could have practically loaded himself in a slingshot and launched himself clear across the country just so he could land in L.A. first. This was the kind of high-profile, byzantine case that Special Circs was designed to investigate.

But Special Circs was in deep trouble.

Dark himself had pulled the plug when he saw there was nowhere else to go but down. He wished Riggins and Constance the best, but he couldn't stomach the bullshit anymore.

He wondered how Riggins had been able to put up with it for so many years.

chapter 10

RIGGINS

Quantico, Virginia

Agent Tom Riggins rinsed out his mouth, spat into the sink, ran cold water over his face, checked his tongue, and wondered if this was it—if this was the day the job was going to kill him.

From the inside out.

Bumps were still there. Bumps were *definitely* still there. His GP must be blind. Maybe he needed a new doctor. Maybe he *was* dying, no matter what the doc said. Dying from the inside out, and now the rot had simply reached his tongue. He washed his face again, this time with water as hot as he could stand, then scooped a handful into his mouth. *Take that you little fuckers.* After drying his face with a paper towel, Riggins went back to his office. Which was still and dark, and not just because it was after hours on a weekday at Special Circs.

Special Circs: Riggins's pride and joy, the office he'd nurtured since its birth. The toughest, most elite law enforcement unit ever created on U.S. soil. His baby.

Special Circs: now in a death spiral.

The unit had started out as something amazing. But years of bureaucracy and muddled directives from above had turned Circs into a shadow of its former self. "Elite" in press release only; now in real danger of becoming just another random fiefdom in the byzantine empire of Homeland Security.

Riggins was the head of Special Circs since the beginning, when it was created as a humble side project of the Justice Department's ViCAP—Violent Criminal Apprehension Program. ViCAP was the computerized think tank that tracked and compared serial killings. It was a vital resource for law enforcement. But sometimes ViCAP tracked cases so violent, so extreme, that local cops or even the FBI weren't quite equipped to handle them. That's when Special Circs would step in.

But five years ago, the secretary of defense—Norman Wycoff—took a special interest in Special Circs. Tried to force its agents to cover up some of his own indiscretions.

Succeeded.

And once he'd wormed his way inside, he never really left.

Normally the secretary of defense would have absolutely zero sway over any Justice Department agency. But now Riggins, due to a series of circumstances that still made his stomach turn, found himself as Wycoff's errand boy. And Wycoff saw Special Circs as his personal squad of bagmen and fixers.

Just when Riggins didn't think the situation could get any worse, it did two weeks ago, after it was revealed that Norman Wycoff was under federal indictment for abuse of his office.

Well duh, Riggins thought. *You pencilnecks just clueing in to this now?*

But it was the worst possible thing for Special Circs. Because the only thing worse than having an evil overlord questioning your every move? The sudden lack of an evil overlord. A patron, even if it's Satan himself, is better than no patron.

With the serving of the first subpoena, Special Circs—already on the verge of being irrelevant—was now tainted goods. Whatever Wycoff had touched had turned to shit. Wycoff had his fingerprints all over Special Circs. The headlines touched off a mass exodus of the best and brightest manhunters and forensics experts in the world. Riggins had already held good-bye parties for three of his best agents and two lab techs. And the worst personnel blow of all was yet to come. . . .

So as Riggins ran his tongue around the inside of his mouth, he could not help thinking that it would take an act of God to turn Special Circs around.

Or—if the early rumblings were any indication—the act of a madman named Labyrinth.

Riggins read about the case last night, and he half-expected his phone to ring any minute. Years ago, in the era Riggins liked to call B.W. (Before Wyckoff), Special Circs would have easily been the go-to agency for something like this. Are you kidding—a cunning psycho engineering the double homicide of two very prominent Los Angelenos, and dropping clues off at LAPD headquarters like he's the fucking Joker or something? Special Circs all the way. Hell, back in the B.W. days, Riggins was often turning down cases, determined to devote Special Circ's resources to only the most extreme cases, the worst of the worst.

But now, in the post-B.W. era?

His desktop phone was a useless lump of plastic on his cluttered desktop. No e-mails, no FedExes, no texts, even.

Nothing.

Riggins chided himself for thinking they'd be calling him.

You fool.

Much as Riggins hated to think along political lines, what Special Circs needed to save itself was to bag this Labyrinth fuckhead early. Look where no one else was looking. Riggins wasn't worried for his own job. They could shitcan him tomorrow and that would be fine. But *Special Circs needed to exist.* The country needed it. If anything, the world was an even more insane place. In fact, insanity had been adopted into the mainstream like never before.

Look at the reaction to this Labyrinth fuckhead. Riggins scrolled through the comments on that YouTube site and saw more high fives and attaboys than he did expressions of grief or shock. The whole country was losing its goddamned mind.

If he had Steve Dark and Constance Brielle on this guy, they could . . .

Riggins stopped himself, chided himself again. *Stop thinking about what you don't have. Concentrate on what you do. What you've always done.*

Catch this son of a bitch.

Riggins had done it before; he could do it again. Namely: Put together the top crime-fighting minds on the planet and catch a monster. They'd caught the worst of the worst before. And while the Sqweegel case was one of the more tortured takedowns in the history of the department—they got it done. Special Circs may be down, but it was not out.

They could still cut through the bullshit red tape and catch this Labyrinth psycho before things escalated.

chapter 11

DARK

West Hollywood, California

Two days later, Labyrinth's identity was still a mystery.

On the plus side, the killer hadn't sent any new packages or uploaded any additional video clips.

On the minus side, he didn't have to. The media was still in the middle of a full-on Labyrinth/Elizabeth/Loeb feeding frenzy.

The FBI, following the media's lead, seemed to be focused on the Hollywood angle. Two dead detectives were tragic, but the members of the LAPD put their lives on the line every day. Celebrity murders, however, seized the public imagination like nothing else. People invested parts of themselves in the lives of the famous. When something awful or thrilling or shocking or embarrassing happened to them, it was a form of vicarious living.

Dark, however, didn't pay attention to any of that. Over the past six days, he'd turned his attention to the homeless man—the walking time bomb.

Who was just as much a mystery as Labyrinth himself.

No I.D. of any kind, no print match, no DNA match on any known databases. Eyewitness claimed he just walked in off the street and remained fairly calm as he was forcibly separated from the box. The man was trembling, and he reeked like the inside of a tomb, but he was not a man under duress, eyewitnesses claimed. He appeared to be resigned to his situation.

But nobody knew who he was.

People didn't just materialize out of nowhere. The cutout had to be born *somewhere* to end up in the middle of L.A.

One thing was clear: "Labyrinth" wasn't a one-off. The whole thing was too elaborate, too carefully planned. The clock, the art theft, the little maneuver with the LAPD stationery. This was him showing off: *Ooh, look what I can do.*

Nothing would make Dark happier than to catch this guy right now and tell him, face-to-face:

Here's what I *can do.*

While the LAPD had come up with zero hits on the homeless man, they were also severely hampered by the number of databases in the world. There were more databases in the world than the ones accessible by law enforcement. There were extra-legal and so-called black databases that had existed even before Sir Alec Jeffreys made his DNA profiling breakthroughs at the University of Leicester back in 1984. Aggressive sampling and reporting and outright genetic theft had filled in the gaps to create a truly rich database of nearly every living being on the planet, as well as many of the dead.

That was the kind of database Dark would be accessing—again, thanks to his guardian angel Graysmith, and her nebulous intelligence sources.

Josh Banner had smuggled him a piece of the homeless man's DNA out of LAPD HQ this morning. Dark had processed the sample, and now was awaiting a hit.

Praying for a hit, actually.

Dark's phone buzzed.

Graysmith again.

She'd been away somewhere in the world—and as usual, she wouldn't divulge where, exactly. But now she was back in California and wanted to stop by and talk about Labyrinth.

Six months ago Graysmith had seemingly materialized out of nowhere and acted like a guardian angel to him—offering him access, weapons, intel, even goddamned planes that would slingshot him from coast to coast in pursuit of the monster. She told him she had access to a discretionary budget from deep within U.S. intelligence channels, and not to worry about where it all came from.

You've seen, firsthand, what kind of resources I can offer you, she'd said.

But what do you want in return? Dark had asked.

I want you to catch the monsters.

Special Circs does that.

But Special Circs isn't as good as you. And they're not able to follow the job through—to give the monsters out there what they deserve.

Which would be what?

Death.

A guardian angel—with a bit of the devil inside her.

Dark harbored serious doubts about Graysmith during that first case—the hunt for the so-called Tarot Card Killer. For a time he suspected that she *was* the Tarot Card Killer, and was worming into his life just to fuck with his head. Those suspicions were unfounded. She'd been vital to the investigation. She had given him exactly what she'd promised—nothing more, nothing less.

By the end of their first case, Graysmith had hinted that she was going to quit her unspecified job in U.S. intelligence and join him full-time.

And then do what? Catch serial killers in our spare time? Dark had asked.

Yeah, she'd said, squeezing his hand.

For the past six months, that is what they did. Whenever Dark wasn't being a father. They used a sophisticated database program to track all unusual murders worldwide and looked for patterns. Graysmith still apparently had her access to both databases and funding. When Dark had asked her about that, she told him not to worry and keep looking for monsters. There had been promising developments in Europe, but then the killer had tripped himself up and was caught by Interpol. Dark continued to search, to study the patterns.

But all along, Dark wondered: Who was funding her? Where was this all going? He'd done some digging and found some answers.

And soon, they were going to have a little talk about all of this. Because the answers he'd uncovered brought up even *more* questions.

As usual, Graysmith let herself in, coffee in one hand, beer in the other. She handed the bottle—Shiner Bock—to Dark. He twisted off the cap and took a sip and tried to figure out where she'd been by her appearance. Her smooth skin was slightly tanned, and her hair had been trimmed. Otherwise she looked the same. Her bright eyes always had the same look of bemusement about them—that slight detachment that Dark could never figure out.

"My boss is very interested in Labyrinth," Graysmith said. "Where are you on the case? I want to be able to tell him something."

"Or else?"

Dark was keenly aware that his access to databases, forensic tools, parking hangtags—*everything*—could vanish in an instant. He almost expected it to happen. He was a man who had been given wonderful presents throughout his life, only to have them ripped from his hands when he least expected. So if you always expect it, you can soften the blow.

The way Dark was feeling, he wanted it all to go away. Right now. He didn't need fancy gear to catch this monster.

So he pressed the issue.

"I want to speak to your boss."

Graysmith smiled, with a hint of sadness in her eyes. Dark's gut—normally an excellent barometer for these kinds of situations—felt cold.

"You can't. He values his privacy above all else."

"Introduce me anyway."

"Don't you trust me?"

Every nerve in his body screamed NO. At times they were as intimate as two human beings could be, but Dark was keenly aware of the no-fly zone between them. If Dark wanted the support to continue, he wouldn't ask any questions.

"Lisa," Dark said, "it's not about trust. I want to talk to him. Right now."

"Impossible. If I could, I would. But that's just not going to happen."

"I want to talk to Damien Blair. Now."

That stopped Graysmith cold.

"How do you know that name?"

chapter 12

DARK

Dark wanted to tell her:

Because I'm a motherfucking manhunter.

After the Tarot Card Killer case, his eyes opened up. Dark was through being pushed around like a pawn. He learned to make his own promises, set his own goals. Create his own fate. As long as he could do that, there was hope. Even when everything else was stacked against him.

So Dark did a lot of investigating on his own over the past six months. He skipped electronic resources and went old-school, following a paper trail. Just like Tom Riggins had taught him, back when Dark was a rookie. And over the past few months he'd been able to trace the supposedly untraceable Lisa Graysmith through financial transactions. Simple fact was if you work for someone, they must pay you. Hard as you might try, it is next to impossible to completely eradicate a money trail from the face of the earth.

Dark didn't have all of the puzzle pieces. But he did know the name Damien Blair, who had several addresses throughout Europe, South Africa, and Hong Kong, as well as vast fortunes at his disposal.

Blair was connected, polished, savvy, and secretive. He was also boring to mainstream media. The only Blair news mention over the past year was that he was a regular attendee at the World Economic Forum's annual meeting in Davos, Switzerland—where the entrance fee is a cool half million, not including first-class travel fare, chalet rental, car and driver, helicopter rental, and so on.

Nothing troubling emerged from Blair's public bio, but that could simply mean that he'd spent millions to obscure his life from prying eyes. A man just doesn't go through all of the trouble of wooing and funding a retired FBI agent unless he wants something specific in return.

However, Dark figured that was enough of a wedge to crack open the truth.

"You want to tell me about him, or should I go on?" Dark asked. "Or maybe I'll just call Blair's office myself."

Dark took another sip of beer and waited her out. Watched the bemusement in her eyes turn to annoyance. And then, finally, resignation.

"Let me make two phone calls."

✢

The first call was presumably to Blair.

The second, however, was to Dark's mother-in-law.

Graysmith had met Mrs. Collins in the aftermath of the Tarot Card Killer case, introducing herself as a former FBI colleague of Dark's. His mother-in-law was too smart to take that at face value; she was like her daughter that way. Intuitive, canny, empathetic, almost to a preternatural degree. Dark sensed he and his mother-in-law would soon be having a conversation about who this Graysmith woman was, and what she meant in terms of her granddaughter.

For now, though, Mrs. Collins would keep those thoughts to herself and relish the time she could spend with Sibby.

"It's all arranged," Graysmith said. "Your daughter's covered."

"You called my mother-in-law?"

"Finish your beer. We've got some traveling to do."

Graysmith drove, taking the 101 up through Hollywood toward Van Nuys. Their private plane would be waiting, she explained. Dark realized he was wearing a semi-clean T-shirt, a hoodie, and a pair of severely distressed jeans. No weapons, no phone, not even so much as a pen. Wherever they were headed, he supposed he'd gather what he needed along the way.

"I suppose you're going to draw this out," Dark said. "Make me work for it."

"No," Graysmith said. "I have permission to tell you. But don't make me repeat myself. I'm a scout for a unique and highly secretive group of investigators who have had their eye on you for a long time. Ever since the Sqweegel case, from five years ago. When the Tarot Card Killer emerged, Damien Blair decided to give you the tools you needed to catch him."

"What, like a tryout?"

"No. Like, assistance. I've never lied to you, Steve."

Dark processed this, quickly rewinding the past six months, cross-checking their conversations against this new and oh-so-delightful development.

"We wanted you to accept our help so that you could reach your full potential. And you *have*, Steve. Don't you realize that? Consider where you were even six months ago. Still trying to figure it all out. Still struggling with what you were, and ignoring the potential of what you could become."

"Wonderful," Dark said. "I've blossomed. So where are we going? Specifically?"

"Paris," she said.

Los Angeles Times

Still no further threats from "Labyrinth," no clues as to identity. Police chief speculates: "We think he was a one-off."

chapter 13

LABYRINTH

Right now everyone in the lobby of the fancy oil corporation is wondering:

A giant fish tank? Which of these overindulged, overcompensated suits ordered the giant fish tank?

Yet there it was, being wheeled into the headquarters of the Intertrust Petroleum Corporation (IPC), one of the largest such oil concerns in Dubai.

The unofficial company motto seems to be: Money Is No Object. And that ethos is reflected in every design choice throughout the building.

I watch as a confused assistant signs for the tank, assuming that one of the CEOs had ordered it.

Because, you know, CEOs did whimsical things like this.

When money is no object, you seek out increasingly bizarre toys to amuse yourself.

Well, my next package will certainly amuse them.

Two executive assistants approach the tank, peering in at the lone, ugly fish inside.

The moment the packages were signed for at the main IPC reception area, I received a small push alert on a cell phone, which prompted me to log on to the company's own internal servers.

I eavesdrop, using the hidden cameras and microphones from IPC's own internal security system.

With the right software, you can pretty much stand inside any room in the world, thanks to the network of security cameras that human beings have wired up to watch themselves obsessively.

It is fun to watch them try to figure out this new gift.

One assistant asks,

What kind is that inside the tank? Do you recognize that kind of fish?

The other says,

No idea. It looks . . . sick.

Why order a fish tank this big with only a single fish inside?

Like I said, no idea. Maybe it's somebody's idea of a joke. Maybe in a few minutes, somebody's going to walk through the front door with a white cap and a set of knives, and this poor wee fella will end up as sushi.

They stifle their laughter. Don't want the executives to hear them have too much fun.

But jokes helped ease the tension of working for the most high-strung, power-mad people in the known universe.

The executive assistants take their levity where they can get it.

I don't begrudge them that.

The companion package arrives a few minutes later—a small FedEx box.

An assistant jokes,

Probably fish food.

But when the assistant tears off the cardboard strip, they are more than a little surprised to find a gold watch inside, along with a folded piece of the company's own letterhead.

This strikes a chord.

One of the assistants says this all reminds her of something she'd just read on the Internet—about that actress and her producer boyfriend.

She says,

Didn't the LAPD receive all kinds of weird shit in the mail, hours before a bomb went off?

The other says,

Yeah, a riddle. The nutcase sent a *riddle*!

I hope that it is abundantly clear by now that I am not a "nutcase." Every action has a specific purpose and meaning.

It doesn't matter that the world doesn't understand right now.

Those who play the game will pick up the small nuances of what I do.

And those will be the people who help me save the world from itself.

Two detectives from the Dubai Police's General Department of Criminal Investigation arrive at IPC within minutes.

Oil concerns receive prompt and courteous attention from the police.

The shorter of the two is also the wider, and the taller one is balding.

Cheap men, engaged in cheap business, deluding themselves into thinking they are doing something good by protecting cheap lives.

They examine my riddle in a quiet conference room, say that forensics techs are on their way.

With a company as powerful and influential as IPC, the police know to bring out the big guns.

For the time being, these cheap men only nudge the edges of my letter with gloved fingertips, talk about elimination prints from the executive assistants.

They should be poring over the riddle. It will tell them everything.

My riddle, written in English:

I CAN RUN, BUT NEVER WALK,
OFTEN A MURMUR, NEVER TALK,
I HAVE A BED BUT NEVER SLEEP,
I HAVE A MOUTH BUT NEVER EAT.
WHAT AM I?

LABYRINTH

Instead, they examine the wind-up gold wristwatch—a custom-made Patek Philippe that included a perpetual calendar with the phases of the moon.

An expensive item, hand-built, with only the finest materials.

An exquisite piece of craftsmanship, handled by their sausage-link simian fingers.

The cheap cops talk about examining the timepiece for prints, falling over themselves to impress each other with their forensics knowledge, of which they possess very little.

At long last they finally notice the inscription and date on the back of the watch:

To Everette
My Favorite Infidel
10/11/48

One of the detectives calls it in back at headquarters—they need to know who this "Everette" is, what the date means, and if possible, what the hell that line about the infidel means.

The date seems to wedge itself in the fat detective's mind.

He muses out loud,

Nineteen forty-eight.

A significant, controversial, and turbulent time in the Middle East, and something about it bothers him . . .

As it should.

The taller one notices that the watch seems to be running . . . slow.

The fat one times it against his own digital watch—the wind-up is losing seconds here and there.

He asks,

What does that mean?

I want to tell him,

Go on, keep playing, you're doing fine.

I listen as they call and ask for the area's top watchmaker to be brought down to headquarters immediately, and they're about to transfer the letter and watch back to the lab at headquarters when one of the assistants stops them, says,

Don't you want the fish?

The detectives stop, look at each other.

Fish?

The police are adamant: no details to be leaked to the media.

Not.

A.

Single.

Thing.

The expectations of the Dubai Police are as unreasonable as they are unlikely.

Just as I anticipated.

⁂

They are guilty of forgetting that many employees of the Intertrust Petroleum Corporation are expatriate Americans, and Americans are a nation of loud people who tend to overshare.

The assistants who'd received the fish tank and the package?

No exception.

Even their iron-clad nondisclosure agreements are not enough to dissuade them from bursting at the seams to share what they had experienced. As if events in real life didn't actually happen unless they were noted and "liked" in the virtual world.

⁂

IPC executive assistant Lauren Sandovsky is the first to leak information about an hour and twenty three minutes after the arrival of the packages.

My information virus begins with her, in a short, private direct message to a former boyfriend:

> Hey. You're probably asleep but you will never guess what happened to me at work today.
>
> *3 hours ago*

> No, beautiful, I'm up. I'm always up. So okay, I'll bite. What happened to you at work today? Did a sheik invite you to join his harem?
>
> *3 hours ago*

Racist. NO. I think I opened a package sent by a serial killer!!!

3 hours ago

WHAT?

2 hours ago

You know that Labyrinth thing—the Bethany Millar murder? Well we got this weird package today, and the police think it's the same guy.

2 hours ago

That is insane. Did you take a photo of the package? Can I use it?

2 hours ago

Um, yeah . . . but NO you cannot use it. Do you want to get me fired?

2 hours ago

Come onnnnnnn . . . I'll be your best friend. . . . :)

43 minutes ago

Seriously, Lauren, how can you NOT share this with me? I live for this stuff!

40 minutes ago

Don't make me get down on my knees and beg.

19 minutes ago

FOR YOUR EYES ONLY. Understand, tough guy?
[PIX ATTACHMENT: 43728.23.jpg.]

7 minutes ago

Oh . . . wow. And yeah, I promise.

1 minute ago

Brad Rayner works as a content manager on an alternative news Website based in Chicago, Illinois.

The photo appears on that site approximately seventeen minutes after Brad received it.

I am surprised it takes that long.

chapter 14

DARK

Over the Atlantic Ocean

Dark was drifting off in a semi-dazed state when the laptop on the table next to him went *ping*. He blinked, looked around, and instantly remembered—oh yeah, I'm inside the plush belly of a Gulfstream G650, racing at Mach 0.9 to meet a man who's been secretly recruiting me.

The laptop *ping* meant that the DNA sample of the homeless man matched with an identity. Again, Graysmith's clandestine databases had come in handy. This man did indeed exist. Dark spun the ultra-thin laptop so that he could see the screen, then tapped a few keys.

"So who is it?" Graysmith asked from the other side of the plane.

"Coming up now."

This short, seven-word exchange was the only conversation they'd had since boarding the Gulfstream. She pointed Dark in the direction of the laptop and perched herself on a seat opposite with a cup of herbal tea, earphones, and a tablet computer.

Dark waited for the results.

And their mystery homeless man turned out to be . . .

. . . nobody.

Not literally. The man had a life, a background. Just not a terribly distinguished background—certainly not one that would cause his fingerprints and identity to be stripped from every known law enforcement database worldwide. His name was Aldi Kutishi, and he was an Albanian shopkeeper who was thought to have been killed during a looting spree in the early 1990s. Only Graysmith's underground resources revealed this tiny piece of biographical data. His whereabouts for the past two decades?

Unknown.

It was as if the man had stepped into a pocket alternate universe, contracted an untraceable disease, then manifested in L.A. on a balmy fall day, living long enough to deliver a strange package to the police.

So this . . . "Labyrinth."

For starters, he'd given himself that moniker. That was significant. Most killers were branded by the media or law enforcement, but Labyrinth had identified himself from the beginning. Did Labyrinth see himself as the master at the center of a dizzying and hopelessly confusing maze? Or was he trapped inside as well, and killing people was his only way out?

He was careful to use a courier who had no background. Therefore, Labyrinth must have some kind of access to law enforcement databases around the world to ensure that his man was a proper, untraceable nobody.

Labyrinth also had access to, or could forge, LAPD stationery, as well as a rare sketch of a Hollywood starlet. He was either an expert thief, or employed one, or several of them. Not unusual for someone to parcel out a job.

Why would he pick this courier, though? What about Aldi Kutishi made him the ideal human bomb?

"Does the name mean anything to you?" Dark asked.

Graysmith shook her head. "Not a thing. But the people you're about to meet may have some ideas."

"How long have you worked for them? Or are you just a freelancer who goes around worming your way into people's lives?"

"I've worked for Damien for a long time. By the way, I understand what you're doing. You've felt like you've been betrayed or abandoned by most of the people in your life. Naturally, you're taking some of this hostility out on me. I not only understand it, but I expected it. Because I used this sense of betrayal and abandonment to enter your life. But this was carefully considered, and we saw no other way. You had just left Special Circs. You were not about to join another organization, no matter how appealing it may have sounded. I had to lead you to it, which is all I've done. If you hate me for it, I'm prepared to accept that."

"I don't hate you," Dark said. "How can you hate someone you don't even know?"

Graysmith said, "Oh, I don't think you really believe that, Steve."

Dark turned his attention back to the laptop. How he got here didn't matter; the fact remained that there was another monster out there. And Graysmith had touched on the truth. The idea of an organization with unlimited resources and access—and no red tape—*did* appeal to him now. As long as he got to take this monster out.

When they deplaned it was night, and very cold. A wind from the north picked up a chill from the ocean and slammed it into their bodies. Dark tried to compute the time difference, and wondered what his daughter was doing right now. Getting ready for school?

As they walked down to the tarmac a black limousine rushed toward them, intent on arriving at the bottom of the staircase the very moment they'd reached it. Graysmith rummaged through her bag and pulled out a fabric hood. Wordlessly she held it out for Dark to take. He just stared at it.

"You're fucking kidding."

"Sorry, it's a requirement. I told you, Blair values his privacy. Unless you want to turn around and fly back home?"

"This is insane."

"Blair insists. He operates in total secret, and the existence of his organization depends on it. There's always the chance, however slim, that you're a wildly brilliant sociopath who's seen through my cover all along, and in fact have been hunting me to get to them."

"Gee, you've figured me out."

"I thought as much. Now please, indulge me? It won't be for long. You'll hardly know you're wearing it."

But he took the hood anyway. The fabric was soft and breathable, at least. He slipped it over his head.

The hood turned out to be a diversion. For the moment he slipped the hood over his head Dark felt a sting in the side of his neck, and then his vision went black for real.

⁂

AP News

Breaking: Norman Wycoff under indictment, accused of abusing Defense Department powers.

chapter 15

RIGGINS

Quantico, Virginia

The restaurant was quiet, dim, empty. Just the way Riggins liked it.

"Come on," he said. "It's *me*. Don't you think I could find out anyway?"

Constance Brielle smiled. "Well, I *could* tell you . . ."

"But you'd have to kill me, right?" Riggins smiled, swirled the ice around in his drink. "Well, sweetheart, many have tried, and somehow I'm still walking around."

"Yeah," she said. "Me, too."

Riggins had spent a lot of time with Constance in the hospital in the aftermath of the Tarot Card Killer case. She had gone head-to-head with a psychotic ex–Navy Seal in a fire tower of the largest building in San Francisco—the Niantic Tower. She had barely survived the encounter. Her arm had been broken in two places. She had been choked and then finally driven headfirst into a concrete wall, giving her a concussion. The fact that she had survived meant that Constance was tougher than any of them realized—including Constance. But it was Riggins who had carried her out of the burning Niantic Tower. Riggins who had stayed with her, holding her hand, telling her how tough she was. How if it had been him, he would have been curled up into the fetal position crying for his mommy. Constance had smiled, even through the morphine-drip haze, and Riggins knew she'd be all right.

Riggins turned out to be wrong about that. Constance was not okay.

And now, just six months later, Constance was quitting Special Circs.

"Guess we're born survivors," Riggins said.

They'd met up at a joint not far from Quantico—a dark, old-school chophouse with huge wooden booths and white tablecloths. Riggins liked it because it was quiet. It was also a good place for drinking. Constance ordered a bourbon, Black Maple Hill, neat, her first alcoholic beverage since getting out of the hospital. Riggins ordered a crème de menthe with pineapple juice on the rocks. Which was absolutely disgusting. And, which was the point. Riggins needed a drink, but he figured that sipping something disgusting would keep him from getting too drunk. He didn't want to go bad on himself now, of all times. He eyed Constance's bourbon, though.

"Any news from King Asshole?" Constance asked.

King Asshole = code word for Wycoff.

"No. The man's going down in flames, that much is clear."

"What's that mean for you?"

"Going to ignore it, do my job."

There was a sudden brightness in Constance's eyes. "You're on this Labyrinth thing, aren't you?"

"Yeah," Riggins lied.

Truth was, in the week since that first creepy video had been uploaded, nobody had said *boo* to him. Riggins decided to pursue it anyway. No evil overlord meant no accountability. At least in the short term.

"You should be working this one with me," Riggins said. "I need someone like you on this."

"Tom . . ."

"I know, I know. And I lied. I don't need someone like you. I need you, and I know I can't have you."

"I just feel like I . . ."

"You don't have to explain. I understand better than anybody."

And she did. Tom Riggins knew the crush of the job better than anybody. The fact that he was still in it, after all of these years, was either a miracle or a statistical anomaly. Special Circs agents lasted anywhere from forty-eight hours to six months, tops. An unusually long career might mean a year or two of service. Somehow Riggins had lasted a quarter of a century. Only Steve Dark and Constance Brielle came in at a distant second and third spot on the longevity list.

Dark had quit earlier in the year; Constance was pulling the plug now.

She was headed to a job in the intelligence community; she'd been scouted. Riggins did some intradepartmental digging. Turns out, Constance had been scouted quite often over the years, but turned down all offers flat. She preferred to stay with Riggins. And, of course, Steve Dark, her unrequited paramour.

Dark, who hadn't visited her in the hospital.

Not once.

They'd never spoken about it, but Riggins knew it bothered the both of them.

Riggins thought about the last time he saw Steve Dark. Six weeks ago, on the westernmost edge of California, in the wake of a bloodbath. For a period of time, a horrible, excruciating length of time, Riggins had worried that Dark had gone to the place of no return. That he might even *be* the Tarot Card Killer. Riggins knew things about Dark's lineage that not even Dark himself knew. So when Riggins had the gun in his hand and pointed at the closest thing he had to a son . . . he was fully prepared to pull the trigger. And what an awful moment that had been.

I'm not crazy, Tom. I'm as sane as I've ever been, Dark had said.

What have you been doing? Riggins asked.

My job. Just not for you.

Was he still doing the job, out there in L.A.?

❧

The truth was—and here was the horrible truth he could never, ever reveal to anyone, especially Steve Dark:

Riggins half-expected Steve Dark to completely snap at any given moment.

When it happened, Dark would not be to blame. Not entirely. Not when that kind of thing is in your blood.

In the aftermath of the Sqweegel case five years ago, Dark had completely destroyed the body of his nemesis, chopping it to pieces before personally pushing it into a crematorium. Hours later, though, Dark realized his mistake. That they should have kept some of Sqweegel's DNA for future reference, to match against unsolved crimes. And then Dark remembered the one place where he still could find a DNA sample. Riggins had volunteered for the job.

Hours later, Riggins was picking up the dead cold hand of Sibby Dark and gently ran a stick under one fingernail like he was wiping a tear away from the corner of a baby's eye. He thought about how hard Sibby Dark had clung to life, gouging away at her tormentor, ripping through his latex suit and tearing at his flesh.

Riggins ran the sample personally, and waited for the results in the empty trace lab. When they came back with a CODIS hit, Riggins wasn't surprised. Sqweegel hadn't just sprung up from the bowels of hell to terrorize mankind. Even monsters had relatives.

But Riggins had no idea that one of those relatives would be *Steve Dark himself.*

According to the results, the two were brothers.

So for the past five years, Riggins had swallowed the truth and kept it in a lock box inside himself, and he drank a little more booze to keep it shut. He couldn't let it slip, he couldn't let on.

But he kept a careful eye on Dark, watching for any signs of psychosis or instability. Not that these things always ran in families, but it certainly explained a lot about Dark's inclinations. He was the world's best manhunter because he was a very short distance away from being a Level 26 killer himself.

The very thought terrorized Riggins beyond belief.

That someday, he'd have to hunt down his own surrogate son . . .

"Riggins, are you still here on earth with us?"

Constance smiled at him, but it was for show. Riggins could tell she'd been thinking about Dark, too.

What he wanted more than anything was to gather Dark and Constance together and work this one last case, this one last time. But you couldn't always get what you want, and living in the past was the surest way to give up your future.

"Yeah. I'm here."

Riggins raised his hand, summoned the waiter, and asked him to bring over another Black Maple Hill, double, neat.

Told Constance, "I'm not going anywhere."

But she was, and Riggins knew it.

chapter 16

DARK

Paris, France

When Dark woke up he was lying on a settee in the middle of a very large room. The world seemed like it had tilted to the left. Graysmith was next to him on the settee. She put a hand on Dark's shoulder as if waking him from a gentle nap, not the injection of a knockout drug.

"Steve, meet Damien Blair, the head of Global Alliance."

Blair, standing in front of them, had about ten years on Dark, as well as graying hair at his temples. Handsome features. Bright eyes. Blair didn't extend his hand. He stood there, fixing an icy stare on Dark.

"How did you know my name?" he asked.

Dark took a mental snapshot of his surroundings. Ornate columns, painted over dozens of times with a pale primer. A high, vaulted ceiling in badly need of some of that primer. To his left, a stage. All at once he realized why the world felt like it was tilted on its side. They were in an old movie palace, only with the seats removed, leaving the floor pitched at an angle toward the stage.

"You live here alone, or with a roommate?" Dark asked.

"Just borrowing this for our meeting. Which will be brief, because the situation is rapidly evolving, and I don't have much time to hold your hand." Blair looked at Graysmith. "Let me ask you again—how did you know my name?"

"The old-fashioned way," Dark said. "I looked for it."

Blair smiled—or what passed for smiling. The man's face seemed genetically incapable of expressing true mirth.

"You're the first candidate to uncover my name, which is very impressive."

"So was that another tryout? If I guess your weight and height, will you let me join your little super club?"

This time Blair didn't even pretend to smile. Instead he turned to face Graysmith and asked her, "Does he know about Dubai yet?"

Graysmith shook her head. "No. I kept the plane in media blackout mode, as you requested."

"Good," Blair said.

Dark stood up. Blood rushed away from his brain and he had to fight the vertigo. "Now will you tell me who you are, and what you do?"

Blair said, "Your beloved Special Circs was known as the most elite serial killer–hunting unit in the country. Dealing with the worst of the worst. Right?"

Dark nodded.

Blair said, "Imagine a similar unit, only global in scale. Populated by manhunters of your caliber, and in some cases, even more seasoned. And whose prey is much more fearsome than your garden-variety serial killer."

Dark didn't think Blair realized how fearsome serial killers could be—such as the worst killer Dark had ever faced. A being that didn't even qualify as a human being. A living monster with pure hate running so hot it burned the blood in his veins, reducing it to tar. They called him Sqweegel. He had taken away the only woman Dark had ever truly loved. It had taken a special friend to guide him out of the fun house of horrors that was his mind.

You create your own fate, Dark had told Riggins just a few months ago. *As long as you do that, there's hope.* And he'd come to believe that.

If Blair had spent just thirty seconds inside a room with Sqweegel, he wouldn't be dismissing him as "garden variety."

Still, Dark said nothing. He was here on Blair's dime; let him make his pitch.

"You've spent your career chasing what you call Level 26 killers," Blair continued. "But there are worse things out there—worse than even Special Circs realize. I created Global Alliance, with the support of major governments around the world, to neutralize these burgeoning threats."

Dark stared at him. Was this meant to impress him? The monsters *I* chase are bigger and badder than the monsters *you* chase.

"Funny," Dark said, "that I've never heard of you, or these *worse things* you talk about."

"Because thus far, we've stopped them first," Blair said, deadpan look on his face. "Mr. Dark, I could show you some interesting case files—and you should peruse them at some point, should you choose to continue. I think you'd find them intellectually fascinating. But as I mentioned, there's not much time for back and forth, so let me explain what we do."

The way Blair explained it, Global Alliance was an all-star team of international agents, bringing together people with the top skill sets in the world: forensics, combat, interrogation, technology, mind ops, and so on. There was no home base; each Global Alliance agent lived in his or her own country, yet came together as needed. Blair was no cop himself; he explained that he was merely a facilitator, with the funding to be able to move anything, to anywhere, no questions asked.

"Why bother with me?" Dark asked. "You seem like you've pretty much got the planet by the balls."

Graysmith sighed audibly. "Told you I needed a little more time."

Blair smiled. "No, he's doing just fine."

Then he turned his attention back to Dark.

"Before being invited to join the ranks of GA, each agent is carefully monitored and tested on various cases. We noticed you when you apprehended and dispatched the killer known as Sqweegel. We carefully observed how you handled the Tarot Card Killer. Ordinarily, we would have invited you in a more controlled, leisurely way. Wooed you, even. But now that Labyrinth has appeared, there's no time. We need your expertise, and we need it now."

"Again, why me?"

"The members of Global Alliance are highly skilled—the best at what they do. But I've never encountered someone who can truly climb into the mind of a killer like you can. And if we're going to catch Labyrinth, I need you on my team."

"Why does Labyrinth demand the attention of Global Alliance?" Dark asked.

Blair's eyes narrowed. He ran his tongue around his mouth, as if he'd bitten into something unpleasant and wanted to scrape it off his tongue immediately.

"Labyrinth is the *reason* I created Global Alliance."

"He only emerged last week."

"True," Blair said, "but I've been aware of his existence for quite some time. Think about that software you've grown so fond of—the program that collates disparate materials from the fat spurting stream of electronic information? That was my design. Genius is nothing more than the ability to put together two disparate pieces of information to create something new. An insight, a song, a revolution—it doesn't matter. My software is a crude approximation of the potential of human genius."

"You seem really proud."

"You've used it," Blair said. "In fact, if I'm not mistaken, you've come to rely on it. Anyway, as you know, the program seeks patterns and attempts to make sense of them. Well, I've been sensing rumblings for the past decade—just like meteorologists sense a superstorm is forming. Indications that someone like Labyrinth would appear. All the signs were there. So I spent my time assembling a team to deal with that threat once he emerged."

"So far he's killed a couple of people and uploaded some creepy shit onto YouTube."

Blair said, "You just think he's another serial killer, don't you? You don't see the larger battle being waged?"

Dark asked, "What happened in Dubai?"

chapter 17

DARK

Graysmith quickly briefed Dark on the riddle, the fish tank, and the gold watch. Everything the Dubai Police had gathered was silently uploaded to her own tablet, and on the flight she had digested and analyzed each piece of evidence as it appeared.

"Why didn't you tell me about this on the plane?" Dark asked.

Blair answered for her. "Frankly, if you had turned us down, we wouldn't want you getting in our way."

"You people are just bursting with trust, aren't you."

Dark knew that the parallels between this new package and the original Labyrinth case in the United States were unmistakable. You had the riddle hand-printed on company letterhead. You had the strange objects that didn't seem to fit any obvious pattern. What did a gold watch given to an oil executive have to do with the fish? Was it some kind of crude joke?

More important: Who was the intended victim?

Any oil executive working in 1948 would be either elderly or dead. Even if the executive was eighteen years of age at the time he was given the watch, he would be eighty years old by now. Was this "Labyrinth" threatening to kill a man who did not have much time left to live?

Because if this case followed the same pattern as the U.S. homicides, then when the timepiece stopped, a new murder victim would be revealed to the world.

"So, what do you make of it?" Blair asked. "Do you know the answer to the riddle?"

I CAN RUN, BUT NEVER WALK,
OFTEN A MURMUR, NEVER TALK,
I HAVE A BED BUT NEVER SLEEP,
I HAVE A MOUTH BUT NEVER EAT.
WHAT AM I?

"The answer," Dark said, "is a river, which can run, murmur, lies in a bed . . ."

"Exactly," Blair said.

"The riddles aren't exactly complex, are they?"

"You're right," Blair said. "They seem to be the first part of a message with a deeper meaning. With the attacks in Los Angeles last week, the riddle seemed to point to the murder method—the hanging, the shooting, the drowning. But there was no real revelation as to the who or why. The real meaning is hidden within the other items."

Dark nodded. "Right. The riddle isn't the point. They're solved easily enough. He wants us to look beyond them."

"So what do you make of the golden wristwatch?" Blair said. "Or the fish? What do they signify?"

"The watch tells us when," Dark said. "The alarm clock in L.A. went off just as Elizabeth and Loeb were being forced to kill each other. This is Labyrinth's way of giving us a deadline."

"How much time do we have left?" Graysmith asked.

Dark turned to face her. "You said one of the detectives in Dubai noticed that the watch seemed slow. Whenever it stops completely, that will be when he strikes again. I'd send a watchmaker to police headquarters immediately to give us his best guess. Someone like Labyrinth would have it timed to the exact second."

Blair smiled. "So this means you'll join us, Mr. Dark?"

"Let's call it a trial run. Get me to Dubai, and let's see if we can stop this maniac from killing somebody else."

"Fair enough," Blair said. "Wheels up in thirty minutes. The rest of the team is on their way to the plane."

Graysmith held out a hand. "Well, this is good-bye."

"This is it, huh? Moving on to your next assignment already?"

"I work freelance. I always have. Not really a team player, though I am extraordinarily good at helping build teams."

"What's your real name?"

Graysmith—or whoever was behind her face—smiled. "Maybe I'll tell you someday. If you're lucky."

"Right."

"And Steve, take care of that little girl of yours. She's special. Dads sometimes forget how much their daughters look up to them."

Dark tried to read her eyes. He couldn't tell if she was finally opening up to him, and speaking from personal experience—or if she was still on the job, and trying to plant a seed in his mind that could be exploited later. Didn't matter though. Dark reached out, took her hand, then pulled her close to him.

"I'll see you again," he said.

"Not if I see you first," Graysmith said.

[To enter the Labyrinth, please go to Level26.com and enter the code: oil]

chapter 18

LABYRINTH

I hang up the phone.

Now that wasn't too difficult at all.

In record time, Charles Murtha is reborn, rehabilitated, and ready for the next step.

I think about how he shrieked when he first heard my voice in his ear. Maybe he thought God was speaking to him? So-called captains of industry could be so easily spooked.

And true, my voice was distorted electronically. Which can sound frightening. But I needed him to take me seriously—and we've all been raised with the expectation that people who abduct other people speak to you in electronically distorted voices.

It's all about expectations.

So I focused on sounding as reassuring as possible. Hope is a powerful analgesic. If you have even an ounce of hope, you can survive virtually any experience, no matter how traumatic.

I told him not to worry, that people were coming to save him right now.

I told him, This really is out of your hands, so don't waste time focusing on that. What you *should* focus on is slowing down your breathing. There's not a lot of air down there. You'll use it all up.

Oh fuck . . . Oh God . . .

No.

No time for panic.

Instead, I told him to focus on the lesson.

It's not long before Charles Murtha, one of the richest oil executives in this region, has it right and can recite it from memory. He seems absurdly grateful to appreciate the chance to actually *do* something after hanging in that pipe for so long. Like so many executives he is eager to please, to prove his worth in some kind of arena, even one as dingy and desperate as this.

So before long he is saying it with true gusto, as if he believes the words coming out of his mouth.

Oh, from your lips to the world's ears, Charles.

I am glad Charles Murtha learned his lesson.

For soon we would be past the point of no return. Even if any member of local law enforcement were to figure out my riddle, there wouldn't be enough time to get a maintenance crew down to the bowels of the resort to free poor Mr. Charles Murtha before . . .

Well, I didn't want to tell him any of that. Especially considering what would be happening to his body.

He was pretty touchy as it was.

chapter 19

DARK

A burly driver raced Dark away from the abandoned movie palace and back to the airport, pausing only to flash his cell phone at a security checkpoint before being allowed to drive directly onto the tarmac. Seems that Blair really got off on those things, because he apparently passed them out like party favors.

There was no question as to which plane he'd be boarding. A Gulfstream was finishing up its fueling sequence. Dark stepped out of the car and saw another man approaching the stairway at the same time. His thin frame was wrapped in a dingy wool Irish Garda coat. Even though he had a youthful face, his skull was topped with unruly white hair, like a Q-tip that had been sent to the electric chair. The man slowed his pace when he saw Dark, and switched the duffel bag to the opposite hand.

"At long last, Steve Dark, in the flesh," the man said, extending his hand. "I'm Deckland O'Brian."

Dark nodded, shook the man's bony, rough hand.

"Hey, didn't you bring any luggage from L.A.?"

"I travel light."

"Not even a book for the flight? I can't go anywhere without a good read. Anyway, after you, my friend."

Dark ascended the stairs and stepped into the wildly expensive

Gulfstream jet. All luxury details, however, had been stripped away in favor of utility: workstations outfitted with touch-screen computers, racks of weapons and uniforms, and even a small forensics lab.

Standing in front of a weapons bay was a tall, broad man with a head that looked like it could be used as a battering ram. Instead of hair, an elaborate gothic tattoo ran over his bony pate and down the back of his neck, disappearing behind his flack jacket. He was assembling a Heckler & Koch MP5A3 with a tactical tri-rail.

"Dark, this is Hans Roeding. He speaks some English, but not much. Even if he did, he wouldn't say much at all."

Roeding nodded, then went back to what he was doing.

"That's just his way of saying, 'Charmed, I'm sure.'"

"Right," Dark said.

"Far more sociable, and able to speak in *many* tongues," O'Brian continued, "is the lovely Natasha Garcon."

As Garcon spun around in her chair to face them, Dark realized that O'Brian hadn't been joking. She was beautiful. Blue-gray eyes, lips that looked like they were forever on the verge of blowing you a kiss. Even with her hair pulled back in a no-nonsense ponytail and no trace of makeup, Garcon would step into any social situation and be the most stunning woman in the room.

"Are we ready to go, then? I'll inform the pilot and get us cleared." And with that, Garcon spun back around, placed a bud inside her left ear, then began to speak in crisp yet hurried French. She'd barely glanced at Dark, which struck him as a little unusual. Was he being dismissed as a member of this team even before he formally joined it?

O'Brian slapped his back, gestured to the workstation. "All yours, buddy. Make yourself at home. Next stop, the Middle East."

So this was Global Alliance.

The "best of the best."

How had Blair put it?

Manhunters of your caliber, and in some cases, even more seasoned.

And whose prey is much more fearsome than your garden-variety serial killer. . . .

These people, however, were not former cops. Their specialties lay elsewhere. They were also virtual ciphers—and for the past decade, had existed off the grid.

Before Dark had left for the airport, Blair had transmitted brief dossiers on each team member to Dark's smartphone. Deckland O'Brian was former IRA and a tech freak. On the surface, he appeared to be nothing more than a software engineer from one of the larger computer companies that had roared during the days of the Celtic Tiger. Beneath that cover, he was renowned as an expert on extracting pieces of electronic information from essentially anything with a memory chip, online or otherwise.

Hans Roeding was a former member of German Special Forces Command—Kommando Spezialkräfte, or KSK, for short. Top-of-the-line soldiers trained in insurgency, counterterrorism, black ops, and a host of other unofficial activities that never end up in the history books. Roeding was the best KSK had produced since the fall of the Berlin Wall, having led secret operations in Kosovo, Bosnia, Afghanistan, Pakistan, Iraq, China, and Libya.

So that meant the team had brains.

And muscle.

Natasha Garcon, meanwhile, was the face of Global Alliance. Not just in terms of beauty. According to her dossier, Garcon was a linguist beyond compare, a prodigy who was speaking a half-dozen languages by first grade and three dozen by high school. Beyond mere translation, she understood the culture and idioms of dozens of nations, as well as states within those nations. If there was a division of law enforcement, foreign government, or intelligence operation to be dealt with, Garcon was first on the scene, clearing the path for the others. Blair had also named her team leader for this mission.

Many years ago, Dark had more or less begged for a chance to join Special Circs. He wanted to be part of Tom Riggins's team more than he'd wanted anything else in the world . . . before he lost himself in it, and ended up losing everything he'd ever loved in the world.

As he sat down, strapped himself in, and looked around at this new "team," Dark couldn't help but wonder if he was about to repeat that mistake.

chapter 20

DARK

Dubai, United Arab Emirates

Commercial flight time from Paris to Dubai can be as swift as seven hours, depending on weather and airport conditions. The weather out of France was horrible, but still Blair's private Gulfstream made it in just under four. A waiting van whisked the team directly from the plane to Dubai Police HQ, where Natasha Garcon spoke to the department chief. Within minutes they were led directly to the evidence room, the fish tank, and the gold wristwatch.

While O'Brian and Roeding seemed transfixed by the creepy-looking fish, Dark put on rubber gloves and examined the watch. Like the sketch of Bethany Millar, this watch was most likely a stolen object of a personal nature. The meaning wasn't in the craftsmanship or the material; the important thing seemed to be that it was given as a gift, back in the 1940s, to an oil executive.

Dark noticed the second hand was moving slower, and slower, and slower, like a dying insect. Eventually, it would grind to a halt.

At which point Labyrinth would kill his next victim.

Blair had arranged for a retired watchmaker to be hastily flown in from nearby Abu Dhabi, and he examined the watch under an X-ray machine. The watch was indeed slowing down. And if his calculations were correct, there was one hour, maybe less, until it stopped completely.

Dark began to build the profile in his head. This was a pattern killer: two separate scenarios, two different parts of the world, but they still fit a pattern. Each time, Labyrinth had sent a riddle, a timepiece of some kind, and a stolen object. The timepiece told them how much time they had left to figure out the puzzle; but what did the riddle and the stolen object point to? The victim? Dark thought about the victims in Malibu. The actress and her producer boyfriend, completely unaware they shared a bloodline. The nude sketch was what had pointed to their identities. The who. But how did the riddle fit in?

The second hand, slowing down even more . . .

Labyrinth was saying:

I have all of the pieces. I'm so brilliant, I'll even share them with you—tip you off early. But I still think you won't be able to catch me, because I'm smarter than you all.

Dark knew that this arrogance would be Labyrinth's undoing. Even the most brilliant sociopaths can't keep up the cat-and-mouse game forever. Being caught is part of the thrill, in some sick way.

But how many victims would Labyrinth rack up before then?

chapter 21

DARK

The fish pissed off Deckland O'Brian.

Big-time. The Irishman hated not having the answer to something *immediately*. O'Brian plugged his tablet computer into the police Internet and started a mad search for the origins of this fish. Within minutes, he had an ichthyologist examining the specimen by Skype, and tentatively identifying it as a "tecopa pupfish." The strange thing was not that the fish was halfway around the world. The strange thing was that it existed at all. According to the ichthyologist, the United States Fish and Wildlife Service had declared it extinct thirty years prior—it was one of the first to be included on the then-new endangered species list. Yet here it was, swimming around the tank. The fish guy begged them for the chance to examine it in person, saying that he could be there the very next day, if they could just . . .

"Yeah, yeah," O'Brian said. "Thanks, buddy."

Extinct was a government term, nothing more. Just because a government labels something extinct doesn't mean it has absolutely, positively disappeared from the surface of the earth. There were black markets for exotic animals, and of course, O'Brian knew how to tap right in to their (allegedly secret) message boards.

"If Labyrinth purchased this little guy," O'Brian said, "somebody *else* had to own him first."

Sure. That made logical sense. Still, Dark thought it was looking in the wrong direction. They should be tracing the clues forward to the next victim, not back to something that the killer may have done months ago. Someone's life was on the line right now. But who?

The clues would tell them.

Maybe . . .

Dark said, "Tell us about this pupfish. Where does it come from?"

O'Brian nodded and tapped the screen in a frenzy.

"Huh. Riddle me this, now. Seems the pupfish were native to your home state. California." Then O'Brian began to sing, off-key: "I wish they all could be Cal-i-for-nia . . ."

Dark ignored him. The fish was from California—a literal transplant here. Just like American oil executives. The watch told them as much.

"Do we have a list of oil executives here in Dubai?" Dark asked.

Natasha shook her head. "Everyone at Intertrust has been accounted for. There's nobody missing. It's one of the first things I checked when we landed."

"What about the other companies?"

"Oooh yes!" Deckland O'Brian cried, then started tapping his screen furiously. "Good idea, Steve-O. I'm on it."

Which was when alarms sounded all throughout Dubai Police HQ.

Immediately Natasha Garcon darted into the fray and pulled aside a detective and hurriedly spoke to him in Arabic. The detective was clearly horrified, wearing a stunned look that told Dark the man had never experienced anything quite like this.

"What's happened?" Dark asked.

"They found a body at a resort on the other side of the city," Natasha said.

"Where in the resort?"

"Um . . . all over the place."

Deckland O'Brian looked up from his tablet. "I ran a search, and okay, let the records show that I'm calling this now. I'd bet a thousand quid the victim's name is going to be Charles Murtha."

AP (Middle East)

Breaking: Man found dead in luxury resort in Dubai.

chapter 22

DARK

On the other side of the city, the river turned to blood.

It was an artificial river in the middle of a luxury resort, built during Dubai's boom days just a few short years ago. Back then, simulacrum environments were all the rage—for example, ski resorts in the middle of the desert. Here, in this resort, you could sip cocktails by the artificial banks of a faux Amazon river, complete with animatronic wildlife and "authentic" natural sound.

When the blood started to flow, half-drunk guests assumed it was some sort of special effect, meant to commemorate a holiday, or perhaps even promote a new film. That is, until one underage guest saw a dismembered hand floating along the shoulders of the mighty river.

"What the hell . . ."

"OH MY GOD!"

"Is that . . ."

Other body parts soon followed, bobbing along in the foamy, crimson-tinged waters, and the police were quickly summoned.

Some guests had enough wits about them to snap a few photos with their smartphones and upload them to social networking sites. It didn't take very long for the Internet to make the connection.

Holy shit! Just heard this "Labyrinth" nut case sent a riddle to Dubai!

2 minutes ago

Did he kill someone famous? #labyrinth

2 minutes ago

Seriously, what's this guy's deal? Is he flying around the world, using up frequent flyer miles, killing people 4 fun?

1 minute ago

Hope he visits my ex-husband in Miami #labyrinth

1 minute ago

The news was already trending around the world (#labyrinth) by the time Dark and the rest of the team—Global Alliance—arrived at the resort. O'Brian was tracking it from his cell phone.

"I've never seen a hashtag so active," he said excitedly. "People are really jumping on this thing."

Dark said, "He's probably watching. Getting off on the attention, the publicity. Is there any way of tracking him through the social network?"

"Are you kidding?" O'Brian asked. "There are going to be millions of people following this stuff."

"What about tracing it backward? Find out who first started talking about Dubai?"

"Easy enough, but what would that prove?"

"I think he's the one giving these things a push," Dark said. "He's spreading the word like a proud parent."

Natasha said, "Tweet him later. We're almost at the scene."

The team divided according to their natural abilities. Deckland O'Brian hit the resort's computer and surveillance network while Natasha Garcon liaised with the resort owners to open up everything else. Hans Roeding went on a hunt through the resort, in case Labyrinth was still nearby. Steve Dark, of course—the only actual cop among them—joined the forensics team already on-site.

Dark found the hand in a little artificial eddy near a riverside bar. Borrowing an ice bucket and plastic bag, Dark scooped up the appendage and contained it. He had no mobile kit, but he had everything he needed (and more) back in the Gulfstream.

Though he had no doubt that this was the body of oil executive Charles Murtha—who'd called out sick four days ago, according to Garcon. Following O'Brian's lead, she'd contacted his company as they raced across town and spoke to Murtha's executive assistant. She presumed he was off on a little boozing/drug-filled desert holiday, pressures of the job and all of that.

At some point, however, "Labyrinth"—or one of his associates—had abducted Murtha and kept him alive until this moment, when the gold watch ran out of tension, and the hands stopped moving.

Hands, like the one in Dark's borrowed ice bucket.

The management had turned off the artificial river. Dark jumped in and splashed up the path to its source. Garcon helped him find a maintenance crew who would open up the underground network of pipes that supplied the water. Halfway up a backup supply pipe, Dark found the snapped chains—and not much else. But this was clearly where Murtha had been bound, waiting for thousands of pounds of rushing water to come pouring down the pipe, blasting him apart in one messy gush. And at the same time, power-washing all forensic evidence from the pipe itself.

Dark knew this because O'Brian yelled for everyone to report to his tablet computer immediately.

Labyrinth had uploaded his next video.

The executive is suspended in the tunnel. He says, "My name is . . ." Hesitates. He's scared out of his mind. "My name is Charles Murtha and the Earth we live on is a gift! A gift to its inhabitants! And in return we rape Mother Earth! We take what was given to us and we burn it and soil it and choke it! But no more! Earth was here long before us and we will honor and respect that!"

Then came the water, striking with such force that the on-screen image jumped as the wave blasted into the camera. But if you were paying attention, just a second before the water struck and the screen turned to white foam, you could literally see Charles Murtha, oil executive, being blasted apart . . .

And finally a title card:

I WILL

HELP YOU

OUT OF THE

LABYRINTH

THE WORLD

IS NOT

BEYOND SAVING

Did you see that? Freeze it 2:43 and you can see this fucken guy EXPLODE

Dollarhyde28 19 seconds ago

The guy has a point. Fuck the greedy oil companies

Felding11 1 minute ago

Hey, FosterK777, what makes this different from showing innocent civillions getting shot 2 hell by U.S. army hellacopters?

2Buzz2 2 minutes ago

Can't believe this is still up, and that we're all watching this. I mean, this is video footage of a man dying!

FosterK777 3 minutes ago

You're not the real guy

Dazzaland101010 5 minutes ago

and the best is yet 2 come

enterthelabyrinth 6 minutes ago

chapter 23

Brussels, Belgium

The name on the vibrating cell phone was TREY, and even though MEP Alain Pantin was in the middle of seven different projects and two live conference calls in his cramped office near Leopold Park, he plucked the cell from his desk and held it to his ear.

"Have you been following the news?" Trey asked.

"Which news?" Pantin asked, squinting, trying to recall the major headlines of the past few hours. The revolution in the Middle East? The collapse of health care in the West? The political sex scandal of the hour?

"The *Labyrinth* news."

At times, Trey could be infuriatingly cryptic. Out of seemingly nowhere, he'd reference box-office tallies, or the impurity of water sources in the Middle East, or some other bit of global trivia. But Pantin had learned that when the man was interested in something, it was very much worth being interested in it, too.

"Labyrinth—you mean the killer who's been leaving riddles?" Pantin asked.

"Oh, there's much more to it than that. Have someone on your team put together a summary. No, better yet, I'll have something sent over. It's been fascinating me, this thing. The implications could be huge."

Pantin didn't know what that meant. But then again, his mind could never operate with the speed and precision of Trey's. The two had met at a dinner party in Spain three years ago, and it was Trey who, after just a brief but intense conversation, convinced Pantin that he should consider running for the European Parliament. Pantin politely brushed it off with a joke, then spent the entire night staring at the hotel room ceiling, realizing that yes, this was what his unorthodox career choices had meant him to do. Amazing. It took Trey just minutes and some insightful questions to draw that out of him; Pantin counted it as one of the most profound moments of his life.

The next morning Pantin called Trey and asked if he'd be interested in joining his campaign team. Trey politely demurred, saying he wouldn't be able to commit, but he'd willingly give counsel and advice where he could. Pantin was elected by a wide margin, and Trey was the behind-the-scenes man who'd helped him win—as well as become a leading voice in Europarl.

Pantin was up for reelection, so of course he could indulge Trey his quirks now and then.

"I heard he struck again," Pantin said. "Somewhere in the Middle East?"

"The murders are interesting in their savage and grotesque ways. But if you look past the Grand Guignol and listen to his message, I think you've got someone who is truly seeking to engage with the world on a level we've never seen before."

"Engage?"

"He's a killer who's not in it for the killing. He's trying to send a message to the world. And what this Labyrinth individual needs is someone to reply to him, from the world stage."

"Sure. Interpol," Pantin said.

"I was thinking you."

"What . . . *me?*"

"This is exactly what you need at this point in your career."

As a new Belgian member of the European Parliament, Pantin was viewed as a comer with a promising future. Nobody knew that Trey was quietly helping his young protégé pursue that full-time. Pantin didn't know what Trey did full-time; there were rumors he used to be part of British intelligence, but nothing solid. Trey repeatedly said he would never run for office himself; he liked the backstage wrangling way too much. Being the man behind the men.

"Isn't that playing in the gutter?" Pantin asked. "The man's clearly a psychopath. Seems strange to jump into the conversation, especially since he's not even operating anywhere near Europe . . ."

"Forget the crimes and think about his message."

"Which is?"

"Based on his attacks on the entertainment and oil industries," Trey said, "I'd venture that he has a problem with selfishness and greed. Sounds like the campaign promises of a certain young Europarl member I know."

"Surely you're not suggesting I align myself with a madman."

"No. You condemn, and then seize control of the conversation. This Labyrinth may be psychotic, but his rage is fueled by real concerns. *Your* concerns, actually. This is a way to make your agenda heard in a fairly spectacular way."

Pantin paused. The advice seemed to run counter to everything Trey had taught him.

"I don't know, Trey."

"You don't have to know. I agree, this is a risky and bold play. So all I'm suggesting is that you start paying attention to Labyrinth seriously. Read all you can. Think about his message. Sometimes a revolution begins from the act of a single individual. Look at Tunisia, and that poor son of a bitch who set himself on fire. You could call him a madman, but he had a message, too, and the message went viral. This Labyrinth? I don't think he's going to stop anytime soon, and the world will need someone to respond. Turn a positive out of the negative. I think it should be you."

"Thanks, Trey. You've given me a lot to think about."

"I'll send over a clip file within the hour."

Pantin hung up the phone and politely excused himself from the two conference calls in progress and stared out at the park, visible through his office window. As usual, Trey's advice was the kind that shocked initially, but needed time to worm its way down into his brain.

When, suddenly, the advice would make perfect sense. People liked a leader who could project an air of calm and rationality into the global conversation.

Pantin smiled, despite himself.

Come on, Labyrinth.

Let's see what you've got.

New York Times

Breaking: Is Labyrinth posting on social media?

AP News

Breaking: Texas oil executive assaulted by pack of teenagers quoting "Labyrinth" speech.

Guardian

Breaking: Green organizations call for boycott of IPC gasoline products pending investigation into "Labyrinth" charges.

chapter 24

DARK

Dubai, United Arab Emirates

Dark had been taunted before. Sqweegel—his longtime nemesis, and a so-called forensic-proof killer—had been dispatched over five years ago, but was still partly alive in a secret corner of Dark's mind. Sqweegel had fixated on Steve Dark himself, forcing Dark out of his cocoon, leading him around the country on a blood-soaked trail of savagery and leaving fresh corpses in his wake until a final showdown. A confrontation that took *everything* from Dark. So if there was one thing Dark had grown to loathe, it was the taunts from killers who thought they were stronger, faster, smarter than the cops who chased them.

But Dark had Labyrinth's game now

The riddle gave the *method* of murder. With the actress and the producer, it had been literal: shot, hung, drowned, just as in the riddle. With the oil executive, he had been destroyed by an artificial river.

The artifact pointed to *who*. The nude sketch. The extinct fish from California.

And finally, the timepiece revealed *when*. But it also lent insight to the who and the method. Everything was symbolic. Everything carefully thought out in advance.

Taunting them.

But that, Dark realized, would work to his advantage. Labyrinth's inflexibility was his vulnerability. He was like a madman setting up an overly elaborate Rube Goldberg–style trap. All Dark had to do was remove one piece in advance, and watch it come crashing down around him. It was familiar, in a sick way. If Dark had been sharper, he could have sensed the pattern with Sqweegel a lot earlier. This felt like karma handing him a cosmic do-over.

Still, that didn't explain Blair's—and Global Alliance's—interest in this case.

"I want to talk to Blair," Dark told Natasha Garcon.

"You've got a phone."

"A number would be great."

Natasha sighed. She'd spent the past few hours trying to coax every possible second of surveillance footage from the resort owners, and was weary from the effort. The fact that they obviously had trouble dealing with a *woman* didn't help, either. She made a big show of pulling her cell phone out of her pocket, thumbing through her contacts, pressing the screen, then handing the phone to Dark.

"Thanks," he said, then held the phone to his ear. Blair answered after the first ring.

"What's the latest, Natasha?"

Dark didn't bother with an explanation. Instead he asked, "Something's bugging me."

"Ah, Dark," Blair said. "What is it?"

"From all that you've told me, Global Alliance operates in the shadow world, neutralizing threats before they surface. This has already surfaced. The whole world is beginning to talk about this. What do we bring to the table that no other law enforcement agency isn't already doing? I feel like we're batting cleanup here."

"What do you suggest?"

"Focus our efforts on thinking a step ahead. Forget Dubai for now. It's over, and he's received the impact he wanted. We've lost this round of his game. Let's start thinking about this like chess, and outthink his next move."

There was silence on the line, and for a moment, Dark suspected that he may have pushed back too hard.

But instead Blair told him,

"You're right. Let me talk to Natasha."

chapter 25

LABYRINTH

Now the world is finally rousing from its slumber and starting to pay attention.

I read it all, the

headlines

Tweets

status updates

push notifications

blog posts

comments

And yes, people are starting to pay attention.

Make one bold statement, they can still write you off as an eccentric—the act could be a one-off. The media said as much. People understood, and could deal with, aberrations. Even shock wears off. Consider the lessons of 9/11. Normalcy returns quickly. People want to be normal. They crave it, because it is safe and reassuring.

To truly make a global change you have to follow it up with another statement.

One that shows the depth of your message.

One that shows you are serious.

This is the way you save the world.

One shock at a time.

dark revelations

Not long after landing in Johannesburg I take a taxi to my rented workstation in a nondescript skyscraper and begin preparing my next gift. They know me here. They smile and nod because I am polite and nice and handsome and well-groomed and not in their presence long enough to make any other kind of impression. They may have seen me once, somewhere, on TV perhaps. . . . But they don't comment or gawk—that would be rude.

They say,

Hello.

And make a comment about the weather or inquire about my flight. So I humor them and say,

Did you know they charge for pillows now? Isn't that the craziest thing? I like comfort just like the next guy, but for nine euro I'll stay a little uncomfortable.

They laugh and smile along with me, even though what I am saying isn't very funny.

I look at them and continue,

I hope you'll forgive the wrinkles in my jacket. Turns out it works just as well as a pillow—of course, you have to remember to take the pens out of your pocket!

More laughs, more enthusiastic now, because that's how they're trained.

I could draw them into a corner and say a few words and within an hour they'd be slicing their own throats and drawing pentagrams on the walls with their own blood.

Just by talking to them.

But no.

There is another package to prepare.

I take the elevator upstairs to my private office where my guest is already waiting for me.

All told this is relatively easy; I had the materials shipped here months ago through a series of cutouts and drop boxes, none of it traceable back to me.

Even if someone were clever enough to trace the movements of the boxes, seizing and opening them would reveal essentially meaningless objects:

A book.

A sculpted piece of stone.

But if you understood the game . . .

It would mean everything.

And soon they will.

chapter 26

DARK

Airspace over Europe

By the time the team was flown back to France, everyone was exhausted. For all of that effort, the suspect known as Labyrinth had left no fingerprint, digital or otherwise. No equipment, no gear, no reservations, no shipping orders, no human contact whatsoever. It was as if a ghost had sent the tank of fish and the gold watch and scrawled the riddle on company letterhead.

Now it was time to head back to the real Global Alliance headquarters to plot their counterattack.

"I just realized," Dark said, "that I have no idea where we're going. Where is the Global Alliance HQ?"

O'Brian smirked. "He didn't tell you about it? Oh, you're going to love it."

Paris, France

Almost two hundred years ago, Paris began pulling the limestone from beneath its feet to construct its magnificent buildings. What remained were a series of underground quarries that were later put to use by mushroom fighters, French resistance fighters, Nazi invaders, and more recently—urban explorers who routinely broke into the web of tunnels and pits for parties or just the sheer thrill of it. The French made it illegal to wander through this tunnel back in the 1950s, but that didn't stop the *cataphiles*.

It also didn't stop Damien Blair when it came time to choose a headquarters for his burgeoning Global Alliance.

Access to GA HQ was difficult unless you were Blair or a member of his team. Armed guards staked out the three entrances: a hidden elevator in a skyscraper above, a subterranean loading dock on a secret level of a parking garage (large enough to accommodate vehicles)—and, as an emergency failsafe, a sewage junction a few blocks away. Even if you were to blast your way past the armed guards—many of them as skilled at combat as Hans Roeding, since he'd trained them—the only way to access the tunnels was through a complex series of biometric devices. And once again, unless you were Blair or one of his handpicked team members, the shape of your iris and the curve of your earlobes and the whorl of the skin on your nose and the structure of the veins on the backs of your hands would give you away. Lockdown. Alarms. Entrapment. After that, you would need an extremely good lawyer.

The main complex was six stories beneath street level, which included a briefing room, weapons room, state-of-the-art forensics laboratory, library, gym, and quarters for the team members.

As the newest member, Dark had been given a spartan room along with some basics: clothes (his size, and a perfect fit), a grooming kit, a new smartphone, tablet computer. Blair told him that he could order whatever he needed on the tablet computer; the goods would be delivered to the guards by the loading dock within six hours. If he needed something in a rush, simply mark it as urgent and it would arrive by courier within thirty minutes. *Just like pizza*, Dark thought.

But what Dark wanted most was to call his daughter, Sibby, hear her voice. It was three A.M. at home, however. He couldn't wake her on a school day.

So instead he crawled into the stiff double bed he'd been given and told himself it would be good to grab a few hours' sleep, at the very least. Dark hadn't slept in days, now that he thought about it. Not since hearing about the first Labyrinth package.

And he could not sleep, now, either.

His brain refused to turn off.

Not until he figured out the killer's next move.

When Dark's mind was fixed on a case, there was little else he could do. It was almost as if he went into a fugue state, the movie theater inside his mind playing flashes of the crime scenes *(the bloody river, the alarm clock, the gold watch, the blown-out interrogation room, the finger, the sketch of Bethany Millar)* on an endless loop while the logical part of his mind tried to piece them together. Some sick fuck out there had obsessed over these same objects. . . .

So where had his mind gone next?

What was Labyrinth obsessing over now?

Before the pieces came together, however, the killer struck again.

AP News

Breaking: Reports of a new Labyrinth riddle in South Africa.

Global Alliance gathered in the conference room, everyone bleary-eyed except for Dark, who hadn't been asleep anyway.

"We headed to South Africa, then?" O'Brian asked.

Blair shook his head. "We don't go anywhere until there's confirmation."

O'Brian chased down the rumor online, trying to find its origin. They all agreed that it was more than possible Labyrinth himself was starting the rumors, fanning the flames before actually delivering his package. Meanwhile, Hans Roeding prepared the plane and loaded his weapons. The man was a natural born hunter who smelled blood in the air. Natasha monitored the South African media closely, looking for any suspicious thefts or missing persons reports that could give them an early lead.

Dark, meanwhile, brooded in his unlit room, attempting to fit the pieces together. From Los Angeles to Dubai to South Africa—what was the pattern? He couldn't help but feel like they were being nudged to jump through another hoop.

He'd dealt with killers who used geography as a chessboard, and patterned their crimes from a God's-eye point of view.

Was Labyrinth doing the same?

No . . . he'd be using a maze.

With himself at the center, like the Minotaur of ancient myth. All roads would lead to him. He would delight in seeing everyone else stumble around the musty corridors lost, unable to see the pattern he could so clearly discern. . . .

Within hours, the rumor was revealed to be real. A new Labyrinth riddle, written in Afrikaans, had been delivered to a police station in one of the most crime-ridden neighborhoods in Johannesburg.

Blair stood behind Natasha as she took notes from the South African Broadcasting Corporation's news report while waiting for her call to her police contact to be patched through. Two objects were said to have been included with the riddle, but government officials were refusing to detail them until further investigation.

"I've got it," Natasha said, after a short conversation with her liaison. She typed quickly and put the riddle on the first of three huge flat screens mounted on the conference room wall:

I'M THE PART OF THE BIRD THAT'S NOT IN THE SKY.
I CAN SWIM IN THE OCEAN AND YET REMAIN DRY.
WHAT AM I?

LABYRINTH

"What were the objects?" Blair asked.

"The police are sending us digital images, and they're downloading right now," Natasha said, "but it appears to be a book and a sundial."

"What kind of book?"

"Early edition of a British school primer. At least a hundred years old, in mint condition. An old-timer there says it was one of the first to be distributed under British rule. They're analyzing it for hidden messages, explosives, toxic substances . . . everything."

"The objects aren't the murder weapons," Dark said. "They're wasting their time."

Everyone in the room turned to look. Dark stood in the doorway, eyes transfixed on the three screens as the images on the second and third began to appear.

Blair said, "We know that—but they're playing it safe, considering what happened in L.A."

The image on the second screen began to materialize: the sundial.

"Can you sharpen the resolution?"

Wordlessly, Natasha tapped the touch pad and zoomed in closer on the image.

"What's that?" she asked. "Is that . . . blood?"

"Tell the South African police to bring it outside," Dark said. "That's the only way we're going to know how much time we have left."

"He really likes to change up his timepieces," said O'Brian. "Gold watches, sundials . . ."

"He wants us to know he's thought of everything," Dark said. "And that he's adaptable. Take away his tech, and he can still get at us, with something as primitive as a printed book and the oldest timepiece in the world."

Natasha relayed the message to the South African police. Sundials depend on global positioning—adding minutes here and there, depending on your location. But soon word came back:

They had approximately ten hours left before Labyrinth struck again.

chapter 27

DARK

Blair wasted no time springing his team into action.

"You'll be headed to South Africa immediately. According to Dark, we've got ten hours; the flight will take half that time. Local authorities will be uploading a complete set of photos and 3-D imaging of the contents of the latest package. In flight you can analyze those contents so that when you land, you'll be ready to pounce. He's daring us to catch him. So let's oblige him."

"It's a mistake," Dark said.

Blair blinked. "Excuse me?"

The three other team members stared at Dark. Apparently they were not used to hearing someone question the powerful and almighty Blair. But Dark didn't care. He'd spent the past few sad years of his Special Circs career following someone else's orders instead of his gut.

"A mistake," Dark repeated. "Labyrinth sets the cheese, and we all go scurrying after it like mice. Is that how we're supposed to catch this guy? By following his little maze, just the way he's set it up?"

Blair smiled ruefully. "He's testing us. He wants to see if we can operate on his intellectual level. The only way to catch Labyrinth is to play his games and then outthink him before the deadline passes. He thinks he's smarter than us, and I know he's wrong."

"Here's what bothers me," Dark said. "Can it be coincidence that he's given us *just enough* time to reach the scene and watch another person die?"

"You make it sound like this is personal. Labyrinth has no reason to know of our existence. For all he's aware, we were ordinary outside investigators, called in to assist the Dubai Police. We operate in secret."

"I have a feeling he knows," Dark said. "A sick fuck like this guy will be paying very careful attention to who follows him. That's what the whole game is about."

O'Brian laughed. "So . . . what, Dark? What's your answer? We just let this monster kill someone else? We don't even try? Is that your solution?"

"No," Dark said. "We focus on the next package. The one he hasn't sent yet."

Natasha's eyes brightened. "Have you picked up a pattern? Something we're missing?"

Everyone turned to look at Dark and waited expectantly.

"No. Not yet."

Blair stepped forward. "You know the answer to the riddle, don't you?"

Dark replied, "Yeah, a shadow."

Blair says: "So you have the pieces. Why not work with what we were given?"

"For that very reason," Dark said. "We were given it. Spoon-fed. It's not this riddle I'm concerned with. It's the *next one* that interests me. He's already planned this fucking thing so far out in advance, if we stick to the riddles at hand we'll always be chasing behind. The items he'd sent had to have been stolen or purchased long in advance, and there's no reason to think that he's not thinking ten or twelve moves deep at this point."

Blair strolled the room, seeming to think it over.

"Fair enough. O'Brian, I want you and Roeding to lead the investigation in South Africa. Dark, you and Garcon stay here and game out Labyrinth's next move. Let's see if there's anything to Dark's theory. At the same time, I want you both working on the current package, and share everything with O'Brian and Roeding. Understood?"

The team nodded and split up. As Dark made his way to the door, he found Natasha blocking his path.

"I hope you know what the fuck you're doing."

chapter 28

LABYRINTH

The cheerful assistant stops Labyrinth in the hallway, touches his arm as she asks,

Can I help you?

In that lovely South African accent.

Labyrinth says,

Why, yes, you *can* help me.

Labyrinth has a face that people trust, as well as a demeanor that disarms them. Which was why the assistant doesn't even flinch as he reaches into the breast pocket of his suit jacket and removes a sealed plastic bag containing a human finger. Her mouth opens slightly as he tells her,

My name is Labyrinth, and I want to confess.

Oh look at her.

She knows the name. She's read the news stories. She's watched the footage on cable news. She's media-savvy. She knows that even if this man is not the real Labyrinth, then he is most likely some nutter and that might be just as bad.

Not so eager to be *helpful* now are you?

Eyes

Mouth

Muscles

Tits

Cunt

All tense.

Come on, keep breathing, young thing, you can do it, it's not like it's *your* finger in the bag.

And it's not her finger, of course.

If you were to take a fingerprint from the severed digit, a subsequent fingerprint analysis would reveal that this ring finger used to be attached to the hand that used to be attached to the rest of one Mr. Charles Murtha.

Labyrinth tells her,

Let's go talk to your boss.

chapter 29

Brussels, Belgium

Alain Pantin was known for being good with reporters. Trey had given him a set of tips that had served him well since his first campaign: Answer only what you want, no matter the question. Make sure you insert your viewpoint at least three times, no matter the question. Smile, no matter the question.

With the Labyrinth case, a slightly different strategy was necessary: Say something a little shocking . . . then insert your viewpoint.

Trey contacted (anonymously, of course) an American reporter named Johnny Knack and hinted that some influential European politicians had a surprising take on the case. Knack had asked for a name; Trey quietly mentioned Alain Pantin.

Pantin had been briefed on Knack's background—the reporter had been involved in a case involving a pair of serial killers, and was currently writing a book about it. So it was important to appear to be anti-Labyrinth, of course, while at the same time changing the focus to the man's message.

Pantin thought he did a good job.

That is, until he read the story.

[To enter the Labyrinth, please go to Level26.com and enter the code: politics]

TheSlab.com

Alain Pantin, European Parliament Member, says, "Labyrinth has the right idea."

Alain Pantin, a young rising star in the European Parliament, says that the postal-happy international killer/terrorist calling himself "Labyrinth" has the right idea.

Well, not in so many words. But you get the idea that he's not spilling any tears over the death of Charles Murtha.

"America can't treat the rest of the world like its personal sandbox," said Pantin, known in Brussels for his tireless work ethic—as well as his provocative statements. "Sooner or later, you're going to piss off the wrong person."

Pantin tried to qualify his statements, of course, by expressing sadness at the death of Murtha. "No one deserves to die like that—not the greatest or the least of us," he said. "I prefer to think we can work things out with peaceful discussion. But this individual, whoever he is, seems to think we've exhausted peace options. And I can't disagree with him in the current climate."

Last year Pantin applauded the release of classified intelligence documents, even going so far as to donate money to hosting Websites and offering whistleblowers safe haven.

But an international leader lending support to a cop-killer?

Well, it wouldn't be the first time.

"Knack destroyed me."

"No," Trey said, "he did his job. In exactly the way I thought he would."

"You'll need to explain that to me. Because last I checked, my inbox was flooded with outraged people calling for my resignation."

"They can outrage all they want. You've just earned yourself a reputation as an independent thinker, a man not afraid to express the opinions on the outliers of the conversation. Forget what's being written about in the mainstream press. Look at the reactions from ordinary citizens, all around the world."

Pantin knew what he was talking about. The Labyrinth case, it seemed, had sparked parallel global conversations. On the surface, it was all about condemning his acts of terrorism and calling for his immediate capture. There was the usual hand-wringing and sensationalist TV news pieces that followed in the wake of killers like Zodiac, the Unabomber, and even Sqweegel.

But beneath that conversation was another—a bigger, secret groundswell of support. You saw it on the Twitter feeds and Facebook status updates and YouTube comments on the alleged "Labyrinth" videos.

They liked what Labyrinth was doing.

Who he targeted, and *why.*

He was providing secret-wish fulfillment for the thousands—probably millions—of people who weren't in positions of power, who didn't have the opportunity to speak into a microphone, who didn't have a platform.

"In other words," Pantin said, "you're saying I'm the first to speak aloud what everyone else is thinking."

"I knew you'd come around to it. And the support you're about to receive is going to be huge. People will remember your name, and pay attention to what you're saying. Even if they don't admit to it at first."

Trey's genius was that he could show you the way while convincing you that you would have found it on your own, given the right nudge.

"So what should I do next?"

"Take every interview request you can, condemn the killer but stress the importance of giving voice to his grievances."

"And?"

"Pay attention to South Africa, because I believe our friend is about to surprise us again."

chapter 30

DARK

After Blair left, a team of guards escorted O'Brian and Roeding back to the jet. Natasha set up shop at the workstation—coffee, Turkish cigarettes, mint pastilles to mask the smoke-tinged breath—and began to download the files from the South African police. Everyone so, so busy. Meanwhile, Dark strode off to his quarters. "These will be ready in just a moment," Natasha called after him, but Dark seemed to ignore her. In turn, Natasha ignored him and kept at it, popping a mint pastille every minute or so. When Dark returned to the workstation he was wearing a leather jacket—something he'd ordered, just to see if Blair was true to his word. Blair had not been kidding. The tailored jacket had arrived within the hour.

"Are you cold?" Natasha asked.

"Not particularly," Dark said.

"Come here and take a look at these scans of the school primer," Natasha said. "The detail and print quality is amazing for a hundred-year-old book. . . ."

"That's fantastic. Really, top-shelf work. Keep me posted," Dark said before turning to leave the room.

"Wait—where are you going?"

"To stop Labyrinth."

Natasha stared at him for a moment, uncomprehending. "Isn't that what we're supposed to be doing here?"

"I have a feeling I know where he's going to strike next," Dark said.

"Yes. Johannesburg. We all know that."

"No. I mean after this one. He's got the next threat planned out already—you know that, right? He's methodical. He's been working on this for years."

"I believe you," Natasha said flatly. "He's got something lined up after Johannesburg, no doubt about it. So where would that be?"

"I'll let you know when I have him in custody."

"You can't be serious."

"You can join me, if you like. I'll buy another ticket on our way to the airport."

"That isn't how it works," Natasha said. "You're not a lone wolf anymore. You're part of a team. If you leave without Blair's approval, you're gone."

Dark said, "And that would totally ruin my day."

While Blair's resources were impressive, Dark knew that money or planes or a strike team weren't going to catch this monster. Dark needed to do it the way he'd always done: by tuning in to the freak's wavelength and following his gut. If he had to run every instinct or decision past Damien Blair, then he might as well be back at Special Circs, under the fat thumb of Norman Wycoff. The team didn't matter. For Dark, it was all about catching Labyrinth. Blair could scold him later.

"So where do you think he's going to be?" Natasha asked.

"Look, it's kind of a crazy hunch, but it's feeling right, the more I turn it over in my head."

"Are you going to make me guess, or tell me?"

"New York City."

"Why do you think he's going back to America?"

"Because of the riddles. I have a feeling they don't simply point to the current threat—he's including a little preview of the next one, too. Remember the first riddle? About a photographer, hanging her husband out to dry? That referred to the actress and her producer, but it was a nod to the oil executive, too. A husband, one Charles Murtha, literally hung out to dry."

"It's a stretch," Natasha said. "What about the second riddle?"

I CAN RUN, BUT NEVER WALK,
OFTEN A MURMUR, NEVER TALK,
I HAVE A BED BUT NEVER SLEEP,
I HAVE A MOUTH BUT NEVER EAT.
WHAT AM I?

"The literal answer?" Dark asked. "A river. But I think it's also referring to the victim. Someone who also fits that description. Maybe even a flip side of it. Someone who deserves to be punished for talking too much. Or eating too much. Or maybe falling asleep at the wheel. I have a feeling it's someone prominent. So far Labyrinth has targeted celebrities and symbols of particular industries."

"Did you share this stroke of genius with Roeding or O'Brian?"

"You can tell them on the way to the airport," Dark said. "Though I'm not sure it'll do any good. I meant what I told Blair. He's toying with us, giving us just enough time to jump through his little fucking hoops and . . . oops, sorry, play again. The only way to beat this motherfucker is to jump ahead of him."

"You may be right. So how do you get New York from the third riddle?"

I'M THE PART OF THE BIRD THAT'S NOT IN THE SKY.
I CAN SWIM IN THE OCEAN AND YET REMAIN DRY.
WHAT AM I?

"I'll tell you if I'm right," Dark said.

Natasha, after a moment's hesitation, snapped shut the laptop, wrapped the power cord around its body, and followed Dark outside to a private car already waiting.

"If you're wrong, I'll put a bullet in you myself," Natasha said as the car raced to the airport.

TRANSCRIPT: THE JANE TALBOT SHOW

TALBOT

Hello, my friends. If you don't see the familiar Jane Talbot Show set, don't worry—it's not your cable signal. [Smiles] I'm joining you from a remote studio location, a location known only to me, for reasons that will be clear in just a few moments. As you know, for many years, individuals accused of crimes have appeared on my show to surrender in person. They've feared mistreatment from the police, and often with good reason. Well, today we have another individual accused of the most serious crime imaginable—not here in Johannesburg, but as far away as Los Angeles in America and Dubai in the Middle East.

MONTAGE: Cable news footage from the "Labyrinth" murders—Malibu, Dubai.

TALBOT

He calls himself Labyrinth, and he says that he's a force of good in the world, not evil.

MONTAGE: Police still—items from Labyrinth's packages.

TALBOT

And today, in a worldwide exclusive, Labyrinth is here, live, in the very next studio, ready to explain his actions of the past week.

CUT TO: "Labyrinth," draped in shadow, in a darkened studio, waiting.

TALBOT

I want you to know, home audience, that we did not come to this decision lightly. We do not harbor criminals; we merely want to facilitate a surrender. And the man calling himself Labyrinth insists that he will give up after this broadcast. But first, he wants a forum to air his views. [Pause] Labyrinth, we are granting your request.

LABYRINTH

Thank you for having me, Ms. Talbot. I'm a fan of the show.

TALBOT

Why are you doing this?

LABYRINTH

Why do *you* do this?

TALBOT

You mean this show?

LABYRINTH

Yes.

TALBOT

I try to be a force of good in the world. To show that one person's good deeds can have a larger impact.

LABYRINTH

And that's what I love about you, and your show. That's it exactly. I am attempting to do the same thing.

TALBOT

But you're . . . accused of *killing people*. No matter the justification, murder is wrong. We must believe that, or we descend into savagery.

LABYRINTH

I disagree, naturally, and believe that bold actions are the only way to produce bold change. But I can appreciate your position, so let me make a deal with you. I'll stop killing. In honor of you and your show. Perhaps I'll spread my message without bloodshed—thanks to your generosity.

TALBOT

Let me make sure I'm understanding you. You're willing to stop killing, and surrender yourself on this program?

LABYRINTH

Oh. . . . [Chuckles] I didn't say anything about surrender.

TALBOT

But I don't understand. I'm offering you a forum to explain yourself to millions of viewers around the world.

LABYRINTH

Millions, Ms. Talbot? Really? Seems you're inflating your reach just a touch.

TALBOT

Let's get back to you, Labyrinth.

LABYRINTH

In a moment. I'm fascinated by you, actually. All of the work you do. Especially for children. You're known for it internationally, aren't you?

TALBOT

My viewers would much rather hear about you, and your mission.

LABYRINTH

You're really keen on helping schools, aren't you? Especially here in South Africa. Such a worthy cause.

TALBOT

Yes, I would agree. But again, we're not here to—

LABYRINTH

I've spent a lot of time looking at your process. Specifically, how you help these schools. It is a fascinating model—one I briefly considered adopting myself. See, what you do, and what the viewers at home may not know, is that you'll do a show on a struggling school, right here in Johannesburg, perhaps. And you will solicit contributions from major corporations—*shame them*, really, into donating computers and books and other educational supplies.

And you'll skim just enough cash off the top to not quite do the job.

TALBOT

I'm sorry. We're done.

LABYRINTH

If you or any members of your production team touches a single fucking button, the bomb under your chair will fucking explode. You will die on live TV, Ms. Talbot. *Is that what you want, you vile cunt?*

TALBOT

W-w-what? You did . . . what?

LABYRINTH

You graciously allowed me to inspect the studio before I agreed to this interview. While doing so, I left a little present under your chair. Surprised no one noticed it.

TALBOT

James, kill the feed now.

LABYRINTH

Kill the feed, James, you kill your boss.

TALBOT

Don't do this. Please don't do this. You're making a big mistake.

LABYRINTH

I could have said the same to you. Don't do this, Jane. Don't pretend to help children while keeping them struggling the whole time, just because it will help your ratings, help you reach those millions of viewers you so covet.

TALBOT

No, I don't—

LABYRINTH

Don't you fucking lie to your viewers, Jane. Poor show. I've collected the evidence into one document, and your viewers can see it for themselves . . . why, right now, as I've just released it into a thousand different servers and download sites. Just search for the terms "Jane Talbot" and "Child Abuse" and you'll be on your way.

TALBOT

Labyrinth, you don't have to do this. We can still talk. You promised me you'd stop killing.

LABYRINTH

And you promised those children so much, didn't you? Hand them a scrap of bread while pressing the heel of your Manolo Blahniks into their dirty little faces.

TALBOT

You bastard.

LABYRINTH

I don't blame you, personally. You're just a symptom of a larger disease. The education system for our most precious resource, our children, is not serving their needs. It's serving the needs of the administrators, the government, by putting the focus on test scores in order to get more funding. Why no creative schools? Why is it all based on one assembly-line system? The current education system is based on Henry Ford's idea from the turn of the century. Education shouldn't be a business. It's outdated and doesn't help our kids. It's a shadow of what it should be.

TALBOT

But . . . I agree with you, I'm trying to fix it.

LABYRINTH

Still clinging to your lies? Let's leave it to your viewers then, shall we? James, I'd like you to open the lines, phone and Web. If you've downloaded the documents, and you wish to see Janey here punished for her crimes against the children, then let your voice be heard. Thy will be done . . .

TALBOT

Talk to me. Please talk to me. Don't do this. Whatever you're planning. We can talk it through.

LABYRINTH

James? Are we rolling? You be sure to keep me updated on those calls, James. Patch them through.

TALBOT

Please. . . .

LABYRINTH

You're right in the middle of what will become the most-watched television show in the history of the medium. You do realize that, don't you? They're going to watch this and read about you forever. It will be bigger than the moon landing. Enjoy it, Jane.

TALBOT

I'm begging you. . . .

LABYRINTH

Don't fucking beg me, you bitch. Beg them. Beg your viewers. Beg the children!

chapter 31

LABYRINTH

I love it—

The sound of a human mind snapping when you trap it and it realizes it has nowhere left to go—no more turns, no back-tracking, no do-overs. . . .

Just wall.

Poor sweet Jane Talbot, listen to her hem and haw and stutter and stop—so inarticulate all of a sudden. It's not just me who enjoys seeing that pig sweat. News of my first three messages, on opposite ends of the globe, excites the media like nothing since the Unabomber or that clown prince Assange.

Jane Talbot, I wasn't lying—you and I are going to make history together.

Stop glancing at the space under your seat.

You can see it from where you are.

I guarantee it.

Already the worldwide Internet chatter is cranked up to unreal levels, beyond my greatest expectation.

Who knew the world cared so much about the education of poor South African children?

Amazing what the populace will care about once you give them a reason.

Some call for me to run for president; others want to give me Jane Talbot's old talk show slot.

I wouldn't take either if you paid me.

Because you can't save the world if you're Jane Talbot.

You can't save the world if you're the president of the United States.

But you can save the world if you follow me.

chapter 32

DARK

Dark and Natasha looked like any average couple catching a flight from Paris to New York City. No luggage to check in, but what did it matter to a young couple in love? However, even casual observers would have picked up on the body language. The male seemed indifferent, while the woman seemed to be realizing that she'd just made the biggest mistake of her life.

"Why are we doing this?" she asked.

"I don't have a gun to your head."

"How sure are you?"

Dark smiled. "A mentor of mine—the guy who taught me how to do this? He was famous for playing his gut hunches. Most of the time he was right. It used to frustrate me, until I learned to follow my gut, too."

"I'd love to meet this mentor of yours," Natasha said, "so I could punch him in the face."

"He'd probably like it."

About an hour into their flight, as they were cruising thirty-five thousand feet above the icy Atlantic, Natasha received a text message from Blair. The plane featured Wi-Fi, but from the sound of Natasha's voice, it was clear she preferred it didn't.

"Fuck," she said.

"What?"

"Blair knows we're on our way to the U.S.," she said, "and he's not happy about it. Not in the slightest."

"No?"

"I'm actually softening his language."

"He told us to investigate. So we're investigating."

"You and I both know what he meant. I was a fool to follow you. Is this what your mentor also taught you? How to nuke the careers of your colleagues?"

"Blair will cheer up when we catch this son of a bitch."

"I don't think that's going to happen."

"And see, I thought you were beginning to trust me."

Natasha shook her head and dropped her cell phone to her lap. "This has nothing to do with trust. Labyrinth's on live TV right now, confessing everything to Jane Talbot. *In South Africa.*"

Hans Roeding loaded his weapons while Deckland O'Brian used his tablet computer to watch *The Jane Talbot Show* Webcast at the same time he hacked into their billing servers. No matter how supposedly "secret" the remote studio location, if the producers of *The Jane Talbot Show* used it, there had to be a bill for it somewhere. There were only a few places accountants could hide a certain line item, and fairly predictable ways for them to disguise it. O'Brian had seen it all before.

"Got anything?" Roeding asked.

"Patience, my steroid-addled friend, patience . . ."

"Give me direction at least."

"Straight for now. Until I tell you to turn, big guy."

O'Brian tried to keep a playful exterior, but inside he was seething. This was not the way Global Alliance was supposed to work. Blair should have stuck to his guns and at least sent Natasha along—a third team member would have made a huge difference on the ground. A fourth would have been brilliant, too, but so far Dark was a crushing disappointment. All this talk from Blair about how the American manhunter would complete the team and take it to the next level. Platitudes and shite, that's what it was. O'Brian would rather shoulder an extra part of the burden than have to deal with that prima donna.

On-screen, O'Brian's search yielded three remote studios scattered throughout Johannesburg. He ruled two of them out for being too large; his gut told him Labyrinth would want to control all aspects of the production. Someplace small.

"Okay, Hans. Turn right."

"Right where?"

"Right *here*, right fucking *now*!" O'Brian yelled. His partner made a hairpin turn. O'Brian tightened his grip on the tablet. He saw how many miles were between them and the studio. A ridiculous number of miles. But he didn't want to depress Hans. Not yet, anyway . . .

But it would be *so good* to be the team that apprehended Labyrinth. Just the two of them.

chapter 33

Johannesburg, South Africa

O'Brian and Roeding made it to the station while Labyrinth was still on the air.

They didn't go ask permission or liaise with local police or any of that nonsense. Roeding smashed in the front door of the studio with a boot, submachine gun in hand; O'Brian covered him. The staffers at this tiny remote studio—little more than three rooms, no bigger than a fast food restaurant—looked pale and terrified. O'Brian knew that questioning the staff would result in unreliable information. They'd be either too nervous to be of any real help, or they'd lie, thinking they were protecting the life of their boss. So as Roeding had raced that last mile through the streets of Johannesburg, O'Brian found a schematic of the building, and based on old production notes, knew which studio would contain Jane Talbot, and which would contain Labyrinth.

Plan?

There was no plan, other than the Global Alliance standard operating procedure in these kinds of high-tension, no-time-left-on-the-clock situations:

Stop the maniac.

Roeding would pounce on Labyrinth and incapacitate him before he had the chance to detonate any bomb.

O'Brian would forcibly remove Jane Talbot from the studio as quickly as possible, in case Roeding was a few seconds too late.

O'Brian also knew they'd need at least two seconds to blind Labyrinth right before the strike. With a press of a button on his cell, he jammed the signal, both externally and internally, with a microwave blast. *Yes,* O'Brian noted to himself drily, *they have an app for that.*

Then he smashed through the studio door.

Inside the main studio was Jane Talbot, wet hot tears streaking down her cheeks and looking like she'd just been involved in a major collision on the highway. She fought O'Brian, too, God love her, clutching the edges of her chair in a death grip. O'Brian had no choice but to punch a nerve bundle in her upper chest, numbing both arms so that he could pry her loose. They stumbled backward into the hallway, Talbot screaming the whole time. O'Brian dragged her toward the exit.

By that time, Roeding had subdued Labyrinth.

The man looked strangely normal. Handsome, except for all of the blood and the contusions on his face.

Over the Atlantic Ocean

"They have him," Natasha said, "as of five minutes ago. He was captured at a small television studio in Johannesburg. Roeding and O'Brian made the arrest, and the Johannesburg police arrived shortly after. They're bringing him to another location for questioning."

Dark listened to her silently.

"Did you hear me?" Natasha said. "It's over. We can go back now to get properly reamed out."

"No. This is not over."

"What do you mean, not over?"

"I think we should keep going."

"Why?"

Dark looked at her, thinking of Riggins. If it didn't feel right, it wasn't right. How many times had he said that? While Dark preferred to ponder a case in a dim, cold, quiet room, Riggins had been all about fire in the blood, breaking down doors, pushing further and further.

"My gut," Dark said.

chapter 34

As it turned out, there had been no bomb under Jane Talbot's chair in the studio. Labyrinth, apparently, had been bluffing.

Still, damage far worse than any bomb had been done. In the frenzied hours that followed, reporters began to pick apart the evidence that Labyrinth had posted online in a thousand different places. Every few minutes a new piece of evidence would surface, spread by curated news orgs and social network posts—fodder for endless discussion and snide comments and sarcasm. Labyrinth's on-air allegations were just the beginning. Jane Talbot was finished, and immediately went into seclusion while her lawyers sprung into action. Even though Talbot's show only syndicated in South Africa, the UK, Australia, New Zealand, and a handful of European stations, the worldwide impact was huge. If you hadn't heard of Jane Talbot before, you'd certainly heard of her now.

She was worse than infamous.

She was *Internet-infamous.*

Unbelievable! Never heard of Jane Talbot until now, but . . . what a scumbag.

3 minutes ago

Anyone else notice that he promised not to kill her . . . and he didn't?

2 minutes ago

He should have killed her. I would have enjoyed watching that.

2 minutes ago

I really thought it was going there, but didn't. Maybe Lab has a heart?

1 minute ago

She's worse than dead—she's been exposed as a phony. Help me expose others.

1 minute ago

Labyrinth himself was brought to Johannesburg Metropolitan Police Department HQ by a military elite response unit and a bomb squad detail. The lessons of Los Angeles would not be forgotten. The mass murderer couldn't be trusted, and might have packed his own body with the same explosives that had been packed inside the homeless man in Los Angeles. Instead of the usual cells, Labyrinth was brought to an empty police vehicle bay—reinforced concrete walls, no windows, and a good distance away from any civilian structure. Doctors, paired with bomb squad techs, stripped Labyrinth naked and gave him a full exam, from blood work to MRIs, to detect anything that could be considered explosive.

There was nothing.

Labyrinth said nothing the entire time.

Despite being verbose in the studio, the man refused to speak or ask for legal representation. Instead he gestured for a writing instrument. When he was supplied with a dull pencil, he wrote three words, block-style, on a piece of legal paper:

I WANT BLAIR

No one knew who he was talking about—except the head of the JMPD, who had been working with Global Alliance since the delivery of the South African package. The man wanted to speak to Damien Blair, in person.

After they landed at JFK, Natasha relayed the news to Dark.

"Blair's going to Johannesburg to interview the suspect. He wants the complete team together as soon as possible. We're to fly down there immediately—tickets are waiting for us at the gate. All is forgiven if we leave now."

"Why the hurry?" Dark said. "Blair's convinced he has his man. What else can we possibly do?"

"Blair doesn't know if this is the real Labyrinth or not—either way, he may not be working alone. Other threats may already be in the works, and squeezing him is our only chance."

"Good luck," Dark said. "I'm staying here. Because there's definitely another package coming to New York City, if it's not here already."

Natasha squinted, as if trying to read Dark's mind. "What makes you so sure?"

"Did you hear what 'Labyrinth' said on the Talbot show? *Education shouldn't be a business*. Right there, he's telling us where he's going to strike next. The heart of the business community."

The public shaming of Jane Talbot nailed it for Dark. So far, Labyrinth had tackled the entertainment industry, then the oil industry. With Jane Talbot, he'd tackled the media and the education system—a two-for-one deal that was already dominating headlines around the world.

The next industry, and most obvious: the financial.

Labyrinth would try to strike at the very heart of it.

"What about the riddle made you think of New York City?"

"The imagery. The birds flying, the shadow over the water. What came to mind repeatedly was 9/11—the last time someone attacked the financial heart of the world."

"What if you're wrong?" Natasha asked. "There are many financial centers in the world. Not just New York."

"But think about Labyrinth's targets so far. He has a thing for America—or what he perceives as the American empire. He kept hammering her on the word *business*, and that was no accident. What's the heart of the American empire? Wall Street."

"So why Jane Talbot in South Africa?"

"She was the ideal target. Labyrinth discovered that she was hiding something. He wants us to believe he's only targeting the guilty, remember? People won't jump on his bandwagon if he starts targeting people believed to be innocent."

Natasha said, "You stay here and chase shadows all you want, but I'm off to Johannesburg. We've got a suspect in custody. Even if he's not Labyrinth, he's obviously part of this. That's the best chance we have."

"I'm going to go find something to eat," Dark said. "A beer would be great right about now."

Natasha just stared at him, but after a few moments, she followed him down the terminal to a bar catering to weary travelers who wanted to numb their senses with enough booze to last a long flight.

Dark ordered beer for both of them. Natasha said she didn't drink beer. Dark said fine, he'd have hers. The bar was practically empty,

as it was the middle of the morning, and only the heartiest travelers would consider an alcoholic beverage at this hour.

"Why do I have the feeling you know more than you're letting on?" Natasha asked.

"You think I'm Labyrinth?"

"No," she said. "You're even *more* cryptic."

"Thanks."

"I'm being serious. You seem so dead sure that Labyrinth's going to strike here, and your reasoning doesn't exactly seem logical."

Dark took a long pull of beer, then eased back into the booth. "Blair sees Labyrinth as this ultimate nemesis. Back in Special Circs, we had a category for killers that went off the charts in terms of depravity and skill and general inhumanity."

"Your so-called Level 26 killers," Natasha said.

"Right. I know what it's like to go up against the worst. I also know how easy it is to follow one of these monsters right down into the darkness to where you're blind. That happened to me years ago."

"You think this is happening to Blair?"

"I *know* it's happening to Blair. He's got a hard-on for this killer, and it's very familiar."

Natasha smiled. "You know, he was incredibly excited about you joining the team. You were all he talked about for weeks."

"I'm just the new guy. And the honeymoon's over."

"No, it's not that. I've been with Global Alliance since the early days, and Blair was never like this with the others. He sees you as a kindred spirit. And he was relieved that you were on the scene from the first Labyrinth package."

"He likes me, he really likes me."

Natasha frowned. "Now you're being an ass."

Dark looked mock-hurt for a moment, then took another pull of beer. Natasha reminded him of Constance Brielle, his former partner at Special Circs. Knew how to deal with people just as well as she did forensic evidence. He wasn't sure if she was sitting here in this booth to humor him or to report back to Blair that he should be dismissed from Global Alliance.

"What do you think?" Dark asked. "Is Blair thinking with a clear head?"

She averted her eyes for a moment, then said diplomatically, "I think he's been focused on the hunt for Labyrinth for a long time."

"So are you going to stay here in NYC and help me catch this guy?"

"Are you going to stop drinking beer at nine thirty in the morning?"

"Pretty sure I'm still on California time. Which makes it six thirty."

"Which is even worse," Natasha said. "Come on. Blair has a Global Alliance safe house downtown."

"Really?"

"We've got places everywhere. You'll never have to pay for another hotel room ever again."

She reached out, took the beer from his hand, and put it down on the table. Then she rubbed her thumb across his bottom lip and smiled.

"Shall we?"

chapter 35

Brussels, Belgium

Alain Pantin obsessively flipped through all of the Labyrinth footage he could find online. The reaction to the latest attack was stunning. It wasn't a violent attack at all; instead, Jane Talbot was given a public shaming.

And if the public seemed shy about embracing Labyrinth before, the shyness was quickly forgotten.

The news orgs were full of essays about Labyrinth and Jane Talbot, with the majority of them expressing more shock and outrage at Talbot rather than the diabolical killer. "Yes, we already knew *he* was bad, but Jane Talbot?" seemed to be a running theme.

There were pro-Labyrinth looters running wild in Johannesburg, smashing bricks through the plate-glass windows of various businesses and institutions that Jane Talbot had supported and promoted over the years. The graffiti was clear: JANE THE LIAR.

And all around the world, reports of street taggers spraying Labyrinth's earliest messages on the sides of banks and government buildings:

I WILL

HELP YOU

OUT OF THE

LABYRINTH

And

THE WORLD

IS NOT

BEYOND SAVING

Trey had given him no time to rest. Pantin essentially halted the business of his office for a full media cycle, granting print, phone, and on-camera interviews about Labyrinth.

The message now: Uncover the phonies.

Pantin told one CNN reporter, "No, you don't have to hold someone hostage to make them confess to their sins. We need more accountability in all areas—I'm talking government, media, education, business."

He told someone from *The Guardian*: "This is a bad time to be a public figure with something to hide. Sure, Labyrinth's actions are deplorable. But it makes you think about accountability, doesn't it? The need for a higher standard among the people who claim to want to lead us?"

By the end of the day Pantin was so punch-drunk from the endless stream of interviews that he started to fantasize about someday meeting Labyrinth, shaking his hand, maybe even convincing him to turn himself in for the greater good, and then going about his public rehabilitation in a series of concert and lecture tours. . . .

Stop it, Pantin told himself. *You are talking about a killer here.*

But a killer who'd breathed new life in his political career. You couldn't ever forget that.

As he stared out at Leopold Park, mind fuzzed over and adrenaline still racing through his blood, a push notice sounded on his cell phone.

AP World

Breaking: Sources claim "Labyrinth" is in custody in South Africa.

chapter 36

BLAIR

Johannesburg, South Africa

The bomb squad techs offered Damien Blair everything from a blast suit to a Kevlar vest, but he waved them away. Instead, he asked to be taken directly to where they were holding Labyrinth—the humid, rusted-out police vehicle bay. As he was led down a too-bright corridor, Blair quietly yet sternly informed his hosts that he was to see the suspect completely alone. No guards, no other police officials. Some of the officers began to protest, but their commander knew better. The man was a career politician on the force, and he knew who backed Global Alliance—more important, knew better than to get into a turf war with the rest of the world. The commander told his men that Blair would be allowed access, exactly as requested.

Blair stepped into the room, heard the door lock behind him, then walked to the gurney where the suspect had been triple-strapped. He was positioned at a forty-five-degree angle. Wordlessly, Blair approached, took the suspect by the chin, and turned his head *this way*, and then *that*, before crouching down to look into his eyes.

"Are you looking into my soul, Damien Blair?"

"You're not him," Blair said quietly.

"Of course I am," the suspect said. "But are *you* the real Damien Blair? They didn't send down a body double, did they? That would be so disappointing, because I've been wanting to meet you for a long time. Your handsome mug don't show up much in the newspapers. In fact, not at all. Where's the rest of your team? Your *Global Alliance*?"

"I want you to tell me everything about Labyrinth."

"I am Labyrinth."

"No, you're not. This is your only, and final, chance to cut a deal."

"Can't we just talk a little? What's the American expression—shoot the shit?"

"I don't think you understand your position," Blair said, then took a Glock out of his jacket pocket and aimed it at the suspect's heart. "My organization is one of the few international police agencies that has the power to accomplish things. Interpol? They investigate, make recommendations. We're different. We act. We investigate and remove threats. Dozens of signatory nations give us three things—funding, secrecy, and autonomy. They trust us to do what is right."

"That's good, that's really good."

"That means I could shoot you now and nobody would even blink."

"You've been chasing me for years. You're not going to kill me now. You're going to want answers. Explanations. Rationales. You're going to want me to show you where all of the bodies are bur—"

Blair lowered the gun, almost casually, as if he couldn't care less about what he hit, and squeezed the trigger. The shot echoed through the vehicle bay, followed by Labyrinth's screams. Loud. Pitiful. Confused. Blair had been aiming, after all. A precision strike: The bullet ripped through the prisoner's Achilles tendon, which caused his foot to curl up in a hideously painful way, as if his entire leg were trying to roll itself up into his torso.

"I'll take you apart," Blair said, "one bullet at a time. The tendon's just for starters."

"NO!" the suspect shrieked. "T-t-that's not how it works. You're a c-c-c-op . . ."

"No," Blair said, "I'm not."

Then he positioned the Glock directly over the suspect's scrotum.

"Please, NO!"

"Where is he?" Blair demanded. "The next bullet takes away your manhood."

"I don't know I don't know please believe me oh God I don't know!"

❖

The suspect talked, of course. At great length, especially after he'd been given enough painkillers.

He continued to insist that he was Labyrinth, that's the only name he'd ever known, swearing on the lives of his mother (who he didn't remember, either), and begging to be believed. He didn't know about any other attacks—God, he wouldn't kill anybody! Didn't they understand that? Blair was good at reading people and was surprised to find himself believing the suspect. That this man truly thought he was a mastermind avenger who called himself "Labyrinth."

The man's been turned, Blair thought to himself. *Turned so deep that he's lost all traces of his former self.*

Still, when a fingerprint match came back with the name Anthony Biretta, and Blair spoke the name aloud, you could see the pieces begin to shatter behind the suspect's eyes. Yes, that name was familiar. Why was that name familiar? The suspect shook his head, as if that would assemble the pieces into the right order. Why *was* that name familiar?

Gradually the full story would emerge, but Blair could already fill in the gaps. Biretta was probably an aspiring actor who was granted the role of a lifetime. Labyrinth would have spent a long time with him—months, maybe even years, for this single performance.

But during all of their time together, the real Labyrinth wouldn't have shown his face, or given any indication of where he lived, how he behaved, even what his voice sounded like. In Anthony Biretta's shattered mind, there would be only fragments of his past life. For him it would be like waking from a long dream, and the horrible idea that his real life, the one he would have sworn was *tangible reality*, had been contained in that dream. And he could never return to it.

"Get his leg fixed," Blair told the police on the way out.

chapter 37

DARK

Manhattan

The area around One Police Plaza had been locked down since 9/11, much to the long-term dismay of nearby residents. The police argued that it would be far too easy for someone to roll down the four-lane Park Row in a white van packed with fertilizer bombs and take out the central hub of the NYPD. Residents complained that blocking Park Row turned an already insufferable traffic headache into an eternal nightmare—not to mention their feeling like they were living in a demilitarized zone.

The Park Row blockades didn't stop bike messengers, of course. Specifically, one bald messenger with a bushy beard that nearly reached his gut. He stopped out front of One Police Plaza, locked his bike, then raced toward the front doors—where he was immediately intercepted by a new delivery detail. What happened in L.A. had sent shock waves through police departments around the world, and the NYPD refused to take any chances. The bald messenger, whose T-shirt read ALABAMA CORN SNAKE, seemed bemused by it all . . . until the security office looked at the name on the return address (Bryan Hilt) and the team was slamming Mr. Corn Snake down to the concrete, Glock at the back of his head, another Glock at the base of his spine, cuffs cinching around his wrists before he even had a chance to expel the air he'd sucked in on the way down.

The security team had been prepped: Anything that even remotely seemed like it could come from that nutcase Labyrinth—pounce now, let lawyers sort it out later.

And "Bryan Hilt" was on a short list of possible anagrams for the name "Labyrinth."

Instant red flag, motherfucker.

The box was immediately transported by armed guard down to a police warehouse near the Brooklyn Bridge for inspection.

Mr. Corn Snake could only sniffle blood and watch as his entire life was ripped apart, from his shitty apartment up in Jamaica, Queens, all the way back to Alabama, searching for a connection to the package's sender.

Dark and Natasha keyed into the Global Alliance safe house in the West Village. The place was well stocked, modern, with several bedrooms around an open living room. The loft was full of the latest technology, flat screens and computers everywhere. Much like the plane, it seemed that Global Alliance HQ could be anywhere Blair needed it to be. As Natasha fired up the computer systems, Dark—still very time dislocated after so many days of travel—thought a shower sounded like a good idea.

"Hey," he said. Natasha looked up and locked eyes with Dark.

"I'm, uh . . . I'm gonna find a shower," he told her.

"Okay," she said.

"Okay." He pulled his gaze from hers. What was that?

Natasha watched and smiled as Dark awkwardly found his way to the bathroom.

Dark peeled off his clothes and fired up the hottest shower he thought he could stand. Under the intense spray in the tiled shower stall, Dark allowed himself to linger in the moment, just letting the water do its job. He was surprised to find that when he got his mind off Labyrinth, he thought about Natasha, could not get that look out of his head. It's not to say he had sworn off women since he lost his wife, but he also hadn't been looking. His life was work and Sibby. But now, like any normal man, Dark was thinking about the incredibly beautiful woman in the other room, wondering what she might be doing. He was about to shrug off the thought when he heard the shower door open.

Dark turned as Natasha slipped inside the shower stall next to him, completely naked. He had to wipe his eyes to make sure he wasn't seeing things. Then, she stepped up to him, put her hands on his chest, and looked up at him expectantly.

"I thought I annoyed you," Dark said.

"You do," Natasha replied, running her fingers down his chest and farther still. She kissed his neck and his chest. "You really, really annoy me."

"So why are you here?" he said playfully.

"Would you rather I not be?" she said as she nibbled on his ear. "Do you need a reason other than we're both here?"

Dark did not. Dark pressed her against the warm tiles of the stall, arms pinned to her sides. She climaxed with a muted cry and then slammed Dark back into the wall and began to exact her revenge, her hips slamming into his with an aggression that only aroused Dark even more.

He refused to give in easily, though, and reversed positions once again before deciding that they were clean enough and there was a bed in the safe house and it would be a shame to not use it.

Afterward, as they lay in bed, heavy breathing punctuating the silence, Dark couldn't believe this had happened . . . in a good way. Natasha stretched her naked body, giving Dark an amazing view, and then rolled over next to him.

"I—um . . ." Dark stammered. Then turned to Natasha and laughed. She smiled . . . an amazing smile. Then saved him from himself.

"It's not easy . . . to meet people doing what we do," she said. "We all have needs."

"So it was just about fulfilling needs then?" he asked.

Natasha hesitated.

"You're a good guy, Dark. I like you."

"But . . . ?"

"But let's not let this be the last time, okay?" Natasha smiled and then slid off the bed, grabbing her clothes. "Oh, and for the record, you still annoy me."

Dark was about to retort when a dual *ping ping* emitted from both their phones.

New York Post

Breaking: Inside sources claim the NYPD has received a package from "Labyrinth"; city braces for attack.

"Please don't be the I-told-you-so type," Natasha said, gathering her clothes from the floor. She didn't put her clothes back on right away, however. Instead she recovered her cell phone from the counter and started to type.

"I'm messaging one of my NYPD sources right now," she said.

Dark took the opportunity to dress and, he wasn't ashamed to admit, wondered if they could have gone again if their cell phones hadn't interrupted.

"It's legit," Natasha said.

"When did the package arrive?" Dark asked.

"Looks like ten minutes ago."

"And it's already out there, in the media. Labyrinth's tipping off reporters just to make sure nobody misses his messages."

"Let's go," Natasha said. "I'll coordinate with my NYPD contact on the way over."

"You may want to put on a shirt," Dark said, turning his back in faux modesty.

"To be continued," she said.

One cab ride later they were being escorted into the police warehouse where the NYPD forensic teams had set up an impromptu workstation. They were all still skittish about explosives after the LAPD attack. Natasha made quick introductions and asked to see the contents of the package. A tech handed Dark the latest riddle, sealed in a plastic evidence bag:

MY BODY TAPERS NICE AND NEAT
WITH BUT ONE EYE I AM COMPLETE
YOU'D JUDGE ME BY MY EQUIPAGE
THE GREATEST WARRIOR OF THE AGE
FOR WHEN YOU HAVE SURVEYED ME ROUND
NOTHING BUT STEEL IS TO BE FOUND
YET MEN I NEVER WAS KNOWN TO KILL
BUT LADIES' BLOOD I OFTEN SPILL
WHAT AM I?

Dark nodded, then handed the riddle to Natasha. "What else came with it?"

"A really old laptop. I mean, a piece of gear I haven't seen since grade school."

The tech pointed to the machine, which was resting on the table. Almost two decades old, if Dark had to guess. The thing looked like a giant slab of hard plastic.

"The worst thing is, he doesn't seem to be giving us any time at all," the tech said as he lifted the screen to reveal a crude digital timer, ticking down. . . .

2:28:41 . . .

2:28:40 . . .

2:28:39 . . .

"What was the starting time?" Dark asked.

"Three hours exactly," said the tech.

Labyrinth was giving them the smallest window yet to prevent his next act of violence. This troubled Dark. The other time periods—relatively generous. The more time you gave the police to solve the riddle, the more fun the taunting. Why was he now playing this one so tight?

Because he knows you're close. He sped up the clock to keep things interesting.

"What was the third item?" Dark asked.

"A legal document from the 1840s. We've got a pair of guys from NYU on their way now to analyze it, but apparently this thing claims that the City of New York once paid thousands of dollars—which was a lot back then—in exchange for protection from a Bower gang. The Knife Boys. The historians said the gangs sound real, but they've never heard about the city paying them off."

Dark pondered this. Protection money. A government made to look bad. A riddle that mentioned ladies' blood. A document from the 1840s, and a laptop computer from twenty years ago. What connected them all?

Natasha approached, riddle in her hand.

"You know the answer to the riddle?" Dark asked.

"At my liberal arts boarding school I was required to take a sewing class," she said. "And nothing pricks like a needle. Question is, who will Labyrinth be pricking in a little more than two hours?"

"If he continues his pattern, then he's going to find someone in the financial world guilty of some perceived sin. We need a list of Wall Street types who have made a fuckload of money thanks to some shady backroom deal."

"Great," Natasha said. "Our victim list now includes thousands of people."

"We can narrow it down. Think about the first four victims. All of them had secrets that Labyrinth exposed. The actress and producer—guilty of incest. The oil executive—guilty of spoiling the planet. Talbot—her embezzlement. This will be someone who hasn't been caught yet. Maybe there are investigations under way, which is how Labyrinth heard about it and chose his victim. But the public won't know about it."

"I'll have O'Brian spin through the files of the SEC. How else can we narrow it down?"

"Don't forget Labyrinth's love of celebrity. He chooses his victims because they'll make great examples. He's hoping people will cheer him on because they'll hate the victim, too, and love to see them suffer. So his victim will be prominent. Not a household name necessarily, but on Wall Street, he'll be a virtual rock star."

"One thing keeps tripping me up in that riddle," Natasha said.

"What's that?"

"The part about never killing men, but spilling ladies' blood. Maybe the man we're looking for is a notorious ladies' man?"

Dark nodded. "Could be. Or it's the opposite. A prude who keeps his kinks in the dark. And Labyrinth's trying to drag them out into the light."

chapter 38

LABYRINTH

Show me a man without a vice and I'll show you a liar.

Shane Corbett is a liar.

He's proud of the fact that he doesn't drink.

He doesn't smoke.

He doesn't do drugs.

He doesn't consort with whores.

He doesn't watch online pornography.

He doesn't eat junk food.

He doesn't even cheat on his taxes.

Nonetheless . . .

Shane Corbett has a vice.

He's just very, very good at hiding it from the world.

But not from me.

I can pry secrets out of anyone.

I'm sitting at a table near the front of the restaurant, alone, sipping a latte, when Shane Corbett enters, black umbrella tucked under his arm, slender white phone in his hand. He looks impatient. He's here for an important business lunch. I know this, because I'm the one who arranged this lunch, through one of my many false identities.

I called and made the reservation.

I chose the specific table—the most high-profile one in the place.

And just a few minutes ago, I walked by that table and squeezed an untraceable liquid into Shane Corbett's water goblet.

Shane Corbett, having no vices whatsoever, is an absolute fiend when it comes to water, drinking it compulsively, as if the fluid can wash away at the evil corroding his veins.

Ha.

Shane Corbett is shown to his table and chooses the exact seat that I predicted he would choose. (Shane Corbett hates having his back to the entrance of any eating establishment.) After handing his black umbrella to the hostess without so much as glancing at her, he smooths out a few minor bumps in the tablecloth with his long, manicured fingers and compulsively glances at his watch.

And then he takes a large gulp of water.

Even a little would have been enough.

I suppose that if something as simple as murder had been on my mind I could have taken his life at this very moment.

But I have something special in mind for Shane Corbett, the man with no vices.

Look at him.

Fist up to his mouth, as if to stifle a burp.

No, not a burp.

Something worse.

The rumbling in his stomach has started in earnest now, the panic flits across his face—

He's not sure he's going to make it.

He bolts from the table, his hips knocking into other tables as he goes, rattling goblets and silverware, but Shane Corbett doesn't care about anything right now except getting inside a toilet stall immediately.

I put down my latte, stand up, straighten my trousers, stretch my back a little, then casually follow him into the men's room.

The sound of Shane Corbett's retching assaults my ears as I open the door. There is an embarrassed executive at the sink, pumping pink foam soap and pretending like he doesn't hear the pitiful hurling and gagging.

I shrug my shoulders and roll my eyes a bit. I tell the executive,

Some people just can't handle their Bloody Marys.

The exec relaxes, returns a polite smile, takes a paper towel from the basket.

I call out,

Come on, Charley. Let's get you to your room.

I find Shane Corbett in the third stall, the one closest to the tiled wall. He is delirious, vomit and drool hanging from a trembling lower lip. He doesn't know me, but he's so far gone he'll trust anyone who can possibly take away his suffering. So it is easy to guide him to the sink, wipe his mouth, then guide him back out into the lobby toward the elevators.

I tell him,

We'll take care of you.

The elevator doors close silently.

[To enter the Labyrinth, please go to Level26.com and enter the code: revenge]

chapter 39

LABYRINTH

I leave the hotel room, listen to the door quietly *snick* shut in my wake. I check the sleeves of my suit to make sure none of Shane Corbett splattered on me. Vomit, blood, or otherwise.

I kept my distance the whole time, but the ladies were *quite* motivated.

Things got a little out of control, I must admit.

Understandably so, from the viewpoint of the ladies.

You see, Shane Corbett *does* have a vice. He's had it since middle school and it almost sidelined his academic career. Now that he's older and has piles of money to burn, he can afford to indulge it and no one ever has to know about it.

Except me.

And the women he's destroyed.

I worked with these women for quite a long time.

A few months, actually, on and off.

They were not hard to find or befriend. Their minds opened up to me willingly, almost eagerly, because their confidence had been shattered at a very young age, leaving them impressionable and constantly seeking those who purport to keep them safe. Truth is, they end up gravitating toward the opposite. Those who exploit their weakness and manipulate them into playthings.

I do not exploit them.

I remind them of how strong they once were.

How they once lusted for life instead of running away from it.

And now, after all of these months, they're good.

And they're *ready to set things right.*

⁂

The women in this room had every reason to repress it.

The parents.

The lawyers.

The money the lawyers gave to the parents to keep them quiet.

As they got older they buried it deeper still, but it was still there, gnawing away at the insides, and once a month they received a vivid reminder of their one and only date with Shane Corbett.

Bury it deeper.

Repress it.

I helped them dig those memories out.

I taught them how to harness it and channel it into pure unadulterated rage.

I even paid for their flights, hotels, and incidentals.

They were ready.

⁂

This wasn't personal, Shane Corbett. Plenty of others in your line of "work" have similar vices. Is it an accident that the most corrupt, vile men run one of the most corrupt and vile industries? An industry that clearly has no right being in private hands?

But rejoice, Shane, because I've made you a part of the solution. It may have hurt, but in the end you're making the world a better place. You won't be around to see it . . . but you can die knowing that you got in on the ground floor.

chapter 40

DARK

"Think I've got a contender here," Natasha said.

She'd been hunched over her tablet computer and cell phone for a solid thirty minutes while Dark continued to examine the riddle and clues. Now he looked over her shoulder at the image on her tablet screen, which displayed DMV info for one Shane Wesley Corbett, twenty-eight, who had a penthouse apartment on the Upper West Side as well as a six-bedroom home in Scarsdale. Smug, handsome, fit, clean-cut.

"Who is he?"

"Corbett's a Wall Street liaison to the U.S. Federal Reserve—one who brokered the bailout of a commodities corporation that built the system with cooked books and bilked their investors and the public out of billions. But because a total collapse would have been catastrophic to the economy, the Fed had no choice but to help. Corbett was the inside whiz kid who helped broker the deal. His name was never made public. So the only people who knew he was involved were the other insiders, of course, and my friend at the SEC."

"Labyrinth's good at knowing people's dirty secrets," Dark said. "That just doesn't sound dirty enough. Hell, there are probably dozens of assholes who fit that description."

"I agree. And that is not Corbett's dirtiest secret."

With Deckland O'Brian's help, Natasha found that Corbett also had a set of juvenile criminal records dating back thirteen years, to when Corbett was still a sophomore in high school. Sealed by the court, but Natasha had encountered sealed records before. Seals had a funny way of opening when Global Alliance made the request.

"Twenty-seven counts of statutory rape," Natasha said. "You were right about keeping things in the dark."

"And Labyrinth knew about this, too. Damnit. Can we find out who else may have cracked open these records?"

"That's O'Brian's department. He's doing some more digging on the plane back from South Africa."

"Let's find Corbett now."

"One thing in the riddle makes sense now."

"What's that?" Dark asked.

"The riddle talked about ladies' blood. Well, according to victim testimony, Corbett had a thing for virgins. It was a fetish with him. He only raped virgins, and never raped the same girl twice. One victim said he got off on looking at his own penis after the act, when it was slick with his victim's blood."

chapter 41

DARK

A call to Corbett's secretary—along with the threat of immediate arrest—yielded Corbett's top-secret lunch plans. He was meeting a potential client at the Epoch Hotel, directly across from the World Trade Center site. Dark and Natasha took a cab to the hotel lobby, where a confused hostess said that yes, Mr. Corbett had been here, in fact she still had his umbrella—but he disappeared after sitting down.

Natasha said, "Time's almost up, Dark. Where is he? Where did he go?"

"He's gotta be somewhere in the hotel," Dark said, then ran toward the front desk, showed the nervous clerk the Global Alliance badge on his cell phone, then moved around to the back and commandeered the registration computer. Dark wished O'Brian were here—computers were not his strong suit.

"Can I help?" the clerk asked.

Dark nodded.

"Do you keep records of guests who asked not to be disturbed?"

"The maids might know. They keep a cleaning schedule on their carts."

Within minutes Dark and Natasha were in touch with the head of housekeeping, who in turn was compiling a list of rooms that had not been made up yet. Dark reasoned that Labyrinth would choose the biggest rooms available, so they narrowed down their search to suites, starting with the top floor, knocking on some, bursting through others to find either confused occupants or empty rooms.

"Is it possible he took him somewhere else?" Natasha asked.

"Possible, but why meet in a hotel?"

The search continued until something in Natasha's bag *ding*ed. A new push notification. She pulled her tablet out and looked at the screen.

Natasha said, "There's already a new video posted."

Open on: high school yearbook photo of Shane Corbett. A voice tells us: "This is the man in charge of the American economy." Cut to: Corbett now, in the hotel room, being confronted by the trio of angry women. "Shane Corbett. He's a man overcome with lust. For money. For material possessions. For even the most intimate of possessions."

Cut to: a woman, blond, twenties, slicing the adult Corbett across his outstretched palms. Blood begins to seep from the wound as he screams.

"Shane Corbett thought he could take it all . . ."

Cut to: another woman, brunette, stabbing Corbett in the back with a broken champagne glass. Corbett falls to his knees, pleading for his life, trembling.

"Witness the corruption of business. It is easier for a rich man to walk through the eye of a needle than to enter the kingdom of heaven. The politicians sold you out . . . to men like Shane Corbett . . ."

Dark and Natasha watched the video in the hallway of the thirty-sixth floor, with Natasha rewinding the footage whenever a new detail appeared.

"Look at the digital clock on the bedside table," Dark said. "This video was shot just a few minutes ago."

"He uploaded it from his camera," Natasha said. "Must have prerecorded the yearbook photo, but he's doing the narration almost live."

The women, Dark thought, must be the women Shane Corbett raped in high school. The ones who promised their silence in exchange for a payoff. Somehow Labyrinth had found them, just like he found his other delivery boys and stand-ins. Found them and messed with their minds and brought them to this hotel—where they could exact their revenge upon Corbett as Labyrinth taped it.

But where were they?

Was Corbett still alive? And could he identify Labyrinth?

"Look," Natasha said, freezing the image. Behind the mayhem you could see the outline of a building. Construction on the new Freedom Tower, still under way across from the Epoch Hotel. Which meant the room was facing west. And though the sun was bright through the window, almost blotting out the details, you could still make out some beams and half-finished floors. You could pinpoint the position of the room.

"Let me see that for a minute," Dark said. Natasha handed over her tablet, then Dark put a boot through the nearest doorway and ran to the window, much to the shock of the occupants of the room, who were engaged in an act you might describe as biblical.

"Sorry," Natasha said, then followed Dark to the window. He drew back the curtains, looked out on the construction scene, down at the tablet, then back at the construction scene again.

"Who are you people? What are you doing in here? I'm going to call security."

Natasha, with her back to the bed, tried to calm them down.

"We're the police, there's been an incident, just stay where you are."

"Police? You can't just kick down the door, this is America!"

Dark grabbed Natasha's arm and said, "I know where they are."

"YOU CAN'T DO THIS!"

They were two floors up, three rooms down. By the time Dark kicked down the door and drew his gun, it was too late. Shane Corbett was on the floor, bleeding out from countless gashes and wounds, the worst of which centered on his groin. Dark kneeled down to check the vitals, but already his skin was cooling. His body felt like death. Your fingertips know it better than your brain. They immediately sensed that something was . . . missing. Blood splattered the carpet in every direction. On the bed and the couch were the women, dazed, looking out at the construction.

Natasha ran to the nearest one—a blonde—and eased the half-broken champagne glass out of her hand before asking, "Where is he?"

"He's dead."

"No, the man who brought you here. Where is he?"

"I came here to take it back."

"Listen to me. A man brought you here. Checked you and the others into this room. He had a camera. Where did he go?"

Dark knew it would be no use. Whenever Labyrinth used a stand-in, he messed with their heads and their memories. Confused them into believing they were in some alternate reality, one that Labyrinth himself controlled.

They'd come within minutes of catching him—but as usual, Labyrinth had left just enough time for himself to escape.

Of course, that was assuming it *had been* Labyrinth in the room, recording the brutal murder of Shane Corbett.

The monster himself might be thousands of miles away, preparing his new package.

chapter 42

Brussels, Belgium

Seconds after the phone rang, Alain Pantin realized he had fallen asleep in his office.

He'd been so keyed up the night before, surfing Labyrinth clips and videos deep into the night, wanting to prepare for the next morning's wave of interviews and appearances. People were already starting to build elaborate Labyrinth-related Websites, including a Wikipedia rundown of his victims, linking to documents that "proved" their guilt. Other sites expanded on Labyrinth's nuggets of "philosophy" from his YouTube video clips. There were also sites dedicated to guessing Labyrinth's identity, and Pantin was more than a little amused to see his own name floated as a possibility.

Midday, after a crushing round of interviews, Pantin retreated back to his office. He'd leaned back and closed his eyes . . . and simply never surfaced.

Until now, an hour later, to a phone call from Trey.

"You've got a flight reservation, leaves in two hours."

"Oh?" Pantin asked, rubbing his eyes. "Where am I going?"

"Edinburgh. I've secured a time slot for you at the WoMU summit this weekend. You can thank me later."

"I want to thank you now. I almost want to kiss you."

A speaking slot at World Minds United—a much-ballyhooed global think tank summit scheduled to begin tomorrow in Scotland—was huge. Pantin hadn't even been able to secure a seat at the session, let alone the chance to appear before it. The eyes of the world would be on Edinburgh; political careers were born at events such as these.

"Look, I wouldn't recommend mentioning Labyrinth overtly, in this case—you've already established yourself as on the record as condemning his acts, and you don't need to rehash that."

"So what, then?"

"Take advantage of the world stage. Everybody claims to be wanting to hear from the rest of the world, but the truth is, the American representative will try to dominate. This is your chance to pull some of the spotlight away from him and promote your agenda."

"I don't know what to say."

"Say nothing. Cancel the rest of your media appearances and start working on your speech on your way to the airport."

Adrenaline banished all signs of fatigue. Pantin stood up, stretched until his fingertips nearly reached the ceiling. Sleep was overrated. Sleep too much and you miss your chance to rule the goddamned world.

chapter 43

RIGGINS

Quantico, Virginia / Manhattan

All of these years had gone by and Tom Riggins was still doing the same thing. Rushing to crime scenes. Not getting enough sleep. Not eating right. Popping antacids. Thinking about the crime, as well as thinking about his next drink. Wondering where all of the years had gone and wondering why he was still doing this.

The moment the news broke about the latest "Labyrinth" attack, Riggins had an assistant booking a Metroliner to Penn Station in New York City. The roads along I-95 were unpredictable—the train was the fastest way to go.

Not that Special Circs had any official reason to be poking its nose into the case—the FBI and Interpol had made that clear, a former colleague even telling Riggins to back the *fuck off*. His requests to travel to Dubai and South Africa—denied. Special Circs was not welcome.

Riggins never let that stop him before.

So he took the Metroliner to Penn Station, caught a cab down to the World Trade Center site to the Epoch Hotel, where the NYPD already had barriers. Riggins remembered the Epoch from the news reports during 9/11. The luxury hotel had been finished just a few weeks before the attacks. While it had been left standing, the entire place had to be gutted and remodeled. Just across the street, the Freedom Tower construction was well under way, reaching to the upper limits of the sky. *About damn time,* Riggins thought.

Inside the hotel lobby, Riggins flashed his Special Circs badge and made it about halfway across the room when he saw Steve Dark.

Riggins swallowed his shock just as Dark turned and noticed him.

"Dark," he said.

A defeated look washed over Dark's face—as if Riggins were a teacher, and Dark had just been caught writing obscenities on the playground.

"Riggins."

"I'm kind of surprised to see you here. Here I always thought you hated New York."

Riggins noticed there was a pretty dark-haired woman standing next to him. More important, it was obvious she and Dark were together. She glanced at Riggins, frowned in disapproval, turned her attention elsewhere.

"Aren't you going to introduce me to your lady friend there?"

"It's not a good time, Riggins. We have to go."

The last time Riggins and Dark saw each other, at the scene of another murder, Riggins and Dark had reached an uneasy peace. The kind that could be shattered in a moment. And this seemed to be one of those moments.

So his former protégé, Steve Dark, was working the Labyrinth case, too. Josh Banner had told him that Dark was working the L.A. bombing and the double homicide in Malibu, but Riggins assumed it was a backyard interest thing. Something Dark, a born manhunter, couldn't resist. But now he was here in NYC, just hours after news of the threat. He didn't fly here on a whim. He knew something had been up—in advance.

"So it's safe to assume you're still freelancing," Riggins said. "Still working for that evil shadowy bitch I warned you about?"

"No," Dark said.

"Well then, who? What, is it a state secret or something?"

"Seriously, Riggins, I'm not messing around, we've got a plane to catch," Dark said, brushing past him. The pretty dark-haired woman with no name followed in his wake.

"Well," he called out after Dark. "See you next crime scene."

Riggins couldn't help but wonder why he was still trying, still doing this, after all these years.

chapter 44

LABYRINTH

I have many things on my checklist to accomplish, but nothing I can't do by remote—and this is too great an opportunity to resist.

It's been a while since I followed a man spontaneously.

I enjoy it.

I decide to follow him while sitting in the comfortable lobby of the Epoch Hotel watching all manner of police officers try to work out the details of my "crime."

Two investigators, in particular, interest me. They're not NYPD, they're not FBI, nor Interpol nor anything else. They're not the usual suspects. Thinking back on the mental footage I have of the scene of my second gift in Dubai, I realize these two were there, too, picking over the scene. They're with some other agency.

Could it be . . . the agency? Blair's secret unit?

As I ponder, an FBI man—you can tell by the ill-fitting suit, the way he hunches, the shoes, the look that practically screams BURNOUT—approaches them and says,

"Steve Dark."

Why, thank you, Mr. FBI man. Nice to put a face to a name. I've read about Dark. Extremely disturbed individual.

Dark himself gives me a name for the bearlike FBI burnout: Riggins.

And a simple search on my phone reveals his identity: Agent Tom Riggins.

Their meeting isn't pleasant. There's some salacious history here. They act like parent and prodigal child.

For a few seconds, it's a coin toss—follow Dark or Riggins?

My gut tells me Riggins. If Dark is to be my hunter, then it would pay to know as much as possible about him.

Perhaps he can be turned.

So when they leave . . .

. . . I follow.

A cab drops Agent Tom Riggins off at Penn Station, where he catches an Amtrak train bound for Washington, D.C.

On the train I sit across the aisle and one seat back so that I not only have a view of his profile and facial expressions, but the ability to see what he reads or who he calls.

He calls no one, however.

The man just sits there and broods.

Closing his eyes every so often, pushing his fingers into his temples.

The pretty brunette next to me who smells of rosemary tries to chat me up—no doubt my suit and my haircut and the quality of the watch strapped to my wrist arouses her interest. Just like they are designed to do. My sheep's clothing.

So I engage in mild conversation, nothing deep, just polite chatter about absolutely fucking nothing.

All the while I'm—

Watching Tom Riggins.

Rosemary asks me,

What do you do for a living?

I tell her, smiling,

Insurance.

Thinking,

I could just lean over and start whispering into your ear right now and by the second sentence you'd be stumbling into the Labyrinth and by the third you'd be hopelessly lost and by the time this train pulls into D.C. you'd be totally mine, you fucking whore, ready to do whatever I tell you to whomever I tell you, including yourself. We could settle in for a long evening of degradation and self-destruction.

And the temptation is there, believe me. When you're on a mission to save the world, you still have the urge to blow off steam now and again.

But it's Tom Riggins I'm after.

Yes, Tom Riggins will provide the most pleasure this evening.

⌖

Tom Riggins disembarks at Union Station, where he's left his car—boring sedan, FBI issue.

I have no car, and cannot offer immediate pursuit.

I do have a tracking device, the size of a postage stamp, which I affix to the body of the sedan, which will give me time to research Tom Riggins's home security system.

Surprise—Tom Riggins has next to nothing A simple home alarm that's easily bypassed with a phone call and the pretense that I am the condo manager and need access to Tom Riggins's bathroom. My voice is authoritative and slightly bored. They believe me.

By the time I arrive in a stolen vehicle thirty minutes later, Agent Riggins has started to settle in for the night.

There he is now, staring into space. Look at him. Pathetic. He's spent most of his life chasing monsters and has absolutely nothing to show for it but a hollow space within his soul.

As if to prove my point.

Tom Riggins moves to his refrigerator, scoops stale ice into an oversize coffee mug, then tops it off with poor-quality scotch and retreats to his living room.

I take advantage of the distraction—kick in the front door, knowing that no alarm will sound. In my left hand, a Taser pistol. The prongs fly through the air and catch Tom Riggins in the chest. I squeeze. There's a crackling sound and then Agent Riggins is on his knees, the cheap contents of his mug spilling on a poor-quality rug that hasn't been cleaned since the day it was installed. I kick the door shut behind me, because we are going to need some private time, Tom Riggins and I . . .

Look at him crawling across the rug, wires still in his chest. Fingers clawed into rakes, pulling himself along the carpet, going for . . .

Oh, he must have a gun hidden in this room.

Tom Riggins, the last of the true hard-boiled men.

But there's no time for any of that. I have a plane to catch in the morning and I have the feeling it's going to be a long night, so I decide to get started. With the toe of my $1,500 A. Testoni, I catch Tom Riggins under his shoulder and flip him around, then quickly kneel on his barrel chest and give him the injection.

I tell him,

You want to know what happened to Shane Corbett?

He attempts to snarl a profanity, unable to even finish the thought.

The drugs are already taking hold, and he's finding it difficult to do much of anything.

I continue,

Soon you're going to learn.

He grunts.

And you're going to tell me all about Steve Dark.

chapter 45

DARK

Over the Atlantic Ocean

"You going to tell me what that was about?"

Dark paused before saying, "It's kind of complicated."

Natasha and Dark were recrossing the Atlantic Ocean. Damien Blair's fury was tempered by the fact that Steve Dark had been right—Labyrinth had struck in New York City, and they'd missed him by a matter of minutes. Natasha watched Dark as he scoured the fresh crime scene, and it was like the man had come alive for the first time in days. Something primal inside the man had been ignited. Natasha had to remind herself that she was investigating the case, too, coordinating with the NYPD and FBI, but it was hard to take her attention away from Dark and his obvious passion for the hunt. It was mesmerizing to watch.

That changed the moment Dark saw Agent Tom Riggins in the lobby. Dark's former mentor—the man who'd seen the same fire in Steve Dark, and tapped him to join Special Circs at an early age. Natasha had read the Global Alliance files.

"I understand," she continued. "I've had my own issues with father figures in the past."

"He's not exactly the *father* type," Dark said quietly.

Natasha knew the truth was different. Dark's foster family had been slaughtered. And his biological parents? No one knew who they were. Tom Riggins was the closest thing Dark had to family.

Natasha let it rest. Better to focus on Labyrinth. She wanted that investigative fire back. When Damien Blair had announced that Dark would be joining the team, she'd had her serious doubts—just like the rest of them. Damaged goods. A lone wolf. Erratic. Emotionally and possibly psychologically compromised. Not exactly what you'd call a good fit.

But now she saw the same blazing element that Blair had seen. And Natasha knew she could help bring it out of him, once again.

She reached out and touched his hand. Dark looked at her, barely, still lost in his thoughts about Riggins. But then all at once Dark *really* looked at her. Dark glanced around, as if only realizing just now that they were in an empty Gulfstream jet paid for by Global Alliance, and there was quite a bit of time before touchdown.

Natasha waited until he caught on, then pressed her lips to his.

Hours later, as the jet cleared French airspace, Dark told Natasha why he thought that Labyrinth would be striking in Scotland next.

The word *politicians* in the video tipped Dark off.

In two days, Edinburgh would play host to the so-called WoMU summit—World Minds United. The media had been buzzing about it for months now. A super–think tank aimed at solving no less than the problems of global inequality—all streaming live on the Internet.

"It's a huge stage," Dark explained now. "Labyrinth couldn't resist something like that. In fact, this may be what he's been building towards the whole time."

"You're saying he's a press-hungry killer. That this is all for the headlines."

"Why else would he be doing this? I don't think it's about the thrill of murdering someone. The deaths are incidental. The message means everything. He even told Jane Talbot that he was done with killing. Don't forget, though, he was saying that on live TV. That was the key."

"But that just proves that Labyrinth is lying," Natasha said.

"How? He didn't kill Shane Corbett. He found other people to do it for him—women who'd have a good reason to want to make him suffer. As far as Labyrinth is concerned, his hands are clean. He's just giving victims a chance to avenge themselves."

"So who does Labyrinth want to make suffer next?" Natasha asked.

chapter 46

DARK

Global Alliance HQ / Paris, France

Back at home base, Blair wasn't exactly falling all over himself to congratulate Dark that his instincts had been correct—that Labyrinth had struck in New York City, and that it was increasingly likely that he was going to hit Edinburgh, too. Dark had presented his case quickly, backed up by Natasha at every turn.

In fact, Blair didn't respond at all. He absorbed the details, but offered no commentary or feedback. After Dark was finished, Blair nodded, then retreated to his personal quarters.

The team sat in silence for a few moments before O'Brian finally spoke.

"Hey, don't take it personally. Big guy's got a lot on his mind. He's had a hard-on for this guy for years."

Dark shook his head. "That's what I don't understand. Labyrinth only emerged just now. I can understand the idea of bracing for a monster *like* Labyrinth to appear, but Blair seems like he's been expecting *this specific monster* the whole time."

"Well, I've been with the team longer than anybody at this table," Natasha said. "We've targeted a lot of threats that no one knows about—and hopefully, no one will *ever* know about. Each time, Blair compares the case at hand to the nightmare scenario in his mind. Each time, the case at hand comes up short. For whatever reason, Blair believes this Labyrinth is the nightmare scenario, and that's good enough for me."

"Doesn't change our tactics," said O'Brian. "Bad, badder, baddest . . . we take 'em out."

Dark stood up from the conference table. He heard what his teammates were saying, and he knew they were right. But there was another piece missing.

"Where are you going?" Natasha asked.

"Be right back."

Blair was at his desk, back to the door, staring at a series of black-and-white photos on the wall. Family, colleagues—whatever. Dark didn't care. He only wanted to know Damien Blair long enough to have him book a flight back to L.A. And if he refused, then fine. He'd be out of his life even faster.

"What is it?" Dark asked.

Blair continued staring at the wall.

"Did you hear me?"

Still nothing.

"Why do I have the feeling there's a lot more to Labyrinth than you're letting on."

Finally, he spoke.

"I was just thinking of a way to admit to you that I was wrong, and I should have trusted you."

Blair spun around in his chair.

"Your instincts are why I was so eager to have you join our team. You remind me of the best operatives I've worked with over the years. Sadly, they're the very operatives who never fail to frustrate me. Because the best seem to work best as lone wolves, and here I am trying to incorporate you into the pack. I do wonder why I'm drawn to such individuals. Must be something in the blood."

Now it was Dark's turn to say nothing. He figured it was better to let Blair speak his mind, and then tell him that he quit anyway.

"What I'm trying to say is, I've had trouble with lone wolves in the past, which is probably why I was determined to break you from the start. But I've been sitting here, trying to poke holes in your theories about New York and the possible attack in Edinburgh . . . and I'm coming up with nothing. I'm forced to concede that you're more finely tuned in to this predator's wavelength than I am."

Dark said, "We just have different methods."

"Exactly. And from now on, we run it your way, Dark. Nothing matters to me except catching Labyrinth. We'll go to Edinburgh, and we'll follow your lead."

Dark nodded, but he didn't step into this office to seize control away from Blair.

"Why do you think Labyrinth's the one?"

"The one?"

"You know what I mean. The threat you've been bracing for."

Blair nodded. "A little while ago, you said you flew to New York on a hunch. That was a leap of faith. I'm asking that you and the team take a leap of faith with me."

A few minutes after Dark left his quarters, Blair picked up his cell phone and thumbed through to the text message he'd received an hour ago.

DO YOU KNOW YOU HIRED A MONSTER?

The message was accompanied by a link. Blair had clicked it, after considerable hesitation. Labyrinth had been taunting him with personal messages ever since the L.A. attacks. Blair had no idea how he found his number, since it was unlisted and untraceable to him or any member of Global Alliance. And with every Labyrinth text taunt—this was the fourth—Blair would dispose of his phone and order a new one.

The link was new. Had Labyrinth come up with some diabolical way to infect his phone, and by extension, the computer systems inside Global Alliance?

No.

Instead, the link caused a small pdf to download to Blair's phone. A DNA report marked CLASSIFIED.

Blair had read the report, and with growing horror, put the pieces together.

Now he was wondering if he had just made the second biggest mistake of his life, or if the two would cancel each other out.

chapter 47

DARK

Edinburgh, Scotland

The package arrived two days later, the morning of the WoMU summit, just as Dark had predicted.

No fancy messengers this time, no homeless couriers. It arrived via next-day shipping from an address in London (that later turned out to be a vacant storefront). Dark and the rest of his Global Alliance teammates—O'Brian, Roeding—were there to watch as the forensic experts carefully picked apart the cardboard shipping box and removed the contents. The team had to watch from behind a thick pane of blast-resistant plastic—for their protection, of course, which annoyed Dark. He tried to remind the Lothian and Borders officials that Labyrinth had not detonated any of his packages so far—just the delivery man for the first one. They merely nodded and ignored Dark, continuing with their excruciatingly slow and methodical disassembly.

"They need to stop screwing around and just open the damned thing," Dark complained bitterly.

"It's procedure," Natasha said, eyeing the Scottish police, who in turn were eyeing Dark.

"We're wasting time."

At long last, the Lothian and Borders police removed another riddle. Same hand printing, same block letters, this time on U.S. Congress letterhead. The image was scanned and projected onto a flat-screen TV.

A MAN WALKS UP TO YOU AND SAYS, "EVERYTHING I SAY TO YOU IS A LIE." IS HE TELLING YOU THE TRUTH OR IS HE LYING?

LABYRINTH

"Good, another twisty little mindfuck," said O'Brian.

"Remember, the riddle's only part of it," Dark said. "Let's see what else he's thrown into the box."

Next, the police removed a modern digital stopwatch—black plastic, common brand name, nothing remarkable about it at first glance. Again it seemed like the Scottish police were moving in slow motion, despite the fact that clearly, nothing had gone *boom*.

"Fuck this," Dark said. "I need to see it up close."

When the door remained shut after a few frenzied knocks, Dark sighed, took a step back, then smashed his boot against it, right near the knob. Wood split and burst. Dark moved into the room, shouldering his way past the hazmat-suited experts, and plucked the stopwatch from the robot arm that was holding it.

"Less than five hours," Dark said, reading the display. "When does the summit begin?"

Natasha, who had followed him into the room, said, "Within the hour."

Dark pushed aside the robot arm and removed the remaining item from Labyrinth's package: a sheath of yellowed parchment paper, incredibly brittle, sealed in a plastic bag.

"What is it?"

The top page looked familiar to Dark, but he couldn't believe what he was looking at. The yellowed, brittle paper. The jagged scrawls. You'd need an expert to authenticate it, of course, but almost anyone could easily identify it.

Did Labyrinth actually just FedEx an early draft of the U.S. Constitution to Scotland?

A historic document expert from nearby University of Edinburgh was rushed down to St. Leonards Street station. The woman blinked as if she'd just woken from a five-year nap, but she tentatively described the document as authentic to the era (late 1780s)—but quickly added this version of the Constitution couldn't be real.

"Why?" asked Dark.

"Well, there is an urban legend going around my circles that there was an early, far more radical draft of the U.S. Constitution debated by the American founders," the expert said. "One that allegedly put much more power in the hands of the executive branch, with ordinary citizens having very few of the rights eventually granted. It was also rumored to have had proslavery elements—instead of the tacit approval given in the eventual version. This, of course, is no doubt an invention of conspiracy theorists, much like this document."

"But the paper and ink check out?"

"Well . . . yes. But there's no way this can be real."

If such a document existed, Dark knew, it would no doubt sell for untold millions on some secret, black market. Yet Labyrinth had found a way to put his hands on it. And he'd sent it, uninsured, by overnight delivery. Almost casually. This was as important as the message itself, Dark thought. He wanted to let them know his wealth was unlimited, and there was nothing he couldn't touch.

Not even the tender heart of the United States of America.

Lothian and Borders did their best to keep the examination of the latest Labyrinth package from the press. But the reporters seemed to know anyway—anonymous tips had armed them with just enough to turn them rabid. They pressed at the front doors of the St. Leonards Street station as Dark and the rest of the team emerged.

"He's tipping them off," Dark said. "Raising the game. It's only fun for him if everybody knows what he's up to."

They walked across the street to the black van that had been transported from Paris. Fully equipped with computers, bug detectors, weapons, a mobile forensics lab, and everything else the team could possibly need. As always, with Blair, money was no object.

"So we've seen the clues," O'Brian said. "We've got a copy of the Constitution and a stopwatch and another riddle."

"Don't know yet."

"Oh come on. You must have *some* idea. Some kind of crazy left-field thinking. That's your trademark, isn't it?"

"Deckland, shut the fuck up," Natasha said. "We're going to have some help, anyway. Blair's already on the scene."

Dark's eyebrow lifted. "He is?"

"These are his people, after all. Aristocrats, the hoi polloi, that whole set. He's smoothing feathers and scoping the scene."

Dark was the product of a foster home and a humble middle-class upbringing. No wonder Blair seemed like an alien to him.

"I thought he never went out into the field," Dark said.

"He seems to have changed his mind," Natasha said.

"Let's go," O'Brian said. "I'm driving. I'm still motion sick from Roeding's driving in J'burg."

The team walked to the van, at which point Dark separated himself.

"Got my own ride," Dark said.

"What do you mean, your own ride?" Natasha asked.

Dark said, "In case you were wondering—yeah, you can pretty much order anything from Blair's little shopping site."

Anything, in this case being a Ducati Desmosedici GP12. Liquid-cooled V4 engine, race-quality, and nowhere near street legal.

He trailed behind the van for a while until he was sure the rest of his team could see him—then he shifted and blazed past them. O'Brian smirked and gave him a one-finger salute as he passed. *Brilliant,* he mouthed. Or at least, that's what Dark thought the man was saying.

To be honest, it was all one vague blur.

chapter 48

DARK

For a meeting devoted to ushering in a new era of global understanding, there was an insane amount of security.

A lot of that had to do with the threat from Labyrinth, of course. But some of it was planned well in advance. All participating nations agreed to a strict no-weapons policy. Even the security guards inside the building were allowed to carry nothing more lethal than Tasers, mace canisters, and rubber batons. The credentials that Blair had sent to each member of the team were successful in getting them past the outer security perimeter surrounding the Scottish Parliament Building, but they were still subject to intensive pat-downs before they were allowed access to the main hall.

Each entrance, no matter how modest, was outfitted with next-generation full-body scanners as well as highly sensitive detectors looking for even trace amounts of explosives, gunpowder, chemical or biological agents—even radioactive matter. Blair had been sent the specs on everything and briefed the team in advance. But they hadn't realized how slowly the lines would move, and that even their Global Alliance credentials could do nothing to breeze them past the security checkpoint.

"More wasted time," Dark said.

"The harder it is for us to get in," Natasha said, "the harder it will be for Labyrinth."

"Is that what you really think? He's already here. Or one of his puppets. And his weapon of choice has no doubt been here for a long time, too. Maybe even when they built this monstrosity."

"Not possible," Natasha said. "Agents have been sweeping every inch of this place for days. And that's on top of the normal security checks. It's clean."

"As clean as a house of politicians can be, anyway," muttered O'Brian.

"Careful," Dark said. "You're beginning to sound like him now."

"Well, this attack may be one I actually agree with. Kill them all, I say."

These words came tumbling out of the Irish hacker's mouth just as they approached the checkpoint. The security detail's eyes turned icy, suspicious, even after Natasha approached and showed them her credentials.

"Whoops," O'Brian said.

There were only three of them. Hans Roeding refused to be weaponless, opted to wait out in the van, parked across the street near Holyrood Palace. This itself was a security breach, but Blair had managed to clear it. If the hunt for Labyrinth did take them back outside, then he wanted Roeding ready to neutralize him immediately.

Back inside, Deckland O'Brian perched himself in a corner with a netbook to scan Internet chatter about WoMU. Labyrinth liked to tease things in advance—there was a chance he'd let a detail slip.

Which left Dark and Natasha to sweep the main hall of the Scottish Parliament Building—thousands of square feet of possible danger.

"What do you make of the riddle?" Natasha asked.

"About the man who tells you everything he says is a lie? Well, he's lying. Even though he's lying when he says that everything he says is a lie, some of the things he says can be a lie. This is one of them."

"I'll take your word for that. So what does this have to do with the threat? Because the method is always hidden in the riddle."

Dark shook his head. "I'll let you know when I see it."

WoMU was purported to be an international "town hall," where new ideas could be discussed minus the politicking and reprisals from hostile governments. An open exchange of ideas for the betterment of all humanity. No idea too great or too small—all were promised an equal forum. The topics: Hunger. Renewable resources. Economic disparity. And more important, the organizers promised a follow-up report and action plan, delivered to world governments everywhere.

But at the same time, delegates could address some of the most powerful world leaders directly, live, after they made a few remarks.

Dark thought that was nice, but he didn't care about any of that right now.

All that mattered was that Labyrinth would consider this to be the perfect stage.

He was here somewhere.

Himself—or one of his avatars.

Damien Blair had followed through on his word. He relinquished Global Alliance command to Dark, who directed Natasha and O'Brian as the three searched the facility.

But there were no weak spots.

No hidden assassin's perches.

Everyone inside the building had been cleared through the security checkpoints.

There were radiation and gunpowder detectors for every ten people in the auditorium.

Guards *everywhere*.

Security was, Dark had to admit, top-notch.

Still, something nagged at Dark's mind. Something felt *off* . . .

chapter 49

DARK

After a few hours of speeches and pleas and even stretches of downright incoherence, the moment viewers had been waiting for had finally arrived: the Q&A session with world leaders. First up: the representative from the United States—powerful Senate Majority Leader Edah Ayres (R-Mo.). The elder statesman, with a big, slightly bucktoothed smile, trimmed beard, and full head of gray hair, took the dais and thanked his hosts.

The conference was being carried live across one global news network and dozens of Internet-based news orgs, and suddenly the media perked up. The rows of camera operators and photographers and reporters down in the media pit roused themselves. Here, finally, truth would speak to power. And they all knew that if they were lucky, they'd catch Senator Ayres red-faced in some misstatement or poorly chosen turn of phrase. Something that could feed the news cycle for the next twenty-four to forty-eight hours, ideally.

"Thank you so much for having me here, with all of you," Senator Ayres said. "I'm blessed and humbled to be with you in this beautiful country."

Dark and Natasha were positioned in the rear of the amphitheater to give themselves the widest possible view; O'Brian, meanwhile, was down in the media pit, just in case Labyrinth had a puppet mixed among the press corps.

"I don't believe this."

Natasha nudged Dark, holding up her tablet. The video image on the screen showed what everyone in the room could see live: Senator Ayres addressing the delegates. But the news feed that Natasha was streaming had something that the live viewers could *not* see.

An on-screen lie detector.

As Senator Ayres spoke, a single word, in bold, red seventy-two-point Helvetica type suddenly appeared on the screen:

LIAR

The small meter in the lower right-hand corner twitched into the red, too.

"Where's that coming from?" Dark asked. "That one site? Is that a parody site, maybe?"

"No," Natasha said, swiping the screen to the next feed. Same lie detector. She swiped again, to another, notoriously conservative news network. Same lie detector, superimposed over their own borders and news crawl.

"How is he doing this?" Dark asked.

Senator Ayres, who of course had no idea his words were being monitored for veracity, continued his opening remarks. "We believe in spreading freedom so that all may enjoy it."

And on-screen, in even larger point type:

LIAR

By now some of the reporters and camera operators—checking their own monitors—realized what was happening. Murmurs erupted, cell phones were plucked from belt holders. Senator Ayres glanced down at the media pit briefly, unable to ignore the slight commotion, but then remembered *where* he was, *what* he was doing, and his bucktoothed smile flashed and his attention returned to the delegates.

"And part of the pursuit of freedom is guaranteeing food security and safe water for all. Over thirty-five thousand people die each day from malnutrition-related illnesses, and this is why my administration has fought from the beginning to better understand the causes and consequences of hunger . . ."

LIAR

The word had spread throughout the hall—the modern media hive mind operating at full speed. Delegates looked at one another confusedly. Camera operators, loathe to turn their equipment away from Senator Ayres, tried sorting through wires to see if there was anything plugged in that shouldn't be. And now the senator's aides had caught wind of what was happening, and a pack of three young men in charcoal gray suits began to hunch-walk toward the dais to interrupt the senator as discreetly as possible.

"Shit," Dark said. "It's coming."

"What?" Natasha said. "Do you see something?"

"No. I feel it."

With that, Dark started running down the center aisle of the amphitheater, guided by the gnawing sense of danger in the pit of his stomach.

He was halfway down when the explosion sounded, echoing off the walls of the entire hall.

And Senator Edah Ayres's face blew apart in a messy red spray.

chapter 50

Alain Pantin watched the attack happen from the wings, and then even he couldn't believe it.

An assassination, live, right before his very eyes.

My. God.

As a history student Pantin used to idly wonder what it would be like to witness a major historical moment—a military victory, a landmark speech, an act of terrorism. Now that Pantin was caught up in the actual thing, and not from behind the safety of a television screen, he felt nothing but icy numbness.

Look at that poor man up on that stage, face dripping with bright red blood that looks positively unnatural, surreal, under the bright lights. Stumbling back, still on his feet, hands shaking, not even able to fall down and die properly. It was a horror show. This maniac had waited until the whole world was watching, and then he'd treated it to a snuff film. . . .

Pantin's cell phone buzzed. It was Trey.

"Don't panic," he said. "This is extremely important."

"Are you watching this?" Pantin asked quietly. He felt goose bumps across every square inch of his flesh.

"Breathe. Keep yourself together. And listen to me."

"Listen to what? Jesus Christ, Trey, are you watching this?"

"Alain, the world's going to want to know what to think of this latest attack, and you are going to be the one to explain it to them."

"*I* don't know what the fuck is going on, Trey. How am I supposed to explain it to the world?"

"Focus on why Labyrinth targeted Ayres. He's only lashed out against people who were hiding something. The world will be reassured to know that he's just like the other targets. Guilty of something."

"Fuck, man . . . You want me to assassinate the character of a man who's just been assassinated?"

"You don't have to make any allegations whatsoever. You should damn this deplorable attack, and invite Labyrinth to air his grievances. Remember to stay focused on the message, not the act."

Pantin hesitated. He watched as pandemonium gripped the room. Several people were rushing the stage, others looking around for assassins' perches.

"Don't give up now," Trey continued. "You're the most tenacious man I know. This is why I've supported you. It may not seem like it now, but this will truly be the moment that defines you."

Pantin cleared his throat, said okay, then put the cell phone in his pocket. After a deep breath, he straightened his tie, wiped his sweaty brow with the side of his right index finger, then made his way toward the stage—toward the sea of reporters falling over one another to capture the moment.

The world will want to know what happened.

I must explain it to them.

chapter 51

After an assassination—successful or otherwise—a certain percentage of any crowd will run for cover, concerned for their own lives. But a surprising majority spring into action. This was the case now. Security, as well as other ambassadors and attendees, began to shout at one another, looking for the shooter.

Dark knew there was no shooter. Not in the traditional sense, anyway. The shooter was Labyrinth, and he had struck from a remote location.

But from where?

How, in a highly secure room where even the security personnel carried nothing more powerful than a Taser?

Dark scanned the room, tracing the velocity of the projectile that had struck. If he had more time, he could use lasers and tape to pinpoint the exact origin of the shot. But he didn't have time. Every second that passed meant that Labyrinth would be speeding away to his next victim.

"Dark."

Natasha had raced up behind him and was now showing him the tablet. A new message was superimposed over the chaos that had broken out:

DYE, SENATOR, DYE

"What does that mean?" Natasha asked. "Labyrinth doesn't misspell things."

A security detail had reached Senator Ayres and was quickly escorting him from the dais and out of the main hall. The politician's arms were pinwheeling around. He was in pain, but he wasn't dying. Not by any stretch. Dark pushed his way through the crowd for a better look. The blood on the senator's face . . . it wasn't blood at all.

DYE, SENATOR, DYE

Labyrinth was being literal. And his promise to Jane Talbot had been kept. He hadn't killed anyone since his appearance on South African TV. Instead, he'd arranged it so that a blast of red dye had struck the lying senator right in his distinguished face in front of millions of viewers. And by the time it was rebroadcast and uploaded and sent around via social networking sites, it would be seen by millions more. Anyone with access to a screen.

The politician had been caught red-faced, after all.

AP News

Breaking: Sen. Ayres attacked with "exploding dye" at Scotland summit; reportedly in serious but stable condition.

CNN

Breaking: Suspect "Labyrinth" on air now.

Within seconds every broadcast had been hijacked.

A man, draped in just enough shadow to obscure his identity, appeared on screens everywhere.

Murmurs throughout the crowd. Shrieks of panic, too.

The figure stepped forward into the light and revealed his face.

The mask was a joke—a plastic Halloween likeness of Richard Nixon. The choice of bank robbers all over America.

"Government is built on and run by liars," he said, his voice distorted mechanically. "Politicians who are out to get as much as they can for themselves, rather than help the people. Politicians who lie about everything. I want a politically free society. Every representative is for the people. Benefits all equally. Not just rich."

Dark stared at the image. There were no more coy videos being uploaded. Labyrinth was speaking to the world, because now he knew the world would be listening. The Jane Talbot "appearance" was a test run. This was another test. Another step into the light. He was teasing the world. Giving them just enough to speculate, to ponder, to wonder.

What's your true face? Dark wondered. *When are you going to show us? When it's far too late?*

Dark watched his body language and had the unerring sense that this was no puppet, no stand-in. This was Labyrinth himself.

And he was still here, in Edinburgh.

I'm seeing RED now. RT: Breaking: Sen. Ayres attacked with "exploding dye" at Scotland conference; reportedly in serious but stable condition.

3 minutes ago

Don't know wether to laugh or go hide under my bed.

2 minutes ago

Well, at least he didn't kill him. He did promise Jane Talbot, you know.

2 minutes ago

The politicians lie to us. I do NOT lie.

1 minute ago

chapter 52

DARK

Deckland O'Brian was already picking through the remnants of the exploded camera by the time Dark and Natasha forced their way down into the media pit. He was squatting and probing the red dye–soaked chunks of metal and plastic with his bare fingers.

Dark said, "Tell me you've got something, Deckland."

"Yeah, I think I've found it—" O'Brian shrieked and pulled his hands away from the smoking components. "Ouch! Jesus fuck! Bloody thing's almost melted!"

"What is it?"

"Well, there's no way to wipe the embarrassment off the good senator's face. But I think we can trace Labyrinth through this wireless triggering mechanism. He'd had to be able to detonate this thing from off-site, and from the looks of this half-melted component here, he can't be too far away."

"So can you trace him?"

"I can try. If I can shock this wee bugger back to life and reestablish a signal, it just might lead us back to our good friend Labyrinth."

"I'm off," Dark said, tapping his earpiece. "Update me on the road."

"I'm coming with you," Natasha said.

"No. I need you to trace the network feeds. Labyrinth didn't just upload a video anonymously this time. He's hijacked the major news networks, and I'm sure they're going to be seriously pissed about the whole thing. Maybe we can trace him that way. I'm sure they're already trying to figure out where he's broadcasting from."

Natasha nodded, then touched his face. "Be careful."

"I'm going to end this thing. Tonight."

Dark pushed his way through the crowds, flashing his cell phone badge when necessary, and pushing people out of the way when that didn't work. Once he finally made it outside the Scottish Parliament Building, Dark ran across the street to the Global Alliance van and Hans Roeding, who saw him coming and rolled down his power window.

"Where are we headed?" the burly ex-soldier asked.

Dark didn't want the extra weight. He needed to be able to move quickly, nimbly. Which is why he didn't want Natasha to tag along either.

"I'm just following a hunch. Stay here in case I'm wrong."

"I can help."

"I know. By staying here."

Roeding didn't say much. He merely broke eye contact and grunted. The soldier had been trained to follow orders, even if he hated the guts of the person giving said orders. And Blair had made it clear: Dark was in charge of this op.

"I need a gun."

Roeding frowned, then plucked a Glock 19 from a console inside the van. He knew that the so-called plastic semiautomatic was Dark's weapon of choice. As Dark tucked it into his waistband, he saw Roeding pull another gun from the console—a silver Derringer. Without saying a word, he handed it over to Dark.

"What's that for?"

"I carry a backup. You should, too."

"Okay. Thanks."

"Sure."

Dark tucked the extra piece in the small of his back.

Evening Mail

Breaking: U.S. senator stable, but doctors fear the dye will leave him blind; skin permanently stained.

Guardian

Breaking: MEP Alain Pantin says that Labyrinth attacks may not stop until "real conversations" start to happen; urges for a new forum.

A few moments later, on his brand-new Ducati, Dark was racing up Canongate, the oldest street in Edinburgh. If Dark followed it all the way he'd end up at the foot of the castle. The ground was wet and the air was misty. Dark could feel the tires almost slipping on the granite sets. But being in charge of his own vehicle was a refreshing change after days of planes and cabs and vans. Nothing worse than relying on someone else for travel.

Just like you, Labyrinth.

You're a man who travels by his own steam, aren't you? Untraceable. Able to slip borders with ease. You're someone practiced at the art of travel. Otherwise, you wouldn't spread your attacks all over the world. You're at ease anywhere. Maybe that's how you were trained. Maybe you're former military or part of a diplomatic security detail. Someone who was always on the move.

O'Brian's voice was in his ear: "Are you there, Dark?"

"Yeah."

"Okay, I see you. Looks like the signal's coming from further up the road, almost near the castle."

Dark's motorcycle raced up the main street. There were people everywhere—on the sidewalks, in the street, not to mention other vehicles. WoMU had sparked impromptu gatherings and parties. Scotland was the focus of the world right now; the Scots were enjoying the chance to preen. The attack on the American senator, of course, had cast a sudden pall on the festivities.

"Stop. You're close."

Pulling to the side, Dark parked the Ducati and checked his Glock. "Tell me where to go."

There was a row of three-story buildings along this side of the street, most of them dating back centuries. Edinburgh's early days were all about building vertically—up a few stories, which was as high as architecture would allow back then. And when the city ran out of room, they'd dig more stories below, a dizzying complex of subterranean levels. The similarities to Paris, and Global Alliance, couldn't be ignored. Dark had never encountered so many labyrinths before.

All at once Dark realized that of course this was it—if Labyrinth were going to hide anywhere, he'd do it in some kind of underground maze.

"Okay, I'm using your phone to lock on your position, and I'm following the signal from the camera."

Dark said, "Just tell me where to go."

"Is there a gate to your right?"

There was. An arched stone doorway with a sign marked BUCHAN'S CLOSE. A gate blocked the entrance almost all the way to the top.

"Go through there."

"It's locked."

"Figure out a way to go through it anyway. There's no other way in, except the long way, on the other side of the block. Which would involve scaling a fifty-foot wall."

Dark pulled his Glock, aimed it at the padlock and chain . . . then hesitated. No. A gunshot might spook Labyrinth if he was still inside. He put the gun away, looked at the drainpipe running alongside the stone building. Dark gave it a tug to test its stability. Seemed okay. Able to hold his weight. Quickly, he ascended the pipe, hand over hand, boots guiding him up the side of the building, until he reached the top of the gate. Right hand, then left—and then he was over, jumping down into the darkness, landing, drawing his Glock.

"I've got a better fix on the signal," O'Brian said in his ear. "It's coming from the roof."

"Check," Dark said, but he knew Labyrinth wouldn't be on the roof, or even the top floors. He'd be down below. Inside the maze of rooms below street level. Somewhere along the narrow streets with modest subterranean tenements on either side.

Gun leading the way in a two-handed grip, Dark descended the stairs, listening for his quarry.

Monsters liked to hide in basements.

chapter 53

LABYRINTH

They'd mark you in the old days.

If you were a criminal.

Anglo-Saxon law had it so vagrants and Gypsies were branded with a large *V*, permanently seared into your chest with a hot iron. Brawlers and fighters were given an *F*; slaves an *S*. Thieves would receive burns on their cheeks so that all may know not to trust them around their personal property.

Even as recently as two centuries ago, disloyal soldiers were tattooed or branded with the letters *BC*—bad character.

Senator Ayres deserves his branding.

I could have burned his face. But this is the twenty-first century, after all. Such tortures are best left in the Dark Ages.

People may think the act was cruel.

That will change when I upload the good senator's real biography, the one they don't hand out in his public affairs office, the one I've been compiling for ten years, the one that talks about his supposed humanitarian efforts to fight disease and hunger around the world, and how these efforts resulted in millions of dollars in contributions. . . .

And how many of these millions went to the good senator's spacious manse in the O'Fallon suburb of St. Louis, Missouri.

And a vacation home near Myrtle Beach.

And lavish buffets of fat-laden foods for your family and mistresses and their families, in and out on a rotating basis?

Did you go to the beach to sun, my dear senator?

Well, I've saved you the effort, haven't I? Your face will appear nice and sunburned for the rest of your life.

I follow the social media hive mind for a while, pleased that the message is getting out.

Then there is a sound.

In the hallway.

Slight.

But I hear it.

I turn—

[To enter the Labyrinth, please go to Level26.com and enter the code: enter the maze]

chapter 54

DARK

No.

Impossible.

Not him.

Not here . . .

⁂

Everything had happened in a frenzied blur—the chase, Dark's shots missing Labyrinth. . . .

Not only missed, but seemed to pass right through him.

The fuck?

Dark had never seen a suspect move so fast, not ever. And he almost didn't see the figure in the robe charging at him, slamming into Dark's sternum with the strength and speed of a sledgehammer.

And in that moment he saw Labyrinth's mask—

A crow-featured plague doctor mask.

Beaked, black, grotesquely inhuman features—but with all-too-human eyes staring at him from cutout holes in the mask.

A glimpse was all Dark had before the fight resumed. Dark nearly fell to his knees but focused on breathing. Just the oxygen and blood flowing. *The adrenaline in the blood will keep you moving. Hurt later. Move now. The monster is getting away. . . .*

Dark charged forward with punches to his attacker's face, his right arm partially numb—but that was okay, because it wasn't really attached to Dark's body anymore. It felt like its own living organism, a slab of bone and muscle designed for one thing: beating the living fuck out of Labyrinth with a series of supercharged blows.

But the man in the mask absorbed every punch without it seeming to affect him at all. And during a brief pause between blows, Labyrinth returned a jab of his own that pained Dark down to the marrow of his bones. Dark wasn't even sure where he'd been struck—only that it hurt far worse than it should have.

Labyrinth took a step back, put a hand to his face, then removed the crow mask.

Revealing *another mask* beneath.

The last mask Steve Dark thought he'd ever see again.

The Sqweegel mask.

The man behind the mask let out something that sounded like a chortle, or a snort, or perhaps even a choked laugh before turning and disappearing into the gloom.

Again: Dark knew it was impossible. It wasn't him. Not here. Not anywhere. He'd watched the bloodied chunks of his body burn in a furnace. There was no coming back from where he'd sent Sqweegel.

So Dark swallowed hard and pursued his suspect. He could hear frenzied slaps of boot heels on stone stairs, so Dark followed him up into the top stories of the ancient building, even though his guts felt like they were lined with razor blades. Dark ascended the central staircase, floor by floor by agonizing floor, until he was almost at the roof level. . . .

chapter 55

LABYRINTH

Oh, Steve Dark.

Ever since seeing you in New York City I had a feeling we'd be meeting up.

And you don't meet someone new without giving them a present.

So I did a little digging into your world . . .

And oh, you won't believe what I found.

It's been difficult to contain myself.

Almost sent it to you directly.

But I thought . . . better to wait.

I knew you'd come along eventually.

And you did.

You found me.

You can be proud of that, at least.

No one's ever looked me in the eye and saw me for my true self.

No one's ever come close.

You climbed up and skittered across the top of the maze just like a brave little dark mouse, didn't you?

More than Damien Blair's ever done.

It took me a little while to find just the right one as described by Tom Riggins, but it was worth the effort and shipping.

The mask:

White latex with metal zippers along the mouth and the top of the head.

Eye holes so its wearer can see perfectly, clearly, no obstructions whatsoever.

You had to keep it greased inside, and that was going to wreak havoc with my hair later.

But it was worth it.

Oh, the look on your face, Steve Dark.

To smash away the visage of your latest enemy, only to reveal your ultimate nemesis beneath.

"Sqweegel."

I don't even have to say anything.

The shock temporarily paralyzes you. This is the face you see in your nightmares, isn't it, Steve Dark? Tom Riggins sees it, too. All the time. He doesn't tell you, but this face is his greatest fear. That someday he's going to wake up in the middle of the night to discover this face looking down at him, only he's afraid he's going to see *your eyes* through the cutout holes, and *your mouth*, curled into a defiant, sickly smile, the open zipper teeth only increasing the effect.

Tom Riggins is afraid of this because he knows the truth about you, Steve Dark. About the blood that runs through your veins.

I know it, too.

Do you?

No.

I don't think you do.

That beautiful moment of Steve Dark's paralysis is all I need. I chose this specific spot. I led him to this point in the maze because I knew it would work to my advantage. Even down below in the gloom of the close I saw it perfectly and knew how it would play out. And Steve Dark followed me right into it, just like everyone else.

Everyone has a secret that can be pulled from deep beneath the flesh, then held up, dripping with blood and viscera, to be examined in the naked light.

Dark's secret is bigger and uglier than most.

I chose this spot because of the window behind Steve Dark. Now I rush forward.

The face of Sqweegel temporarily fries his internal circuits—

So it is relatively easy to push him OUT of the window.

Not all the way.

I hang on to Steve Dark's bleeding arms, watch him twist and turn, trying to break free from my grip, legs kicking, boots seeking purchase.

But he is in my control now.

And I have his next present.

Holding on to him with one hand, I reach up.

Unzip the mouth.

And I say,

Seven out of eleven alleles.

chapter 56

DARK

"Seven out of eleven alleles."

The words made no sense. *None* of this made sense to Dark. Why was Labyrinth leaving him to dangle out of this window, the hard granite of Edinburgh's High Street four stories below? Why hadn't he just killed him? Dark reached out with his boots to find some kind of foothold, something to lean against so he could use the leverage and pull this fucker out of the window, too.

The man above him, wearing the Sqweegel mask, kept at it.

"Seven out of eleven alleles, Steve Dark. Do you know what that means?"

"Fuck you."

"That means there's enough for a genetic match, Steve Dark."

Dark knew that. He was trained in forensic science. But what was this son of a bitch trying to say? This was a hell of a time for a basic lecture on DNA comparisons.

Then he remembered the second gun—the Derringer Hans Roeding had given him. Tucked in his waistband, at the small of his back. He could feel its weight.

Labyrinth continued,

"Tom Riggins ran the test. He told me so. Scraped the sample from under your dead wife's fingernails and ran it through."

Don't listen to him. Just pull an arm free. Yank it free and reach around and wrap your hand around the grip of the gun and bring it up and blow his fucking head apart inside that latex mask. . . .

"Tom Riggins told you there was no match. That Sqweegel was a mystery man. But you know what? Tom Riggins told a little white lie there. He found a match. Seven out of eleven alleles."

Dark ripped his right hand free and felt a jagged piece of glass run up the inside of his forearm. The cut was deep and burned immediately. Didn't matter. *Don't focus on the pain. Focus on the gun.*

"Where are you going?" Labyrinth asked, his face twisting beneath the mask in an expression of mock hurt. "Don't you want to hear who was the match, Steve Dark? Seven out of eleven alleles?"

Don't listen.

Dark plucked the gun from his waistband.

"It was you, Steve Dark."

Dark pointed the gun at Labyrinth's face and said, "Fuck you," before pulling the trigger. At the same moment Labyrinth released his grip on his left arm and Dark began to plunge toward the ground, still pointing the gun, wondering why the shot hadn't whipped the motherfucker's head back, so Dark fell and fired again, and again—*were the bullets just passing through him like a ghost?!*—and then the earth rushed up to meet him.

chapter 57

DARK

Hans Roeding was first on the scene, and found Dark's unconscious body on the sidewalk outside Buchan's Close. He checked Dark's vitals. Still a pulse, still strong, but unconscious. He took the warm Derringer from his hand. The Glock was nowhere in sight. *Must have dropped it inside,* he thought.

When O'Brian and Natasha arrived a minute later, Roeding had already smashed his way into the close and was reporting that Labyrinth—if the person who attacked Dark *was* Labyrinth—was nowhere to be found. Blair coordinated with local police to organize a manhunt throughout Edinburgh, as well as teams checking rails, airports, and all major roadways, but Global Alliance realized such a plan was futile. Labyrinth was a master planner. There was no doubt he had multiple exit scenarios all gamed out, and had simply chosen one of them. They had no description. Even if they did, there was a good chance that Labyrinth had already altered his appearance.

Natasha volunteered to accompany Dark to a secure wing of the world-renowned Pitié-Salpêtrière in Paris. Blair arranged for a private room, which had the advantage of being inside a high-security wing with security supplied by Global Alliance itself. If Dark resumed consciousness, there was a chance he could give some kind of description of Labyrinth.

She sat on the stiff bench in the back of the chopper, staring at Dark's face. His eyes darted back and forth under his lids at a frighteningly rapid pace, so much so that Natasha was at times convinced he was going to have a seizure. His face was bloody and bruised, too. Dark didn't just fall from four stories up—he'd fought with Labyrinth. Maybe he was lucky enough to have gotten a few shots in. . . .

Of course.

Natasha Garcon's area of expertise was not forensic science—not by any stretch—but she had observed enough to know how to take samples for later analysis. She raided the back of the ambulance for a scalpel, tweezers, scissors, sterile cloth squares, and plastic bags. Then she gently held Dark's left hand as she swabbed for samples.

Labyrinth had never left forensic material at any scene, but maybe Dark had pushed him hard enough to make a mistake.

His fingers twitched in her hands. It felt like both yesterday and forever since his hands had caressed her body.

chapter 58

RIGGINS

Quantico, Virginia

The morning after his assault, Tom Riggins woke up and stared at the ceiling, wondering if he should just eat his gun and be done with the whole thing. Or start drinking now to take the edge off the ache he felt from the top of his head to the soles of his shoes. Sure, drinking. Just the thing his fractured mind needed right now . . .

That he wasn't dead was a miracle in itself. He could have been snuffed so damn easily. . . .

But what *had* happened?

Riggins's memory felt like a TV that continued to switch channels every two or three seconds, never lingering long enough on an image to make sense of it. Riggins had experienced plenty of alcohol-induced blackouts, but never anything like this. The inside of his skull felt like it had been cracked open and somebody had scraped his brains out with a paring knife, leaving behind nothing more than some stringy, pulpy tissue.

But the truth was—and this hurt the most:

He'd let himself become a target.

This was the very thing he'd caution Special Circs recruits

against—opening yourself up, revealing something about yourself, giving your prey a reason to turn around and start hunting *you*. Such a fucking *rookie* mistake. As if Riggins needed further proof that his career was over, that he was no longer circling the drain but actually clogged down inside of it, with the rest of the shit.

Riggins climbed off his own dirty carpet, shuffled to the kitchen, turned on the tap, leaned over, cupped some cold water into his mouth. Rinse, spit. The inside of his mouth felt like the striking surface on a matchbook. That fucker had shot him up with something fierce. Some kind of truth serum, because Riggins had a fractured memory of talking. Talking a lot. Nonstop talking. And Riggins was *not* a talker.

It came back to him now. His assailant—if it was this "Labyrinth" freak—had been asking him about Steve Dark.

A billion questions about Steve Dark.

Christ, what had he said?

The drugs were one thing. But not everything. It was the patter, too, the way Labyrinth smacked your brain in one direction, then another. Not torture so much as extremely aggressive therapy. The drugs simply made it difficult to keep your mouth shut and block your ears.

Riggins was halfway to the bathroom when the phone rang. He reversed course and picked up the receiver to hear a woman's voice.

"Agent Riggins?"

"Who is this?"

"My name is Natasha Garcon. We met in New York, at the Epoch Hotel."

"Right," Riggins said. "Don't think we were properly introduced. What happened? Is he okay?"

"No, he's not. He suffered a fall in Edinburgh."

"A what? And where?"

"He's still out. I just . . . I just thought you should know. Dark told me he didn't have any family, besides you. And his daughter."

Even after the events of the past twelve hours, Riggins was genuinely startled to hear that Dark would ever refer to him as a member of his family.

And equally startled to find himself, just a few hours later, preparing for a red-eye to Paris. No official orders, no official okay from the FBI. Just his own plastic buying a wildly expensive one-way ticket. Riggins sat in the terminal bar, slamming bourbons as fast as the bartender could pour them. He opted to drink himself stupid before flights, because in his opinion, there was nothing worse than flying. As he waited for his flight, he called Constance.

"I need to know what Global Alliance is."

"Riggins? Jesus . . ."

"And a check on someone named Natasha. Can you do that for me? I know, you're busy, but . . ."

Constance sighed. "I don't suppose there's a last name?"

"What do you think? Gar . . . something. Garces? Garcin? She said it too fast. But if you find Global Alliance, you'll find her."

"Where are you, Riggins?"

"Trying to do the right thing, but probably making things a whole lot fucking worse. In other words, the usual. I'll call you in seven hours."

chapter 59

RIGGINS

Paris, France

Flying to France was nothing compared with making his way to Steve Dark's hospital room at the Pitié-Salpêtrière. *Hell,* Riggins thought. *I can hardly pronounce the name of the damned place.* When he landed Riggins called Natasha Garcon—who was surprised to learn that he'd traveled all this way. Still, she was able to speak to the staff and put Riggins's name on the clearance list. The guards at the security checkpoint were more thorough than his last colonoscopy. And even then, they insisted on accompanying Riggins up to Dark's room, their guns drawn, ready to shoot to kill if Riggins took one step out of place. They didn't care that he worked for the FBI; they didn't care *how* far back he went with the patient. They were employed by this Global Alliance, and they were paid not to take any chances.

"You guys hiring, by chance?" Riggins asked.

They said nothing in reply. Riggins noted they were wearing serious body armor over their black and gray camos, and loaded up with SIG Sauers and MK23 MOD .45-caliber handguns with suppressors and laser pointers.

"Okay then."

When they finally approached Dark's room, Riggins was treated to one more pat-down—"Seriously, fellas?"—before he was allowed inside. Riggins thought it was a lot of effort for what was sure to be an anticlimax. Garcon had told him that Dark was still unconscious, and Riggins expected to spend the next eight hours sitting next to Dark's bed in a dim room, wishing like hell he could smoke.

But Dark was propped up in the reclining bed, IV tubes still snaked up to his arm. There were heavy circles under his eyes, and Riggins had never seen the man look more beaten or tired . . . but he was awake. That was huge.

"Riggins," Dark said weakly.

"Hey. You're up."

"Yeah," Dark said. "Natasha told me you might be visiting, so I figured I'd better snap out of the coma, otherwise I'd have to listen to you rambling on and on in my subconscious."

Riggins forced a smile. "I'm going to probably ramble anyway."

"Figured."

"So what happened? And what's this Global Alliance bullshit you've signed up for?"

Dark recapped the basics—how he was recruited, and the hunt for Labyrinth thus far, including their encounter in Edinburgh. Riggins listened to the way Dark talked about their battle. How the bullets seemed to pass right through him. How he moved with preternatural speed and strength. Riggins bit his tongue so hard he thought he might sever it. He remembered his attacker—how stealthy he was, and how absurdly powerful. There wasn't a chance to mount a proper fight. The motherfucker was all over him like a wild animal. Shooting him up. Pulling open his brain . . .

"And he was ready for me," Dark said. "Me, personally. Because under another mask, he wore a replica of a Sqweegel mask."

Riggins felt his stomach go instantly cold. "You're fucking kidding. How the hell . . . ?"

"Sqweegel was big news five years ago. It would not take much to dig up that piece of my past. But the way he spoke . . . it was like he knew a lot more about the case than had ever appeared in the papers."

"Huh," Riggins said, but his mind was *racing.* The shattered memories of his assault were making sense now. Oh fuck were they making sense. The attack. He remembered more of it now. *You're going to tell me all about Steve Dark.* Shit, what had he told that bastard about Steve Dark?

Dark continued. "Strange thing was, he didn't want to kill me. He dropped me out of desperation—because I was about to blow his face off. It's like he wanted to mess with my mind, throw me off the hunt."

"Why?"

"Because I'm not one of his targets. He took me seriously enough to try to neutralize me, but he also didn't want to bother killing me. He's extremely precise with his targets, and extremely precise about explaining himself to the world. That's the thing about this one, Riggins. He's not like the other sickos and freaks we've chased down over the years. Look at the people he's targeted so far. All guaranteed to grab maximum headlines."

"We've chased other sick bastards who liked to see their handiwork show up in the press," Riggins said.

"But not like this one. He's ideological more than homicidal. He's not even killing everybody. That's what worries me. A Level 26 killer typically uses a trail of victims to build toward something greater. The question is, what's Labyrinth building?"

"No idea," Riggins said, only half-listening, because the other half of his brain was furiously putting together the pieces of his assault, and the horror and shame were building. There was one awful secret about Steve Dark, and for five years Riggins had kept it buried in an iron vault deep within his mind. Had Labyrinth dug it up and forced it open with a crowbar of truth serum and relentless questions?

"Hey," Dark said, "I am glad you're here. That means a lot."

"What did he tell you?" Riggins asked. "You said he knew things about Sqweegel that weren't in the papers."

Dark was silent for a moment before saying, "It's not important."

Riggins squeezed his fists so hard that his fingernails dug into his palms, drawing blood. Fuck. Labyrinth *knows*. He knows and he told Dark the truth to gain a tactical advantage. And now Dark knows . . . and that's the one thing Tom Riggins swore that his surrogate son would never, *ever* know.

That Sqweegel, their greatest nemesis, and the man who had killed Dark's foster family and beloved wife, Sibby, was a *blood relative*.

What was that doing to his mind? Riggins almost couldn't bear to look Dark in the eye for fear he'd give himself away. The guilt. The shame.

"Riggins."

"Yeah."

"Hey, look at me."

Riggins did. "I'm going to be fine. I'm bruised as hell and that rattled the tapioca of my brains around a little bit . . . but I'm going to live. You're acting like I'm about to check out or something."

"Yeah. No. Sorry . . . look, I'm just hungover and tired. You know me. I can't fly without getting shitfaced."

"Well, down a bunch of coffee. Because I have a favor to ask."

Riggins was again surprised. Dark, like any bitter child, had made a point over the years of letting Riggins know he didn't need him or his help for anything, ever again.

"What do you need?"

"I want you to find Natasha and help the rest of the team catch this son of a bitch," Dark said.

"What, me, join your *superspecial fancy* spy team? You've got to be kidding, right?"

"They've got everything—weapons, money, computers, access.

But they don't have a manhunter. They don't have someone experienced in catching Level 26 killers. They need *you*."

"Hey, they tapped you. They don't want your old boss who's about to be put out to pasture."

"Riggins, I haven't even tried walking to the bathroom yet. And when I get there, I have a feeling that I'm going to be pissing a lot of blood. Meanwhile, this Labyrinth fuck is going to be sending more packages, and he's going to keep going and building toward something that . . . well, that frankly worries the hell out of me. I'd feel a whole lot better knowing you were on the hunt."

Riggins listened to his words, and knew he should feel the slightest bit flattered—the classic pupil praising the teacher. But the shame and guilt blanked all of that out. So all he could say was,

"Yeah, okay, I'll help."

Guardian

Breaking: New Labyrinth threat said to have been delivered to the Vatican.

New York Times

Exclusive: Alain Pantin's call to stop Labyrinth not with guns, but ideas.

chapter 60

TRANSCRIPT: THE CORMAC JOHNSON HOUR, CNN

CORMAC JOHNSON

Joining us tonight via satellite is European Parliament member Alain Pantin, a man who's become known as, for better or worse, Labyrinth's spokesman. Until a few weeks ago, nobody had ever heard of Pantin. He was just one of hundreds of semi-obscure parliamentary members of the EU. That is, until Labyrinth started sending letters and boxes of clues and—allegedly—started killing people, demanding change. I've asked Mr. Pantin on the show to explain why he's hitched his political career to a sociopath and why he thinks Labyrinth's diatribes are worth listening to. Welcome, Mr. Pantin.

ALAIN PANTIN

Thank you, Cormac. I'm a longtime fan of your show, but I'll correct you on one thing, I am not Labyrinth's spokesperson. I have never met this Labyrinth, nor do I represent him in any way.

JOHNSON

But you're taking Labyrinth's messages and running with them.

PANTIN

While I vehemently disagree with his methods, there is something to Labyrinth's messages. Just because a monster tells you that a building is on fire doesn't mean that the building is not, in fact, on fire.

JOHNSON

The bigger question here, though, is whether we should start basing our economic and political decisions on the desires of a monster. Is that a way to run the world? Are you going to base your campaign on the rantings of a madman?

PANTIN

Labyrinth has called our attention to a host of problems in our world that we should ***not*** be so willing to accept, yet somehow we do. We elect people who serve their own interests or those of the highest bidder. I'm sick of it. You should be, too, Cormac.

JOHNSON

You are up for reelection this year, are you not?

PANTIN

I am. And as I campaign, I'm going to remind myself of why I'm running—which is to represent the interests of my constituents. Not just the rich, or the influential constituents. And while the attack on the senator was shameful, look at the allegations that have surfaced in the days since WoMU. Do we want someone morally and ethically compromised to speak for so many?

JOHNSON

Allegedly compromised.

PANTIN

Semantics. And that's what people are tired of. Tired of their courts failing them, tired of seeing CEOs, men who have destroyed the lives of others with their scheming and fraud, given a slap on the wrist and a posh cell in a minimum security prison. People are tired of it. Look at the protests around the world. People have begun to question their leaders and are starting to have frank discussions about accountability. Look at the wave of protests in the Middle East, in London, South America, Greece.

ON-SCREEN: The interview cuts to b-roll of the protests around the world. Many of the groups feature signs with Labyrinth's messages and quotes.

JOHNSON

Why do you think people seem to be getting behind Labyrinth in such large numbers? Police are fairly certain he's nothing more than a serial killer.

PANTIN

I think that people see in Labyrinth . . . a voice. They see someone, at long last, taking up their cause. Most people feel powerless, and they see Labyrinth as at least doing something about it. He is forcing a dialogue that most leaders would prefer to not have. He's giving a voice to all those who can't be heard. People are tired of the corruption. I'm tired of the corruption. [Looks at the camera] Aren't you?

JOHNSON

Thank you, Mr. Pantin. We'll be right back after the break to take your calls. And from the way this board is lighting up, I'd say you good folks still have a lot to say about the matter. We also want to extend an open invitation to Labyrinth himself. If you're watching, give us a call.

PANTIN

If Labyrinth's watching, I'd encourage him to take a rest. Let the people forge their own destinies.

JOHNSON

We'll be right back.

chapter 61

Global Alliance HQ / Paris, France

There wasn't a single new package this time.

There were *five* packages.

All were delivered in late afternoon, which was the perfect time to introduce it into all aspects of the news cycle. Breaking on the Web, covered on cable and network news, and full stories in print the following morning. After the attack at the WoMU conference three days ago in Europe, the media was primed like never before. Not only were they expecting a new package, but they were on tenterhooks waiting for it.

❧

LAB GOES CUCKOO

Targets Five Religious Leaders with New Threat

EXCLUSIVE—The global mastermind who calls himself "Labyrinth" has a new target: major world religions.

Sources tell us that select leaders from five major world religions—Christianity, Islam, Hinduism, Buddhism, and

Judaism—have reportedly been sent a new riddle along with two objects, one of which is rumored to be a small, impeccably crafted cuckoo clock.

Authorities would not say if a deadline had been given, or divulge the contents of the riddle or the third object.

Labyrinth's packages typically contain one riddle and two objects, the combination of which pinpoint his next victim—or victims. . . .

Blair gathered the Global Alliance team in the conference room and presented images and scans of the contents of those packages—just in from law enforcement agencies around the world: The Corps of Gendarmerie of Vatican City. The Saudi Arabia Police. The Indian Police Service in Allahabad. The Indo-Tibetan Border Police Force. The Israel Police.

"The rumor about the clocks is true—we're receiving photos of them now," Blair said. "They appear to be early Black Forest clocks dating back to the eighteenth century, all carefully restored to perfect working order, even though the original life span was thought to be no more than one generation—about thirty years, more or less."

"More antiques," Natasha said. "Just to show us how special he is. Or how rich he is."

Deckland O'Brian chewed a toothpick, asked, "How much time before the little birdies sing?"

"Not much. Four hours."

"Well, fuck me."

Natasha brushed hair out of her eyes. "What else?"

"Each package came with a religious relic."

Hans Roeding raised a beefy hand. "You mean like a cross or a Bible?"

"No," Blair said. "In this case, *relic* means a piece of flesh from a deceased saint or spiritual leader."

"Guess you weren't raised Catholic," said O'Brian. "They once brought a relic of some obscure saint to my local church—I was something like eight years old, and excited as fuck. That is, until I kneeled down and took a gander through the murky glass and saw something that looked like it had shot out of someone's nose. Absolutely disgusting."

"Thank you for that useless detail, O'Brian," Blair said. "What we have are multiple targets spread throughout Asia and Europe."

"What's the riddle?" Natasha asked.

Blair read it aloud:

> IT'S MORE POWERFUL THAN GOD. IT'S MORE EVIL THAN THE DEVIL. THE POOR HAVE IT. THE RICH NEED IT. IF YOU EAT IT YOU WILL DIE. WHAT IS IT?
>
> LABYRINTH

"Well that's creepy, isn't it," O'Brian said.

Blair ignored him. "We have to assume he has other agents working for him. Even Labyrinth can't be in five places at once. I consider this good news. If he has a network, then it stands to reason that there are going to be weak links in his network, so we should choose the four most likely . . ."

There was a noise from the other end of the hall—someone was entering the HQ. Instinctively, Hans Roeding withdrew his pistol from a leg holster and pointed it down the length of the room.

Tom Riggins appeared in the door, hands up in the air, flanked by Global Alliance guards—the same who had escorted him to Steve Dark's hospital room.

"Don't shoot," he said.

chapter 62

"You have no right to be here," Blair said sternly. "Escort him out of here, please."

Riggins lowered his hands, suddenly feeling self-conscious. "Hey, thanks for the warm welcome. I'm touched, really. Look, Steve Dark sent me. I'm with Special Circs back in—"

"We know who you are, Agent Riggins. That doesn't change anything."

Natasha's eyes widened. "Dark's awake? Is he okay?"

"Yeah, Dark's awake but in no condition to move. I think I can help you guys—if you'll let me." Riggins pointed to the armed escorts. "I wouldn't be standing here unless he gave Mutt and Jeff here orders to bring me down to your special little clubhouse."

O'Brian smiled as he leaned back in his chair. "Oh, I like this guy. I really do."

"What makes you think you can help?" Blair asked.

Riggins smiled. "You're chasing the type of guy we call a Level 26 killer. Off the charts in terms of skill and resourcefulness and, for lack of a better term, downright fuckin' evil. So . . . everybody in this room—and I'm just curious now—how many of you have personally bagged a Level 26 killer? Huh? How about it?"

Blair looked down at the conference room table. "Agent Riggins, we don't categorize the people who interest us . . ."

"You, Damien? How about you—you're O'Brian, right? Dark told me about you. Thought we'd get along for some reason. Natasha I've already met. And you—oh, you must be Hans Roeding. I can tell by the way you're stabbing me in the balls with those daggers comin' out of your eyes. How about it, Hans? Ever taken down a Level 26er?"

Nobody in the room said a word. They were all waiting for Blair to respond.

"Look, you wanted Dark to be a part of this little group, right?" Riggins asked.

The team nodded.

"Well, I'm the one who trained him."

Once Riggins was brought up to speed on the riddle and the contents of the packages, he couldn't help but attack the problem like a cop. He thought about the five potential crime scenes, and the five stolen objects—the relics. Like Dark had said: This freak was going for the headline grab. He didn't want to be stopped; he wanted his work to be discovered. Was it a coincidence that there were five members of Global Alliance, including Blair? That it would take all five members, split up, to properly investigate those five crime scenes?

"Five of you, five packages," Riggins said.

"Your point?" Blair asked.

"Labyrinth knew a lot about Dark," Riggins said. "When they fought, he got personal. So you all have to assume he knows about all of you, too. Your skills as well as your weaknesses."

"That's impossible," O'Brian said. "Very few people even know we exist, let alone our identities. Blair, back me up here. I mean, that's the whole point of this, right—that we operate in secret so no one can see us coming? Otherwise, I vote we move out of the bloody catacombs and into some penthouse."

Blair shook his head. "Agent Riggins has a point. If he knew about Dark, then we have to assume our identities are compromised as well."

"I'd bet he was at the scene of many, if not all, of his attacks," Riggins said. "You see that all of the time. Psychos hanging around, watching the forensics teams work. They get off on it. So it's no stretch to think that he spotted you guys early on."

A chill went through Riggins as he spoke those words—because then he realized how Labyrinth had found *him*. New York—the Shane Corbett murder. Goddamnit. He'd been in the lobby with Steve Dark and Natasha Garcon. And *somewhere in the same room had been Labyrinth*.

"Forget ourselves for now," Blair said. "Dark said the key to catching Labyrinth was predicting his next move. Any ideas?"

"I think he's playing with you now," Riggins said. "He wants you to play along with the game, go hopping around the world, scooping up his bread crumbs. That's why I'm thinking these packages were meant specifically for you. Maybe he wants to waste your time. Or maybe he wants you separated, and then he'll pick you off, one by one."

"Damn," O'Brian said. "You really did train Steve Dark, didn't you? You sound just fuckin' like him."

Natasha said, "So what do we do? Do you have an idea about where he might strike next—beyond this current threat?"

"Dark told me that it usually spins out of the answer to the previous riddle," Riggins said. "So how about it? You guys come up with an answer yet?"

O'Brian said, "I was raised Catholic, y'know, so this one came to me pretty easily. The answer is . . . *nothing*. Because nothing is more powerful than God, nothing more evil than the devil. The poor?

They have nothing. The rich? They need nothing. And if you eat nothing, you'll die."

Riggins nodded. "Pretty good."

"So what—we wait and do *nothing*?" Blair asked.

"No. You coordinate with the five police organizations who were sent the packages and have *them* investigate. Tell them to follow the evidence—starting with the stolen relics—just like you would have. And we all start thinking ahead to what he's going to spring on us next."

"You think he wanted to divide us, split us up all over the world?" Natasha asked.

"That's exactly what he wanted," Riggins said. "And won't he be surprised when we catch his sorry ass before he springs his next PR stunt."

Within an hour, the reports began to come in from holy sites, starting with Rome.

The victims were already dead.

Had been for *weeks*, according to initial forensic analysis.

"At least he didn't lie to Jane Talbot," O'Brian said. "He hasn't killed since he promised he wouldn't on live TV."

"Yeah, that's great," Riggins said. "Hell of a guy."

In each case, holy relics had been stolen from specific shrines or sacred places. In Rome, Labyrinth had somehow plundered the Santi Vincenzo e Anastasio a Trevi, notable for being the resting place of the embalmed hearts of twenty-five medieval popes. Once they pried open the resting place, they found the body of a man identified as Lucas Gregory—an American who claimed to be the "true pope," descended from a secret line of authentic popes starting with Saint Peter. No one took Gregory seriously, especially after his numerous predictions for the supposed rapture—when God would call his faithful home, leaving the damned behind—came and went.

"He was no threat to anyone," Natasha said. "Why target him?"

"What was the COD?" Riggins asked.

"Cause of death, they're reporting starvation," Blair said. "In other words, they died from eating *nothing*."

"These religious nuts were spewing nothing—and received nothing in return," Riggins said.

chapter 63

DARK

Dark came up out of a fuzzy nonsensical dream to see that someone had left behind a meal on a plastic tray. No idea if it was morning or night. He lifted the lid and saw scrambled eggs, a triangle of dry toast, and a small cream-colored envelope resting on top of an empty plastic container. Dark opened the envelope with slightly numb fingers and pulled out a card with familiar block printing on it.

I STOPPED BY
YOU WERE SLEEPING
WE'LL CATCH UP LATER

LABYRINTH

Supposedly there were only five people who knew that Dark was in this secret government care facility. The four members of Global Alliance—Blair, Natasha, O'Brian, Roeding—and, of course, now Riggins.

This was another riddle, Dark realized. With Labyrinth, you always had to look for the hidden meaning behind the words.

In this case, Labyrinth's hidden meaning was perfectly clear.

I am a member of your team.

Or at least that's what Labyrinth wanted Dark to think, wasn't it? A man with Labyrinth's resources could probably find a way to dig up a list of supposedly "secret" hospitals near the accident site. From there, some simple, old-fashioned bribery could have yielded Dark's location, as well as entrance to the floor. Dark knew better than to believe that anything was secure.

The larger implications troubled him. Labyrinth's attention had turned, and he was targeting the team specifically. Presumably, other members of Global Alliance had received similar notes. Labyrinth was trying to sow seeds of doubt within the only organization equipped to stop him. GA had stepped up onto the playing field, and Labyrinth was eager to play with them.

Dark pushed aside his scrambled eggs. He wasn't hungry. The smell of them made him nauseous. There was also the fact that a monster could have easily poisoned his breakfast—could have easily killed an unconscious Dark, for that matter.

That's when he saw the edge of the second envelope, hidden under the plate.

This one was pure white, business-size.

Dark opened the flap and removed the piece of paper inside. He recognized the form immediately—a standard Special Circs blood analysis report. The typed name at the top, however, is what stopped him.

SQWEEGEL

When he'd pulled off the mask during their final confrontation, Dark had been surprised by Sqweegel's true face. It had been perfectly . . . unremarkable. Dull black eyes. Shaved bony head. Narrow forehead devoid of eyebrows. Bad teeth. Mottled skin. A geek grown-up. An abused boy.

His *brother.*

This was the blood test that had confirmed it—seven of eleven alleles matching Steve Dark's DNA.

Labyrinth hadn't been bluffing. And now he wanted Dark to know that.

But there was something even worse at the bottom of the page. An insignificant detail that would have been overlooked by most people, because most people haven't had to fill out these kinds of forms. But to Dark, the detail meant everything.

The typed initials: TR.

Tom.

Riggins.

Nothing, Riggins had said, five years ago. *No hits. Fucker was a real nowhere man.*

But the blood test had been run by Riggins.

He knew.

chapter 64

DARK

"Knock knock," Riggins said, flanked by two armed guards.

Dark had been sitting up, waiting. Natasha had briefed him on the killings of the religious fundamentalists—all of whom turned out to be outcasts and heretics of the five religions targeted. All had been captured and stashed in various vaults and tombs and antechambers at the same time Labyrinth had stolen the relics for his packages. Stashed . . . and left to starve to death. It was clear that Labyrinth had killed these men long before he'd sent the first package to LAPD headquarters. Natasha also told him that Riggins was on his way over—he wanted to kick around the riddle with him a bit more.

"Tell him I'm looking forward to it," Dark said.

Natasha could hear the strange bitterness in his voice. "Hey, are you all right?"

Now Riggins was here with a computer tablet in his hand. Dark couldn't think about the case. He wanted to jump out of bed and throw Riggins against a wall.

"You look like hell," Riggins said. "You feeling okay?"

"You fucking knew," Dark said.

"Huh? Knew what?"

"You *knew*, all of these years."

When the realization finally hit Riggins, he looked like someone had just pulled a rubber plug somewhere on his body; the man deflated. He shuffled over to the nearest chair and fell into it, leaning back his head and covering his eyes with his hands.

"Yeah, I knew."

"Why didn't you say something?"

Riggins removed his hands and looked at Dark. He was almost wincing as he spoke.

"Dark, when I found out, you'd just lost Sibby. What, was I supposed to compound your grief by taking away your identity, too? Tell you that a blood test showed you were related to that weird little fuck? No. I couldn't do that to you. You didn't deserve to hear something like that, after all you'd been through. So I took it upon myself to keep watch over you."

"What, in case I went into the family business?"

Riggins shook his head. "I've always known that there's a fine line between us and them. Reason and chaos, good and evil, yin and yang, whatever. It takes a particular kind of mind to be in this game, no matter what side you're playing for. You chose the path of good, and that's all that matters."

Dark considered this. He'd often thought the same thing. What made the best manhunter often made the best sociopath. But that was academics; this was his fucking life. His *family*. His *daughter*.

"How did he find out?"

Riggins exhaled and told him about the attack from the previous week. How he suspected that Labyrinth himself was in the lobby of the Epoch Hotel, watching them all. And how he must have followed him all the way back to D.C., found out where he lived, and . . .

"And what?" Dark asked. "Did you do a couple of shots together and say, 'Hey, you're never going to believe this, this is the craziest thing ever . . .'"

"That motherfucker pulled it out of my skull," Riggins said, his words burning with rage. "I don't know what he shot into me, but it was like I was running off at the mouth, saying whatever popped into my thick head. And he was just fuckin' toying with me, giving me little nudges, to get what he wanted. If I had the use of my hands I would have squeezed his neck so hard his head would have popped off."

"Did you at least get a look at him?"

"No."

Dark and Riggins sat in silence for a while.

"Aren't you going to say anything?" Riggins asked.

More silence.

"Look," Riggins said at long last. "If there's one thing I know, it's that blood doesn't ultimately matter. It's what you do that counts."

"That's a nice sentiment," Dark replied, "but I don't think you believe that. I think it's best if you go back to D.C. now. You're compromised, just like me."

"Steve, look, whatever this is—"

"Didn't you hear me? Get the fuck out *now.*"

A wounded look came over Riggins's face. He opened his mouth to respond, then thought better of it. Instead he dropped the tablet onto Dark's bed and left without another word.

After a while of staring at nothing in particular, Dark picked up the tablet, pressed the power button, flicked the on-screen lock. This was a tablet identical to Natasha's, and it was already opened on a browser page: Labyrinth's latest video.

As footage from various religious wars and crusades and even the Twin Towers falling played across the screen, he spoke:

LABYRINTH

More wars have been fought in the name of God than any others. Religion is a leading cause of man's destruction. Instead of having everyone judge who has the better god, we need to be under one deity that everyone responds to. We shall all share under one god. And the same laws shall apply to all of us . . .

chapter 65

DARK

As Dark stood up from the hospital bed, an icy wave of dizziness washed over him. Every cell in his body screamed: *Lie down. You're not ready for this yet.* Every muscle in his back cried out for more rest.

But that wasn't an option. He needed to catch this motherfucker now.

Labyrinth seemed to get off on knowing everyone's dirtiest, deepest secrets. That told Dark that Labyrinth must have the dirtiest, deepest secret of all.

All he needed was the man's true identity—not his avatars or puppets or stand ins. The real man behind the mask.

And thanks to Riggins, Dark had an increasingly sharper image of that man.

Dark thought about the attack on Riggins, which provided the first hint that Labyrinth was able to control and pry secrets out of people. This had been a thread running through the entire case, starting with the homeless Albanian man in L.A., all the way through the body double he used in South Africa and the women who'd been raped by Shane Corbett.

Labyrinth wasn't cultivating loyal followers like a terrorist mastermind. He was using a blend of drugs and psychotherapy to brainwash them, *Manchurian Candidate*–style. Labyrinth only had a few hours with Riggins, but even that was enough time to pry loose his most closely guarded secret. Give him enough time, weeks or even months, and Labyrinth seemed to be able to completely erase someone's identity or program them for particular tasks.

With the women in New York, Labyrinth would want to be there, nearby—just to make sure the programming stuck. Plus, he wanted to capture Shane Corbett's murder on video for instant uploading, apparently a task he didn't trust to an underling or a stand-in.

That meant the real Labyrinth was in that hotel—and more important, in the hotel lobby at the same time that Dark and Natasha were there with Riggins. He'd watched them, and had chosen to follow Riggins home.

Why didn't Labyrinth follow Dark or Natasha? Maybe he didn't need to. Maybe the note was right—that Labyrinth was already a "member of the team."

He chose to follow Riggins because he could provide something else—a window into Steve Dark's mind. A weakness to uncover. A secret to be exploited.

Again, this couldn't be trusted to anyone else. Labyrinth himself had to be there.

Dark started to call Natasha but then stopped himself. As much as he hated to admit it, Labyrinth's note had given him a shot of paranoia. Who could he trust on the team, if there was even the remote possibility that one of the members was in league with Labyrinth? Or if someone on the team was Labyrinth himself?

So instead he called the contact he remembered from the NYPD directly. In every crime scene, the police take down the names of every possible witness—and that would include the people in the lobby. If Labyrinth had been there, someone would have spoken to him, taken down his name—even if it were an alias.

It was a start.

chapter 66

LABYRINTH

Scotland Yard

My delivery boy is not even three steps toward the front entrance before a rabid pack of antiterrorism agents have separated him from the package in his arms.

My delivery boy is befuddled and he begins to cry.

The agents do not appear to care—they want that package secured, contained, examined immediately.

Then again, I cannot blame them.

The package is wrapped in brown paper and looks like it could contain a toddler.

My delivery boy pleads with them,

Whatid I do whatid I do . . .

But of course, they're not caring much about explaining why, nor do they seem to have much regard for personal well-being—not after the lessons of the LAPD and the NYPD across the Atlantic.

But then he turns the tables on them.

Just like I trained him to do.

First the tears, then the begging . . . and then, just as I instructed him . . .

Utter calm.

A little smile, even.

The tears, so abundant mere seconds ago, seem to evaporate in the wind.

My delivery boy says,

Let me tell you.

The agents are stunned. They ask,

Tell us what?

My delivery boy says,

He made me memorize it.

The agents say,

Memorize what?

My delivery boy says,

The riddle.

And this is what he told them, as they all scurried to write it down verbatim.

> A PRISONER IS TOLD "IF YOU TELL A LIE WE WILL HANG YOU; IF YOU TELL THE TRUTH WE WILL SHOOT YOU." WHAT STATEMENTS CAN HE MAKE ABOUT THE SITUATION IN ORDER TO SAVE HIMSELF?
>
> LABYRINTH

Inside the package, the police will soon discover my gifts:

There is not a toddler, not any other living thing inside.

A giant hourglass, with about three hours' worth of sand left.

And the tiniest sliver of paper with the letter *L* printed on it.

This shouldn't be too difficult for them to figure out.

My delivery boy then closes his eyes and keeps the smile locked in on his tiny face, just like I trained him to do.

He knows he did a good job.

I am across the street, watching him do a good job.

He smiles in the belief I will reward him when this is over. Like all good boys he wants nothing more than to please his master.

I found this delivery boy turning tricks for drugs in Brixton.

I showed him a better life.

Taught him how to act.

How to lie with utter conviction.

I wasn't lying to him, either.

He will continue to enjoy a better life, starting in three hours.

chapter 67

After the Cormac Johnson interview, Alain Pantin found that his star was in ascendance like never before. His press officer was overwhelmed with media requests from around the world, both television and print. The hook, of course, was the ongoing Labyrinth attacks, but it was as if audiences were now prepped to wait for Alain Pantin's analysis of each attack, and the message behind it.

Each interview began to follow a familiar pattern. The public condemnation:

"What he did to that American stockbroker—and those poor women—that was simply hideous, don't you agree, Mr. Pantin?"

Followed by a quick casting of suspicion over the victim:

"If the allegations prove to be true, however, then some might even say that Shane Corbett got off a bit *light*. If what they're alleging is true, of course."

And then finally, an attack on the system behind the victim:

"Isn't this a commentary on certain people believing they don't have to account for any of their actions, no matter how despicable?"

Up until this point, Pantin would nod, condemn, and silently agree that yes, there does seem to be something suspicious about the victims. Tsk-tsk, tut-tut, they really should catch this maniac immediately.

But Pantin would truly shine when unpacking the message, because the message is what everyone secretly wanted to hear.

That unchecked greed and power needed to be punished.

Even if it meant being sliced to pieces with the jagged edges of broken champagne flutes.

Pantin understood the mass appeal. Back in primary school, there was always a certain delight in watching a classroom troublemaker being called to the front of the room for a public chiding (or if the professors were old enough, a public whipping). You would shake your head and pretend to sympathize, but inside you were cheering. Because it was a rare delight to watch the wicked receive their just punishment. It even emboldened you to the point where if the troublemaker turned his attention to you . . . well, you might dish out some of that punishment yourself.

"You don't need a broken champagne flute to take down the Shane Corbetts of the world," Pantin would say. "You need a new system that safeguards against the Shane Corbetts, that doesn't tolerate their greed, nor practically *encourage* it with lavish bonuses and luxuries that most people in the world will never enjoy."

It wasn't a Labyrinth attack until you had Alain Pantin unpacking it for you, sussing out the truth behind the carnage.

And Pantin found himself in a slightly surreal position of having to select the biggest media markets, because . . . well, there wasn't time to speak to them all.

chapter 68

DARK

Dark almost found himself in a fistfight with the guards posted at his door—they had been under strict orders from Blair to not let Dark leave until the doctors had given their complete consent.

"Move out of my way," Dark told the sides of human beef blocking his exit.

"We need to confirm this with Control," one of them said. "Wait here until . . ."

"Oh fuck this," Dark said, pushing himself into the narrow space between them so suddenly that they had no choice but to part.

"Mr. Dark! You can't go!"

A few yards away Dark stopped and turned. "What are you going to do? Shoot me? I need a ride back to headquarters. Are you going to take me there, or do I have to catch a cab? Which, by the way, might really piss off your boss."

The guards saw there was little point in arguing.

When Dark arrived at Global Alliance HQ—against the wishes of his doctor—the team was poring over a high-resolution scan of a sliver of paper.

"Hey," Dark said, walking into the room toward his usual chair.

Blair blinked. "Are you cleared to leave?"

"Yeah. What do we have?"

Natasha quickly recapped: a package to Scotland Yard, containing an hourglass and a tiny fragment of paper.

"What's that?" Dark asked, narrowing his eyes. "An *L*? For *Labyrinth*?"

"Maybe," Blair said. "But it's not the letter itself that is disturbing; it's the source. Experts are telling us that this was clipped from one of the four 1215 exemplifications of the Magna Carta."

"Uh, actually, it's just 'Magna Carta,'" said O'Brian. "At least, in academic circles."

Magna Carta: the foundation of British—and by extension, modern—law.

Dark nodded. "He mentioned the word *law* in his previous video. He's going after the legal establishment, somewhere in London. So where are these four copies kept?"

"Two at the British Library, one at Salisbury Cathedral, and another is a touring copy, though it has been kept for long periods of time at Fort Knox in the U.S.," said Blair. "No one is reporting a break-in. Nor would they, for obvious reasons."

"Well, Labyrinth got in somehow."

"It's a joke," O'Brian said.

The group turned to stare at him.

"No, literally," O'Brian continued, "a joke, from spook circles. I may or not have worked for various intelligence outfits at some period of time in my long and storied career, and I may or may not have had occasion to share a pint or five with various intelligence officers . . ."

"The point, Deckland?" Blair asked.

"Anyway, it's an old joke. What's the ultimate final exam for spy school? Why, breaking into Fort Knox and stealing back Magna Carta . . . for England! This tells me that our Labyrinth, if not a former member of British intelligence, is at the least very well acquainted with their culture."

Dark thought about Labyrinth's skill at "turning" people. Brainwashing drugs. The ability to cross borders undetected. Access to secret documents and letterhead. It would seem to make sense that Labyrinth was a former spook.

Blair, meanwhile, seemed eager to change the subject. "And the riddle?"

> A PRISONER IS TOLD "IF YOU TELL A LIE WE WILL HANG YOU; IF YOU TELL THE TRUTH WE WILL SHOOT YOU." WHAT STATEMENTS CAN HE MAKE ABOUT THE SITUATION IN ORDER TO SAVE HIMSELF?

Dark said, "The prisoner has to say, 'You are going to hang me.' They can't hang him, because that would mean the prisoner didn't lie. And they can't shoot him, because that would mean he didn't tell the truth."

"Brilliant," O'Brian said. "More word games. No wonder this one is pinned to lawyers."

chapter 69

DARK

As the team tried to figure out the method of murder (hanging versus shooting?) and the precise target (which lawyer?), Dark noticed something strange. Everyone in the room seemed unusually guarded, playing their own theories close to the chest. That's when it occurred to him: Labyrinth had sent other messages, too.

"Are we going to just sit around and eyeball each other?" Dark asked. "Or are we going to talk about what's really on our minds?"

Natasha said, "You received one, too, then. A letter, saying that Labyrinth was one of us."

"Yeah," Dark said. "On my hospital tray."

"Mine was in bed waiting for me at my flat," Natasha said.

O'Brian found his note propped on the keyboard of his home computer. Hans Roeding declined to say exactly where his note had been left, but it was clear that it had been a source of great embarrassment. No soldier the caliber of Roeding likes to admit a weakness at his place of residence.

O'Brian smiled. "Look, I'll save everyone some time here. Labyrinth is actually me. Yeah, I thought things were getting a little boring around here, so I decided to create this amazing supervillain just to liven things up."

"Don't joke," Roeding said. "Not funny."

"And see, I would suspect that you are Labyrinth, big guy, but you're really shitty at riddles. Unless . . ." O'Brian narrowed his eyes in faux suspicion. "Unless that's just a cover, and you're going to kill us all!"

"Shut up."

Blair interrupted. "This means nothing. None of you are Labyrinth."

"Sure, easy for you to say," O'Brian said. "For all we know, *you* could be Labyrinth. You've set up this entire operation just to catch yourself." He looked around at his teammates. "That's it, isn't it? Holy shit, paranoia is such an intoxicating drug."

"This means nothing," Blair said, "because I've been receiving taunting messages from Labyrinth like this since the beginning."

"What?" Dark asked. "And you didn't share them? Do you fucking understand how investigations work, Blair? No clue is too small."

"Like you, I was keeping that close to my chest," Blair said, "knowing that he was simply trying to undermine the team. Sharing that with you would have been disastrous for this investigation. I've ignored the messages, so now it seems he's reached out to you."

"How does he even know who we are?" Natasha asked.

"Unless," Roeding said, "he is sitting in this room with us right now. Who is the only person who has claimed to have seen Labyrinth in the flesh?"

Dark said, "You think I faked that fight and threw myself out of a fucking window?"

"It's a good cover, you have to admit," said O'Brian.

"Dark isn't making that up," Natasha said. "I have proof."

"What proof?" O'Brian asked. "The two of you could be in league . . ."

"*Enough,*" said Blair. "Labyrinth is not a member of this team. I've had each of you investigated and background checked to within an inch of your very lives. Which is why I trust the people in this room utterly and completely. He's trying to play us against each other, and I'm not going to let that happen. *None of you are Labyrinth.* End of discussion."

chapter 70

LABYRINTH

I walk through the halls of the most prestigious law firm in all of London. It's a short trip from Edinburgh. Lovely trains, too. I like the sandwiches they serve.

At the office, no one tries to stop me—they smile and nod, even.

They know me, after all.

I'm very familiar with the work of this firm, as I've employed them in the past.

They're superb lawyers.

They're especially good at springing criminals out of investigative and legal traps.

Like the serial rapist who was set free last week, who even winked at one of the victims who'd had the courage to testify against him in open court.

But their specialty is white-collar criminals.

Like the embezzler who happens to be a relative of a prominent member of Parliament. Picked the pockets of a national antipoverty agency and used the proceeds in the most brazen manner possible . . . and wouldn't have to return a dime. Ever.

It's the reason I retained them years ago to handle some of my affairs.

Finally I glide across a plush rug to a corner office, where a lawyer in a bespoke suit is reading over documents.

My own personal lawyer.

Handsome.

Neatly groomed.

The latest stylish cologne from the pages of GQ UK rising from his flesh.

He is perhaps the best here, and I absolutely hate him.

Nothing about my mission is personal . . .

Well, except for this.

(I worked it in.)

The man looks up, confused, but smiling. Says,

My God, I had no idea you were visiting! Would you like an espresso, or perhaps something from the bakery down the—

I interrupt him to ask,

The rope or the gun?

He blinks.

Beg your pardon?

I tell him,

It's not *my* pardon you should be begging.

He says,

Trey, come on, what's this all about?

Then I show it to him—the pistol I have in my jacket pocket, because perish the thought that security would even consider frisking me, one of their most generous clients, but even if they'd found that, I could have produced a (fake) legal permit to carry such a weapon, considering my (fake) diplomatic status in this country, and even if they'd given me trouble with that, there's of course the length of hemp rope inside my briefcase, though I would have been disappointed not to be able to offer my lawyer the choice,

The rope or the gun.

He screams,

OH MY GOD.

I shoot.

His office is in the corner, and well insulated from the warren of cubicles outside. The blast of the shot is muted. Could be a car or could be someone popping a piece of packing material.

My lawyer's face scrunches up and he stumbles backward, almost tumbling into his own desk.

I catch him by his necktie, pull him forward, tell him,

How about both?

And he is helpless, blood seeping through his trembling fingers, as I hold him steady with one hand and reach for the rope with the other.

My lawyer's eyes go WIDE as he sees the hangman's noose.

I don't have to worry about finding a place to secure it, as I've been in his office many, many times and know where the central support beams are, above the drop ceiling and harsh fluorescent lighting fixtures.

I hang him.

Then I stay to record some video.

Upload it.

I'm not in any rush to leave, even though I have a plane in two hours.

I know I'll be able to exit this building unmolested.

These people are my lawyers.

Even if I'm caught—I'll no doubt beat the rap.

Reuters

Breaking: Lawyer shot dead, hung—Scotland Yard confirms there are links to "Labyrinth."

AP News

Breaking: Copycat Labyrinth crimes reported in San Francisco; vandalism at law offices on Market Street.

Montreal Gazette

Breaking: Two lawyers shot near rue McGill—student shooter claims he is "Labyrinth."

chapter 71

Brussels, Belgium

"Alain."

Pantin could hear the concern in the man's voice.

"Trey? What is it?"

"You're going to see something in the news about me. I want you to avoid judgment and instead focus on the conversations we've had. I think you know me well enough to know that I've never led you astray."

"What are you talking about, Trey? What's wrong?"

"Everything we've discussed has been leading up to this. I chose you because you're the man best suited for the task at hand."

"What task?"

"To put the world back together again."

Pantin was confused. He'd never heard his mentor Trey Halbthin talk like this before.

Then again, over the past few days the world Pantin knew had been turned upside down.

Chaos and revolution were on everyone's minds, with acts of protest and vandalism and acts of violence springing up in all corners of the world—not just the usual tinderboxes. You didn't have to be a political prophet like Trey Halbthin to understand that the winds of change were blowing hot, spurned on, no doubt, by Labyrinth's systematic attacks on big business and politics and even religion.

And Pantin found himself at the center of the maelstrom.

"Trey, what are you talking about?"

"Labyrinth has had a serious effect on the world, Alain. After being asleep for so long, people everywhere are waking up to the fact that they're being manipulated by the tyrants. People in the West think they're free, but they're not. They're enslaved by the same institutions, only they have better toys and dental care. It's the same manipulation, all over the world."

The realization started as a tiny cold ball in Alain Pantin's stomach. The more his mentor spoke, the more he realized what he should have seen from the beginning.

"There's a sign coming, Alain. A big sign. Unmistakable. I've chosen you to take the lead when this sign comes."

"Tell me what you're planning," Pantin said quietly.

"You're the doer, Alain. I'm merely the man behind the scenes. It's been about you this whole time. It doesn't matter what I do. What matters is what *you* do with it."

"I can't. . . ."

"You will, because no one else *can*."

Alain Pantin leaned back in his chair and looked out at Leopold Park. The weather was unusually warm, and people were taking advantage of it. Couples. Children playing—many of them the sons and daughters of his fellow Europarl members. They had no idea what was awaiting them. The new world that was slowly coming into being all around them. History not just in the making, but forced into being by the act of sheer will.

His will, if he wanted.

Once again, Trey Halbthin was right. Whatever horrible acts he'd committed to create this revolutionary moment didn't ultimately matter.

It was up to Alain Pantin to turn it into something meaningful.

chapter 72

DARK

Global Alliance HQ / Paris, France

O'Brian found the connection mere seconds before the news broke.

"Long shot here, but Timothy Porter—he's based in London, and over the years he's given many lectures on the Magna Carta, even going on tour with one of the copies. Could that be it?"

Natasha said, "It's definitely him."

"How do you know?"

"According to Reuters, he's just been found dead in his office."

"Fuck me," O'Brian said. "Another hour on the clock and we could have . . ."

"That's how he plays," Natasha said. "There's never enough time, with him just out of reach."

"So was he shot or hung?" O'Brian asked.

"Both," Natasha said.

Within minutes, the now-familiar Labyrinth video was uploaded to the usual mirror sites, spreading and trending globally within minutes. A dead criminal lawyer? This promised to be the most-watched Labyrinth video of all—a virtual snuff film starring the world's most hated profession.

Within minutes . . . Dark had a feeling that this, too, was a hands-on operation. Labyrinth had used one of his puppets to deliver the package, possibly even watching from a safe distance.

Dark, feet on the table, staring at the ceiling, said, "Can you get me a list of Porter's clients?"

"Why?" O'Brian asked. "Do you think you're going to spot someone named L. Abyrinth, or something?"

"Can you do it?"

Of course O'Brian could do it. And when Dark compared the list with the list he'd received from the NYPD, one name popped out: "Trey Halbthin."

Halbthin had been there, at the Epoch Hotel, in New York City, and was even interviewed by the police. The man presented diplomatic credentials, and explained he'd been there to meet "an old friend for coffee." Nothing about him aroused suspicion; diplomats in New York City were common. And Trey Halbthin was also a longtime client of Timothy Porter's, going back at least five years. Why would he kill his own lawyer?

"We might be dealing with another one of Labyrinth's puppets," Natasha said. "O'Brian, dig up everything you can on this Halbthin guy."

"Already on it."

"I think it's him," Dark said quietly, sketching with a pencil on a legal pad.

"Why? Why would he risk putting himself out there where he could risk capture?"

"I don't think he's worried about being captured anymore," Dark said. "He's headed for his endgame. And he's practically announcing his identity."

"How?"

Dark turned the legal pad toward Natasha. He'd written, in block letters:

TREYHALBTHIN

And then directly below it:

THELABYRINTH

"An anagram," Natasha said. "Another fake identity."

"Well, if this identity is fake," O'Brian said, reading from his monitor, "then it's the best and most elaborate identity I've ever seen. It's legit as legit gets, and goes back deep. This isn't some schmo who filed a fake driver's license application. And you want to know something else?"

"What?" Dark asked.

"He's just cleared security at Heathrow, and he's about to step onto a plane."

"Where's he going?"

"Philadelphia."

"Okay, we need a virtual army platoon to intercept that flight when it lands," Dark said. "I want a complete clampdown on the crew and passengers until we get there and sort through them one by one. Where's Blair?"

Blair was in his office, staring at the images of Trey Halbthin that his team had pooled from a variety of databases around the world.

He looked at the chin, and the skin around the eyes, the shape of the ears.

My God.

It was *him*.

Once you trained your eyes to look past the plastic surgery and the makeup and the false hair plugs and everything else a trained agent uses to change his appearance, you could see it.

After all of these years of searching, Blair thought, *there you are, right in front of me.*

Why are you flying to Philadelphia?

What endgame do you have in mind for us?

Are you waiting for me to stop you?

Or do you want me there to watch as you stop the world?

chapter 73

LABYRINTH

Right now at Philadelphia International Airport there are many men in ill-fitting suits who I can only assume are a conglomeration of federal agents meant to detain me. They are looking for a man matching Trey Halbthin's precise description, and right now I look nothing like Trey Halbthin.

Then again, I'm not even on the flight they're tracking.

My "Trey Halbthin" identity did take that flight, but that was a matter of some simple hacking (airlines, like most American industries, leave gaping security holes in the most astonishing places) to attach that name to *another* individual who fit the general height, weight, hair, and eye color.

An individual who, sadly, will probably spend the better part of the next month in a stuffy conference room as Homeland Security agents pick apart his life by the seams.

But one small pawn in a game this large means nothing.

It's important that Blair and his team will be there for the end.

I arrive in Philadelphia via private jet under the cover of another identity.

It was a comfortable flight.

Spent most of it with my eyes shut and my mind preparing my final gifts to the world.

❖

Hello, Damien.

Are you thinking about me?

❖

Snow is falling on downtown Philadelphia as I make my way across Spruce Street and through the doors of Pennsylvania General and to the welcome desk.

I ask,

Can you help me?

They say (of course),

Yes, what can we do for you?

Of course they want to help me. I am smiling and wearing a suit and I am clean and well coiffed and white so of course they direct me to the president's office down a hall and across a gorgeously manicured pathway.

Pennsylvania General was the first hospital in America. It is about to achieve another first.

Ground Zero of the New Order.

I do hope my pupil, Alain Pantin, is paying attention. He holds the key to everything. I simply need to show him the lock.

❖

I hold the package close to my chest.

Inside my package is another riddle, of course, along with a cell phone with a timer app, ticking down the seconds until it all begins.

I've also gifted the hospital president with a small hand-carved wooden box packed with grave dirt. I'm a little disappointed that they won't be able to pore over these clues like the others, because I spent a long time filling that little box with a few ounces of soil from Mount Vernon and Quincy and Charlottesville and Montpelier Station and Richmond and the Hermitage and Kinderhook and North Bend and Louisville and Buffalo and Concord and Lancaster and Springfield and Greeneville and New York City and Fremont and Cleveland and Albany and Princeton and Indianapolis and Canton and Oyster Bay and Arlington and Marion and Plymouth and West Branch and Hyde Park and Independence and Abilene and Stonewall and Yorba Linda and Simi Valley and Grand Rapids where I have even sometimes opened the caskets and looked at those dead presidents. Sometimes I touched their decayed faces. Sometimes let my touch linger for a while.

They were touchable when alive and they are even more touchable now.

I could have done anything to their bodies, absolutely anything I wanted, but instead I just gathered soil for my little box—a gift of presidents for the president.

It will go unappreciated.

Perhaps someday my biographers will try to unpack the mysteries of the coffin dirt, and perhaps they'll team up with an expert or two and start the laborious and time-intensive task of separating the samples and tracing them back to their places of origin and once the familiar towns and cities start to register there will be a moment of shock.

But not now.

Not with less than an hour left on the timer.

As the President of the First Hospital in America shall soon see.

Look at him.
He's smiling at me.
And I smile back.
I say,
Hello.

chapter 74

DARK

Paris, France / Philadelphia, Pennsylvania

Damien Blair had the GA jet fueled and ready for the team's arrival. Takeoff happened sixty seconds after the team's van pulled onto the tarmac. Still, the plane lagged behind Trey Halbthin's private jet by about an hour. Dark and the rest of the Global Alliance team landed in Philadelphia and was transported by another van up to Pennsylvania General, where the hospital president was already in a conference room with the local FBI field office.

Dark showed the president photos of Trey Halbthin that O'Brian had dug up from his identity search—passports, driver's licenses, bank cards. The hospital president confirmed that yes, that was the man who delivered that package.

"Any idea where he went?"

"Not at all."

"We want to evacuate the hospital," the special agent in charge told Dark.

"No. That could just speed up the clock," Dark said. "Even if he didn't, you could spark a citywide panic. What was the timepiece in the package?"

"A digital timer on a cell phone," the SAC said. "Twenty-three minutes left."

"There was also a small toy coffin with dirt inside," the hospital president said. "What does that mean? Is this a death threat against me personally?"

They already had the riddle projected onto a wall:

THE MAKER DOESN'T NEED IT,
THE BUYER DOESN'T USE IT.
THE USER USES IT WITHOUT KNOWING.
WHAT IS IT?

LABYRINTH

"Now we know what our suspect looks like," Dark said to the FBI brass. "Let's start thinking like him—grand, symbolic. He's not going to just mow down a bunch of nurses in the hospital cafeteria. He's making a statement, so he'll want a stage."

The special agent in charge nodded.

"Anybody have the answer to Labyrinth's riddle yet?" O'Brian asked. "Hans, you want to jump into the game, maybe?"

Roeding just stared at him.

"Now there's the intellectual response I'd been hoping for—thanks, Hans! Anybody else want to—"

"You didn't let me finish," Roeding said, wicked smile breaking out on his face. "The answer is a coffin. Maker doesn't need it, buyer doesn't use it, user doesn't know he's using it. Just like you won't know when I put you into the fucking ground, you Irish bastard."

Natasha sighed. "Save the bromance for later—let's find this son of a bitch."

Pennsylvania General was immense. What began as a single building has spawned a dozen others spanning multiple city blocks. If it was a medical procedure, it could be performed here, in one of the multiple centers and clinics, many of them world renowned.

Twenty-one minutes left . . .

The four members of Global Alliance split up—no time to coordinate a plan of attack when Labyrinth could be virtually anywhere. The best thing to do, Dark reasoned, was for everyone to put their own best skills to use and follow their gut instinct. Any sign of Halbthin, they'd hit the panic button and everyone would come running.

After breaking away from the team Dark found a plastic hospital map mounted on the wall. He studied it not as a cop but as a performer like Trey Halbthin. A man who liked symbolic places and grand gestures.

Within a few seconds Dark realized where Halbthin would be.

chapter 75

DARK

The operating theater was state-of-the-art—once.

Once being 1804.

For most of the ninteenth century, surgeries were not private affairs. If you had a limb that needed to be removed—or perhaps an unsightly tumor growing out of your chest, cataracts forming over your eyes, painful, stabbing stones in your bladder—then your procedure would be open to the general public. The hospital, in fact, would hang notices around the city to detail what would be done to you, on what day, and at what time. When it came time for your procedure, you would not be given anesthesia. Instead you would be encouraged to drink yourself into a stupor or binge yourself on opium until you couldn't distinguish angels from surgeons. And then up to three hundred people—surgeons, students, the general public looking for a little bloodletting to liven their day—would sit or stand in this grand amphitheater, looking down as the nation's top medical minds would take their blades to your quivering body.

Yeah, Dark thought. *Labyrinth would love a place like this.*

At first glance, the room appeared to be empty. But that meant nothing. Dark's quarry could be hiding on the upper levels, waiting to pounce.

The phone on Dark's hip buzzed. A text from Riggins:

CALL ME

Great timing, Riggins. Goddamn it. . . .

Dark ignored the phone and continued searching, prepared to shoot at anything that moved. If that *was* Trey Halbthin back in Paris, then he knew the motherfucker could move fast.

Again, the cell phone:

CALL ME NOW

Dark called—Riggins answered after the first ring. "Where are you?"

"Philadelphia."

"I've done some digging into this whole Global Alliance thing, especially after you told me that Labyrinth was trying to point a finger at one of your teammates." Riggins spat out the word *teammates* like a divorcée would say *new husband*.

"Anyway, everybody checks out, except for one thing, which is honestly driving me a little crazy here . . ."

But Dark didn't hear the next part because his brain instantly tuned in to another sound, echoing off the walls of the surgical theater.

The teeth-rattling sound of a blade being unsheathed.

chapter 76

LABYRINTH

I tell Dark,

Welcome back to the maze!

Something beeps, softly—I wonder if Dark hears it.

I say,

I'm going to enjoy working on you. I've got at least fifteen minutes to play. I can do a lot in fifteen minutes.

And then I show him what I'm holding:

A capital saw—

Also known as an amputation saw. Pistol grip ivory handle, eighteen-inch blade, made by a Philadelphia metallurgist during the Civil War.

Dark inches closer, asks me,

Where's your mask?

I smile, tell him,

No need to hide anymore. My work is over. There is nothing you can do to stop me. I couldn't take back my last two gifts to the world, even if I wanted to.

I know what Dark is doing—trying to buy some time, inch closer, keep me talking, all of that banal cop bullshit, until he can pull his Glock and aim it at my chest and squeeze the trigger and watch the bullet slice through my body before I am able to slice through HIM.

I ask,
Do you know what this is?
Dark says,
I don't give a shit.
And then pulls his Glock
Aims it at my chest
And squeezes the trigger
Or TRIES TO anyway.

Nothing happens. Look at poor Steve Dark, confused, wondering why his Glock 19 is refusing to let him shoot the bad guy. . . .

chapter 77

Natasha was moving swiftly past an intensive care unit on the second floor when a patient started to code.

"Code blue, code blue!" someone cried.

Alarms sounded and staff rushed around her. Life in a big city hospital. Familiar turf; she'd spent weeks with her stepfather as he died a slow painful death from pancreatic cancer. Everything about this hospital, from the shade of the tile floors to the antiseptic scent in the air to even the crisp uniforms of nurses reminded her of that time. Natasha tried to keep her mind focused, but a few seconds later another patient crashed, just a few rooms down the hall. More alarms, more frenzy. And then, against mathematical odds, a third patient. And a fourth . . .

Nurses, obviously panicked:

"I've got someone coding over here, too."

"What the hell is going on?"

Over the loudspeaker, a voice struggling to sound calm said,

"Doctor Allcome to floor three, Doctor Allcome to floor three, please."

Natasha knew this was hospital code for a serious emergency—"all come." Meaning, all unoccupied medical personnel were being ordered to report to the third floor immediately.

Which was when she realized they were too late. Time was up. Labyrinth's plan was already under way.

Pennsylvania General was equipped with over 3,200 flat-screen TVs, in hallways and waiting areas and in patient rooms. At the same time, they all began to show the same thing:

Another message from Labyrinth.

Images: Crowded hospital hallways. Patients in cold steel beds pushed up against walls. Wan faces. Nurses weaving in and around the chaos.

LABYRINTH

Health care is the biggest industry in the world and achieved that status by being a for-profit industry. It's far better to keep someone sick, so they keep building up bills and forcing people to fork over their savings for care, rather than actually cure anyone. I will take this industry back and make it about SAVING THE PEOPLE.

chapter 78

DARK

Dark tried to squeeze the trigger of the Glock again—and once again, it refused to budge. The gun seemed like a useless chunk of metal in his hand. What the fuck was going on? By this time, Labyrinth was rushing toward him, impossibly fast, surgical saw held close to his right arm, muscles tensed, ready to strike . . .

NOW.

Dark dropped the gun and threw his body backward.

The blade whipped across Dark's neck—shredding several layers but failing to slice muscle. A fraction of an inch would have made the difference between a nasty scrape and a life-ending severed artery.

As Dark's back hit the floor, Labyrinth was coming at him with a savage backhand swipe. Dark caught Labyrinth by the elbow and twisted. The man's arm felt like steel-reinforced concrete. His strength was unreal, especially on such an average frame.

"Let's start with a hand," said Labyrinth, then head-butted Dark. Savagely. Cleanly. Bright flashes appeared in his vision. Dark struggled to keep his grip on Labyrinth's arm, but felt his muscles trembling. His forehead felt like it had burst open. What was the man's skull made of—iron?

Then Dark remembered the gun, a few inches away. He twisted his body to the right, finally releasing his grip on Labyrinth's arm.

The blade cut through the air an inch above his head. Dark rolled, grabbed the Glock. Firing it may not work. But even an empty gun was a useful weapon. Dark swung it and smashed it into the side of Labyrinth's head. Again. And again. And again. Iron skull, meet gun metal. With every blow Dark could feel the raw hate bubbling up inside of him.

Then Labyrinth seized Dark's hands, clamping down tight. Blood was running down the motherfucker's face, but the monster was smiling anyway.

"Must drive you crazy," he hissed.

Labyrinth increased the pressure, and it felt like Dark's fingers were inside a metal vise. His entire hand throbbed and went numb.

"You have no idea why you couldn't shoot me, do you?"

"Fuck you."

The gun in Dark's hands began to twist around, Labyrinth manipulating his struggling fingers like a lump of clay on a spinning wheel. Too much force, fingers suddenly too slippery, the gun rotating—until Dark was staring down his own barrel.

"Welcome to the maze," Labyrinth said.

There was a soft beep.

In that tiny moment, Dark realized that it was his own Glock making that noise. He pushed forward and twisted his body away at the same time, but it was too late. The gun exploded and a bullet ripped through Dark's bicep.

The pain—unreal.

One hand in front of the other across the cold tile. The gunshot wound throbbing. This wasn't the first time Dark had been shot, but that fact didn't make it hurt any less.

Somewhere behind him, he could hear Labyrinth recovering his saw from the floor.

"Where are you going? We still have plenty of time for some amputation techniques."

One hand . . .

. . . in front of the other.

"I saw police photos of what you did to poor Sqweegel. You must feel pretty horrible, knowing that you sliced up your own *brother* like lunch meat."

Dark told himself,

Don't listen.

Just keep moving.

But the very mention of the name Sqweegel brought it all back—their final confrontation in that monster's basement lair, the ax swinging up and down, his spindly limbs hacked away from his torso. . . .

And now with the awful knowledge the black blood spurting from the wounds ran through *his own veins*. Through *the small strong heart of his baby girl* . . .

Don't.

Don't do this to yourself.

Block it out.

Keep moving.

Keep moving . . .

. . . *to the case.*

"Let me spare you some guilt and show you what it felt like. I think I'll start with a leg."

Ignoring the agony in his shoulder, Dark pulled himself to his feet and threw himself forward toward a display case situated along one curved wall of the amphitheater. His body smashed into it, shattering the glass, which rained down on ancient surgical tools. Scalpels. Hacksaws. Labyrinth lunged at him with his amputation saw. Dark spun and put a boot in the middle of his assailant's chest, knocking the wind out of him. Dark kicked him again as he thrust his hand into the case, cutting his fingertips on the broken glass until they slid across something smooth . . . metallic. Now Dark had a weapon, too.

A scalpel, already stained with blood from Dark's shredded fingertips.

Labyrinth caught his breath and came at Dark, holding the amputation saw low and to his left, gearing up for another vicious swipe. Dark felt like he was already bleeding in a hundred different places.

"Chopped your own brother up with an ax," Labyrinth hissed, then made his move, whipping the saw through the air with almost superhuman power and speed. Dark crouched down. The blade whizzed by the top of his head, missing it by millimeters. Dark plunged the scalpel into Labyrinth's side in a series of jackhammer-like stabs, *stick stick stick stick stick,* until the man cried out and lost his balance.

But it wasn't a cry of pain.

It was laughter.

"HA HA HA HA HA!" Labyrinth exclaimed gleefully as he spun around to face Dark. "You are the equal of your brother! You are *very good* with that scalpel."

"What do I have to do it with?" Dark asked. "I thought you were better than that."

"Nothing," Labyrinth said. "You're just *fun.*"

"You say you want change," Dark said, ignoring him. "What are you changing now by fighting with me?"

"The change has already begun, and there is nothing you or Blair or anyone else can do to stop it. For way too long men like you have steered the masses into false security while raping them blind. Your precious *establishment,* the one you so blindly serve, is designed to *use* people. Used for greed and profit and power . . ."

"Just like *you've* been using people to spread your nonsense. That's the problem. People are smarter than that. They'll see you for what you are. A monster."

"Me? A monster? Maybe. Doesn't matter, though. My role is finished. It's up to another to lead them out of the chains."

Another? Dark thought. *Does he have a partner in this, or just another puppet?*

Labyrinth smiled. "So go ahead, killer. Kill the monster."

Dark looked at him calmly.

"No."

chapter 79

DARK

Dark dropped his scalpel—and saw the expression of genuine bewilderment on Labyrinth's face. A microsecond later, Dark lunged. Labyrinth flinched. Dark grabbed the edges of the amputation saw. Labyrinth redoubled his grip on the weapon, his arms like steel cables. Dark could feel the strength behind it.

"Kill me, killer," Labyrinth hissed. *"Kill me kill me kill me . . ."*

Dark focused his strength on twisting the saw around, violently bending Labyrinth's hands by the wrists, until the blade was facing the opposite direction, however just a few inches above the man's taut and muscled neck.

"Shut up," Dark said, and then brought his knee up into Labyrinth's crotch, followed by a brutal head butt. Dirty street moves—moves a man like Labyrinth, or Trey Halbthin, or whatever the fuck his name was, would not expect. Labyrinth loved to crawl inside his victims' minds to learn which buttons to push. With Steve Dark, Labyrinth was pressing the buttons marked SQWEEGEL, thinking he could goad Dark into a certain set of predictable behaviors.

But Dark wasn't channeling his "inner Sqweegel," or any of that bullshit. He was tapped into his primal self, his *real self*—the scared kid in the orphanage, the moody teenager wandering the streets of downtown L.A. alone, the rookie cop staring down his first psychopath, the tormented father on the beach, missing the love of his life, holding his little girl's hand. But most important, the man who was drawn to catch monsters, not join their ranks.

And that man fought mean.

Labyrinth curled up into a ball, dropping the hacksaw. Dark kept hammering him with punches and kicks to keep him off balance.

"You're not a prophet or a savior," Dark said. "You're a fucked-up, overeducated asshole with too much money and power."

Labyrinth reached up, as if to fend off a punch, but Dark elbowed him in the face, then squeezed a handcuff around his right wrist.

"And I'm a cop. Not a killer."

Dark dragged Labyrinth down to the operating table, wrapped the other cuff around a thick metal leg that hadn't been moved in over two hundred years, and cuffed the left wrist. No matter how strong this son of a bitch might be, there was no way he was moving this table. He'd have to break his own hands first, or snap the high-grade steel links between the cuffs.

He took a step back and gazed down at his prey. As much as his body ached and burned and bled, Dark felt a strange euphoria wash over him. The high of closing a case. No—that wasn't it. This was the high of catching a monster, dragging him kicking and screaming into the light, for all of the world to see.

"You caught him," a voice said behind him, filling the auditorium.

Dark turned to see Damien Blair enter the room, gun in his hand. Blair wasn't a field operative; he prided himself on being the "facilitator." Had he come over on a separate jet? Was he here for a J. Edgar Hoover–style glory moment—the ultimate photo op? That didn't make sense.

"What are you doing?" Dark asked.

Blair raised the gun.

Chicago Tribune

Breaking: Patient records mix-up results in at least four deaths at two area hospitals; hospital officials say "under control."

PBS NewsHour

Breaking: Medical mistakes sweeping big city hospitals; doctors overwhelmed.

AP News

Breaking: New Labyrinth riddle received at Pennsylvania General just one hour before the wave of hospital errors.

Philadelphia Inquirer

Breaking: Spokesperson for president of Penn. General confirms that he received a "Labyrinth" letter.

TheSlab.com

Breaking: Now Labyrinth is picking on the sick—what next? Orphans and the elderly?

chapter 80

DARK

Blair had a slightly crazed look on his face.

"I knew you'd catch him, Dark. All this time, I knew it would be *you* who caught him. There's never been a man-hunter like you."

"Damien, seriously—put the gun down. He's out. And he's not going anywhere. Where's Natasha and the rest of the team?"

"Move aside," Blair said quietly. "I'm not asking. Consider that a direct order. Move aside now."

"Direct order, my ass."

"Don't make me shoot through you."

Dark shook his head, confused. "All this time, and you want to kill him?"

"You don't understand. He can't be allowed to live. He's far too dangerous for that."

Dark surprised himself by positioning his body squarely in front of Labyrinth's. Five years ago, he probably would have helped Blair kill this son of a bitch—held him down and everything.

But five years ago, he had an uncontrollable rage in his blood, and he'd almost lost himself. No matter what any blood tests said—he was his own man. Not controlled by his genes, or his bloodline, or anything besides his free will. That was the difference. Dark was a different man now. He wasn't about to slide back into the past.

He told Blair:

"No. We're taking him in."

"You don't get it. You need to trust me on this one."

"No, you need to explain it to me."

Blair sighed—but kept the gun trained on Dark. It didn't move the slightest bit. The man's focus was keen, unshakeable.

"I wasn't lying to you when I said that I created Global Alliance to catch Labyrinth. That's because only I knew what he was capable of, and I knew that if I ever had a chance of catching him, I'd have to assemble the best."

"You're not making much sense."

"Before I created Global Alliance . . . I created Labyrinth."

Dark couldn't believe what he was hearing. "You what?"

"This was almost fifteen years ago. We were both young and ambitious, working for an offshoot of MI6. You were part of Special Circs? Well, this was something similar—only in espionage. We were tasked with creating the ultimate agent—a man who could go anywhere, anytime, for any mission, with no limitations. Someone who could pluck an eyelash from the face of the sitting president of the United States just to prove he could do it. Literally, a man who could save the world in case of dire emergency. The code name for the project was *Labyrinth*."

"You *created* this motherfucker?"

"As a force of *good* in the world," Blair said. "At first, Labyrinth wasn't a person. It was a concept. We even flipped for who would become Labyrinth."

"I'm guessing you lost."

"No. My former friend here lost. Lost *himself.* If I had known what madness would follow, I would have scrapped the project and burned the files."

"So why the fuck didn't you tell us who we were hunting from the beginning? Knowing his real name would have been a help, for starters."

"Doesn't matter what his real name was," Blair said. "He abandoned it fifteen years ago. That was part of the project. Complete erasure of identity, so that if an enemy agent did capture Labyrinth, no reprisals could be visited upon his family. This project depended on a new name, a new face, and cutting-edge treatments and fierce field-op training. We created a laundry list of what the ultimate agent would look like, then we set about creating it—in *him*."

Dark thought about Labyrinth's movements. The ease with which he crossed borders and thresholds and office lobbies. The way he hid his movements, his calls, his purchases, his thefts. His ability to pry his way into someone's deepest darkest secrets. Seemed to be consistent with the abilities of an "ultimate intelligence agent."

But so much was left unexplained—such as the priceless artifacts, the weapons, and the funding.

"Is he still on the Global Alliance payroll?" Dark asked. "All this time you kept bragging about your unlimited budgets and unrestrained access. That sounds a lot like what this son of a bitch has been enjoying."

"No," Blair said. "I haven't seen him in ten years. We had a . . . *very violent* parting of ways."

"What happened?"

"We came to disagree about our mission, on the whole notion of what it meant to do good in the world. I ran specialized missions to put Labyrinth to the best possible use. However, he began to suffer delusions of grandeur—thinking he was some kind of higher being, meant to single-handedly fix the world's ills. When I realized that the strain had been too much, and that my friend's mind had snapped, I did what needed to be done."

"Which was?" Dark asked.

"I sent a highly skilled hit team after him," Blair said. "The elite of the elite, the military's best manhunters. They never returned. Their bodies—never recovered. And then Labyrinth himself vanished . . . utterly and completely. But I knew he wasn't dead. He'd just gone down deeper than he ever had before—so deep, even I couldn't find a trace of him. *Just like he had been trained to do.* I moved on to other projects, but I knew Labyrinth would be back for revenge. So I slowly built Global Alliance, gathering the best operatives in the world to tackle the worst of the worst. Because I knew that someday Labyrinth would reemerge, and I would need the best possible team to neutralize him. There was no sign of him until a few weeks ago, when he emerged to send his first package to the LAPD. With that, I knew that everything I'd feared had come true. Only it wasn't revenge he was after. All this time he'd been away, working on his plan to save the world."

"Save the world? By what—a campaign of terror?"

"But it's not a terror campaign at all. From that first package, I knew what he was doing. He was trying to *turn the world*."

Dark stared at him, waiting for him to explain.

Blair smiled. "It was Labyrinth's most prized ability—to be able to *turn* an individual. Flip an enemy from their side to your side. Coax a source into surrendering top secret information."

"How?"

"At first it was a joke between us—the idea that we were leading a lab mouse through a series of corridors until he reached the center of the labyrinth. But instead of finding cheese, the poor mouse would offer up his own cheese. Gladly. Willingly. We ran many experiments in Eastern Europe—volunteers, for the most part. Labyrinth here became quite adept at running people through the corridors of their own mind, knowing exactly which buttons to push to make them scurry one way, or another. At first we used a certain regiment of drugs to soften up our subjects, but soon Labyrinth could work just as well without them. Give him a day, and he could turn your life inside out . . . just by speaking to you."

All at once Dark realized what Blair meant by *turning the world*. Labyrinth's entire campaign was about leading the world itself, the hive mind of modern social media, down a series of corridors until they gave *him* what he wanted.

Control.

Domination.

A voice spoke up from behind Dark.

"Well, it didn't work on you, Damien."

chapter 81

LABYRINTH

Oh yes.

I am awake.

I've been awake the whole time.

I know how to take the worst blows any mortal can offer. So I let Dark beat me and handcuff me and think he had the upper hand.

I know that I am in no real danger of being apprehended or killed.

They can't stop my plans now.

No matter how hard they try.

I also admit—I also wanted to hear my old friend DAMIEN's explanation. And I must say, it is not entirely satisfactory.

His version of our association, of our mission, makes our experiment sound like a bad television movie of the week.

Oooh, the noble spy, just trying to do the right thing until his mentally imbalanced friend BETRAYED HIM and left him to pick up the pieces. . . .

Such utter SHIT.

Like everything else in the world, the truth about my origin is far messier, far more complex, far more subtle than what Blair can stammer through in his ham-handed attempt to shoot me in the face and erase what he perceives as the biggest mistake of his life.

We are the parents of the NEW ORDER, Damien, can't you see

that? But you shy away from your parental responsibilities, fearful of the implication, still wrapped up in some misguided religious guilt.

You are the facilitator.

I AM THE DOER.

Just as always.

But instead of a warm powerful glow, you see blood on your hands.

It is not blood

Good sir

IT IS THE AFTERBIRTH OF THE NEW AGE

Yes

Yes

Yes

YOU ARE WEAK YOU WERE ALWAYS WEAK SO EAGER TO OPEN NEW DOORWAYS BUT SO RELUCTANT TO STEP THROUGH THEM, DAMIEN! IF THE COIN HAD TILTED TO THE RIGHT INSTEAD OF THE LEFT IT COULD BE YOU INHABITING MY SKIN . . .

BUT IT DIDN'T

FATE ANOINTED ME!

And that

KILLS YOU, DOESN'T IT?

But I don't speak these thoughts aloud. There is the inner me and the outer me; the outer me moves me through the world and the inner me knows that he will someday rule it.

chapter 82

DARK

Dark turned to face Labyrinth, who was still handcuffed to the operating table. The man was smirking, even with blood running down from his hairline and nasty purple bruises forming on his battered flesh. Labyrinth was *gloating*. Instinctively, Dark knew that meant something else was in play—another attack under way. Labyrinth was still running them around the maze. Which was all the more reason to keep the fucker alive. Killing him would only make it more difficult to stop the death trap he'd already set into motion.

"So I'm going to end this," Blair said quietly.

"No," Dark said.

"Tell me, Dark—what did Blair promise you to make you join his little team? Did he tell you he'd keep the monsters away from your little girl, Sibby? Did he promise you peace, of some kind? Keep you so busy chasing the so-called *bad guys* that you'd have no time to brood over your dead wife?"

"He needs to die now," Blair said. "Step aside."

"We have him," Dark said. "We don't need to kill him. We'll make him sing."

"What, are you going to pour water down my throat, Dark? Make me gurgle until I . . . how did you put it, sing?"

"He's smarter than that," Blair said.

"I am, Steve Dark. Oh, I am! So, so smart. You should listen to the man. He thinks he created me, after all."

"I'll shoot through you if I have to," Blair said.

"Then stop talking about it and just fucking do it."

"Yes!" Labyrinth cried. "Do it! Pull the trigger! Please please please! It will help things considerably!"

And then something exploded above them.

Glass beads rained down as Hans Roeding rappelled down from the skylight, gun in hand, trained on Labyrinth's head. And it stayed trained on Labyrinth all the way down, until Roeding's boots landed with a dull crunch on shattered glass. At the same moment, Natasha and O'Brian came smashing through the doors to the operating theater. The cavalry had arrived.

But then Roeding surprised them all by swinging his arm around so that he was aiming at Blair.

"Drop the gun, Blair," Roeding said.

Both Natasha and O'Brian cried out, confused—what the fuck are you doing? Why are you threatening Blair? What's going on? Dark, however, knew what was going on. The note he'd received in the hospital had been a taunt from Labyrinth, but it also was the truth. He had infiltrated the ranks of Global Alliance. He'd turned Hans Roeding. God knows what it took to run the tough old soldier through the tortured maze of his own mind.

"Hans, no—don't tell me . . . not you . . ."

"The gun. *Now.*"

Blair turned his attention back to Labyrinth, who had a beatific smile on his face.

"Heads, you lose," Labyrinth said.

An anguished wail blasted from Blair's mouth, a cry of betrayal, of frustration, of ultimate rage, and suddenly, he didn't care that he had a gun pointed at his own head. All that mattered was killing his creation.

But when he squeezed the trigger—it, of course, did nothing.

That's because Hans Roeding took care of all weapons for Global Alliance, from blades to handguns to shoulder-launched rockets.

Hans Roeding had been working for Labyrinth all along, which meant he had installed cutoff devices triggered by the sound of his master's voice. Try to shoot Labyrinth with one of Roeding's guns, and the gun would shut down. Revert to a useless lump of iron. Roeding—the Global Alliance weapons master—could also easily fill a Glock 19 with blanks. That's what had happened in Edinburgh. Dark had been shooting with fucking blanks! If Dark had been using a gun with live ammunition, Labyrinth would have been stopped back then.

Blair realized the depths of Roeding's betrayal as his finger and thumb squeezed hard again on the trigger, and absolutely nothing happened.

"No," he said. "No no no, I vetted you, I vetted all of you. . . ."

"Enough," Roeding said and snapped off two shots. Tandem bursts of blood sprayed out of Blair's chest as he was lifted off his feet and thrown backward. The cry that escaped Blair's mouth was surprisingly shrill, like from a child who'd suffered his first pair of skinned knees.

Natasha put her own gun to Roeding's head and squeezed the trigger and—

Nothing.

Roeding spun around, gun now pointed at Natasha's midsection. There was the hint of a smile on his face, the first time Dark had ever seen such a thing. He wasn't just carrying out his master's orders. He was enjoying this.

Dark reacted instantly—crouching down, picking up the bloody scalpel and winging it through the air. It embedded itself in the side of Roeding's throat.

The soldier coughed, took a step to the side. Blood dribbled past his lips.

"Bitch."

Natasha leaped out of the way as Roeding fired anyway, bullets blasting through wooden benches over two centuries old, before he fell to his knees and dropped the gun. A puppet with his strings cut.

Before he bled out, however, Roeding whispered something. Dark caught it on the edge of his hearing:

"Enter the maze."

What did that mean?

Hans Roeding was dead before he could answer.

On the floor, Labyrinth was still gloating. All of this was just too vastly entertaining.

"Well, so much for Global Alliance," he said. "Let's see, we've got one team leader dead, one betrayer dead . . . leaving the emotionally compromised newbie, the fetching linguist, and the drunk geek."

Dark crouched down so that he was eye to eye with Labyrinth. "You're going to be locked up for the rest of your life. That is, until they decide to stick a needle in your arm. All in all, I'd rather be the emotionally compromised newbie."

Labyrinth smiled. "Don't worry. I can still lead you to the promised land. You can still complete your mission, even without Mr. Blair. Do you want the next riddle, team?"

"Fuck you," Natasha said, then checked Roeding's vitals—there were none—before prying the gun loose from his dead hand.

"I'll take that as a yes."

The man who called himself Labyrinth smiled and closed his bruised eyes and recited aloud in a mock stentorian tone:

NEVER WAS, AM ALWAYS TO BE. NO ONE EVER SAW ME, NOR EVER WILL. AND YET I AM THE CONFIDENCE OF ALL, TO LIVE AND BREATHE ON THIS TERRESTRIAL BALL. WHAT AM I?

Dark knew the answer. The riddles were never the problem. Once you started to think in terms of metaphor and code, the answers began to appear more clearly. The keys in the riddle were the words *was* and *to be*. Tenses. Past, and future. The speaker wasn't a person, it was an abstract concept.

Dark said,

"The answer is *the future*."

"Say it, Steve Dark. Tell me I am the future. Say it! I AM THE FUTURE!"

But Dark ignored him.

"Where are the other clues?" Natasha asked. "The who, and the when?"

"Well, you interrupted me before I had a chance to leave them. You'll find *the who* up on the third level. As for the when . . . did you know that all surgeries in this theater used to be conducted in the daylight only?"

Dark glanced over at Natasha, who was already on the move, racing up the creaking wooden stairs to the third level. But was she racing into another trap? Dark was overcome with the horrible feeling that Labyrinth had engineered all of this, every last move, in this operating theater.

Maybe Blair had been right all along. That the only way to beat Labyrinth was to enter the maze with him.

"I didn't know that," Dark said. "Why the daylight?"

"Because there was no electric lighting. Come on, Dark, I thought you were sharper than that. The surgeons had to rely on optimal daylight, streaming in from above. Most procedures were performed from eleven A.M. until about two P.M."

Natasha called from above, "I've got a locked trunk up here. I'm going to open it."

"Don't," Dark said, then grabbed Labyrinth by his throat and squeezed. "I'm going to make him open it for us."

Yeah—enter the maze with him, then kick his ass and *force him* to show you the way out.

"I assure you, Natasha Garcon," Labyrinth said, his voice strained, "that there is nothing dangerous inside that trunk. You may open it without fear."

Never trust the fucking monsters. Never. Dark implored her—

"Goddamnit, don't do it. . . ."

The crack of a gunshot echoed through the amphitheater. "Lock's off. Opening it." Labyrinth smiled, shaking his head gently back and forth. He kept his eyes—which seemed to grow blacker by the second—locked on Dark.

"Well?" O'Brian called out. "What's inside of it?"

Natasha's voice was hesitant, uncertain. "Photographs," she said. "Appears to be hundreds . . . maybe even thousands of baby photographs. Recent, vintage, color, black-and-white, all kinds."

Dark's mind raced. A trunk full of baby photos. The second artifact, beyond the timepiece, always pointed to the victim. Was Labyrinth trying to say that he was going to kill thousands of children? Or already had?

"So . . . what the bloody hell does it mean?" said O'Brian.

Labyrinth rolled his eyes.

"So impatient that you don't even want to flex that fat gray muscle in your skull, Mr. O'Brian? Actually, you'll like this one, since your Irish Catholic mother no doubt squeezed out you and your multiple siblings as often as bowel movements."

"Dark, you're closer. Will you push some teeth down the fucker's throat?"

Labyrinth continued,

"The notion of family has become corrupted. With adultery, divorce, stepfamilies, single families, family doesn't mean anything anymore. The idea of the nuclear family will be reimagined! We'll treat everyone as family! One family under Labyrinth! We should equally love and support each other, regardless of heritage. Wipe the slate clean. Start over."

Start over . . .

Dark realized what Labyrinth had done.

"The photos . . . in random order. He's fucked with the birth records."

"Good, *good,*" Labyrinth said. "How did I do it? What gave me access?"

"Shut your fucking face before I put a bullet in it," O'Brian said.

Natasha said, "The previous attack was just a warm-up. He messed with the hospital systems today—people were coding at hospitals all over the country."

"Ms. Garcon, I'm quite proud. I know our dearly departed friend Mr. Blair here would have been proud, too. Yes, while everyone was scouring their little hospital systems for errors, a team of independent contractors in Indonesia were busy exploiting the security breach."

Labyrinth smiled at them all.

"They took away my name. But I've come to learn that *names mean nothing whatsoever.*"

Thousands of newborns around the world were about to have their new identities erased in a flash. And Dark had no idea when.

Instantly Dark thought about his daughter, Sibby. He couldn't help it. It was involuntary. A baby brought into the world in a monster's dungeon, with no idea that her own mother was dying, or worse—that the monster's blood ran through *her* veins, too. There was something especially horrible about the torment of innocents—the deck stacked against you from the moment of your birth.

Dark couldn't let this happen.

He pulled the scalpel from Roeding's neck, walked over to Labyrinth, crouched down next to him, smiled.

"I've been tortured before," Labyrinth said.

"Not like this you haven't," Dark said, then grabbed the man's face with one hand, turning it to one side. "I think I'll start with the eardrums."

"This won't work. I think you know that, Steve Dark, and you're simply trying to scare me into cooperating. Do you really think I'll succumb to the threat of torture? I've been the torturer! I invented this game!"

"Dark—what the fuck are you doing?"

O'Brian said, "Let the man work."

"Or maybe an eye." Dark pressed the tip of the scalpel against the fleshy hollow under Labyrinth's right eyeball.

"You can stop me at any time."

"Ho-hum."

Labyrinth moved his tongue around his mouth as if he were trying to pry a seed from between two molars.

"See you in a while," he said.

All at once Dark realized what he was doing. The superoperative was engaging a fail-safe—no doubt buried in a tooth. A time-honored spy tradition. If you've been captured and you want to avoid spilling vital secrets under torture, you pop a false tooth and swallow the cyanide capsule inside.

Dark grabbed Labyrinth's face under the nose and around his chin and struggled to pry open his jaws. Nothing. His mouth was clamped tight, his muscles like steel cable, his jaw inflexible. Dark made a fist and snapped a tight, hard punch into Labyrinth's face, rocking the man's head backward. Still nothing. And whatever he had swallowed had already slid down his throat, because a weak smile appeared on his bloodied face.

chapter 83

LABYRINTH

Well.

This is good-bye.

For now.

I wasn't anticipating the need for shutdown at this moment, but Dark is forcing my hand. I recognize that wild, righteous look in his eyes—the willingness to hurt me for what he needs to know. He thinks he's being a hero. I know better. I've looked at the Sqweegel autopsy photos. Brothers, under the skin, latex or not.

There is no doubt that I could withstand anything Dark intends to dish out, but I do not wish to go through the tired old pantomime. *Ooh look, here's your eyeball, look how perfectly oblong and squishy. Now shall we pop an eardrum, or cut out your tongue?*

Boring.

So I take my medicine and prepare for sleep.

Just sleep.

Not death.

My medicine—which cost six million euros to develop—simulates a vegetative state, shutting down higher brain functions but maintaining breathing, heart rate, blood pressure. My body will go on autopilot. Nothing will be able to reach me. Not for six days, after which my brain will resume its normal functions. I will be back. No doubt I will be incarcerated in some kind of secret facility that America is so fond of. But escape will not be difficult. I have escaped from much worse.

And by then . . .

Everything will be different.

There will be a new world around me, and it will have a new leader.

A young, smart, ambitious, tenacious, and extremely malleable European Parliament member named Alain Pantin.

I've been conditioning him for years to step up onto the world stage at this moment, and he has not disappointed me once. He is the perfect man for the job.

Why raise an army when all you truly need is one charismatic man to engage the hearts and minds of those who will be all too eager to be led?

All Alain Pantin needs is the one gift that has yet to be delivered, and it is a gift that the entire world will be able to enjoy.

So.

This is good-bye.

But only for now.

chapter 84

DARK

"Fuck."

Dark checked Labyrinth's pulse. Slow but steady.

"Is he . . . ?" Natasha asked.

"No," Dark said. "He put himself into a coma."

Natasha was on her cell to the special agent in charge, telling them where they were, what they needed, and that she'd explain more when they met up. When she hung up, the sad remnants of Global Alliance looked around at one another.

Dark asked O'Brian, "Can you stop this cyber-blitz?"

"Get me to where the hospitals keep the servers, and yeah, I can pretty much stop anything. How much time do we have left? I need deadlines, man. It's how I work."

"I'll call you when I figure that out."

It was quickly decided that Natasha would stay with the seemingly comatose Labyrinth—through surgery, through everything. Dark, meanwhile, turned his attention to the time. This amphitheater was meant to be Labyrinth's stage. Dark had the riddle, and the artifact—the baby photos. But what about the timepiece? There were no clocks in this room. No wristwatches, no sundials, no calendars . . . nothing.

Only when Dark looked up at the shattered skylight at the top of the dome did it occur to him that the room itself was the timepiece.

The surgeons had to rely on optimal daylight, streaming in from above. Most procedures were performed from eleven A.M. *until about two* P.M.

Dark raced up to the third level to where Natasha had found the trunk full of baby photos. About two feet to the right—as he expected—a beam of sunlight burned softly on the wooden floor.

When the sunlight crawled across the floor and hit the trunk . . . the deadline would be reached.

Dark did some quick mental calculations, called O'Brian, who was on his way to the hospital's server room.

"You've got about a half hour, give or take ten minutes," Dark said.

"Thank fuck. I think I can do a half hour. Was worried you were going to say something like thirty seconds."

"Do it."

Natasha touched Dark's face. "I'm going with him. Be safe."

"You're the one babysitting the monster."

"You still haven't invited me to your home for the holidays."

Dark blinked. "I didn't know you . . ."

"I like to skip to the best part."

She kissed him once before jogging away to follow the procession out of the operating theater.

Dark sat down on the wooden stairs as a pair of EMTs began to work on his arm and hands. He glanced over at Blair's lifeless body. EMTs were trying to work on him, too, but he was long gone. The man had spent his life telling himself he was doing good, only to be punished for it at every turn. He'd let the monster out of the box and struggled to stuff him back inside.

For the first time since he'd met him, Dark realized he half-admired Damien Blair, after all.

New York Times

Breaking: Thousands of hospitals worldwide notified of possible birth records hacking; latest Labyrinth threat.

AP World

Breaking: "Labyrinth" arrested; identity unknown, but one threat remains.

Reuters

Breaking: Birth records breach averted; latest Labyrinth plot "goes nowhere," say officials.

chapter 85

DARK

Outside the hospital in the freezing cold, Dark looked around at the old colonial-era houses. Everything seemed unreal, like something from a dream. He didn't know the last time he'd slept. All he could think about was hopping one last plane—over the past two weeks he'd grown to hate planes more than anything else in the world—so he could be at home in L.A. with his daughter. Tomorrow was Christmas. He hadn't played Santa Claus, but it didn't matter. He just wanted to hold her, smell the sweetness of her hair, try to push the riddles, the death, the bloody splatters . . . everything . . . away. For even a little while. A small break. A rest. A calming-down period while he pondered his next move, now that his would-be employer was dead.

"Mr. Dark?"

Dark turned to see Blair's driver, holding an attaché case in his hands.

"This just arrived, addressed to Mr. Blair. I thought you should have it, considering . . ."

Dark took the case, which was heavier than it should be.

Somewhere else in the world, in a storage locker, a timer came to life with a faint beep. It had been sent a signal from an online cloud, which in turn had been activated by a remote command uploaded from Labyrinth's watch, which had been monitoring his vital signs.

Labyrinth had slipped into a coma, which triggered the fail-safe. Just in case he wasn't awake to deliver his final package.

Kneeling on the cold sidewalk, Dark hesitated before the case intended for Blair. If Labyrinth wanted revenge, then of course he would deliver the final blow to the man who'd tried to kill him. Whatever was inside was most likely designed to shock or kill.

But not right away. Labyrinth was never that direct. Dark remembered Natasha's fearlessness. If they had all waited to analyze the trunk, it would have been too late. So fuck it. Dark flipped the latches with his thumbs and opened the case. Inside was a letter with printed block letters on what appeared to be a piece of Damien Blair's personal stationery. The font style and coloration of the paper suggested it was at least two decades old. Blair would have no doubt recognized it, had he been alive to open the package.

The riddle:

> I AM TERRIFYING AND FEAR INSPIRING, AND THE PHYSICAL WORLD CANNOT TOUCH ME. WHEN I'M FINISHED, YOU MAY NOT EVEN REMEMBER ME. WHAT AM I?
>
> LABYRINTH

The final Labyrinth riddle. Delivered to Damien Blair personally, from his longtime nemesis. His own personal . . .

All at once, Dark knew the answer.

. . . nightmare.

They were beyond metaphors now and into the literal. This was meant to be Labyrinth's final gift to the world, the final turn in the maze. The world would see that the center contained not cheese but a literal *nightmare*.

Dark lifted the page. Below the riddle was a heavy atomic-powered clock, the kind you'd buy at a high-end specialty shop for the man who has everything. These types of clocks guaranteed accuracy within a millisecond. The face showed a digital deadline, ticking down to less than twelve hours from now—midnight on Christmas.

The when.

A nightmare . . . in a little less than half a day.

So who?

Who would be the final victim?

Blair was already dead.

Perhaps the answer was in a small glass vial, secured by a leather loop sewn into the side of the attaché case. Dark carefully slid it out of the loop with his bandaged fingers, then held it up to examine it. There was dark red fluid, no more than an ounce, filling half of the vial.

Blood.

Dark had seen enough of it to know the real thing by sight. Was this the final victim's blood, maybe?

The clock was ticking. He needed a lab—*now*.

Natasha had been standing outside Labyrinth's heavily guarded hospital room when her tablet computer *ping*ed.

The noise jolted her back to reality. Her new reality. For the past half hour she'd been running her life through her head and realized that she'd put every ounce of herself into the team with little left over. She'd been so angry with Dark at first because he seemed to ridicule the very thing she held dear. Now she understood his detachment. Because when the things you hold dear are taken away, it leaves you with a void that aches like crazy.

But the *ping* meant that a new video tagged with "Labyrinth" had been uploaded to the Net.

Natasha checked her screen, clicked through, and saw there was a new video. Apparently uploaded just a few seconds ago by . . .

. . . by the comatose man in the heavily guarded room behind her?

[To enter the Labyrinth, please go to Level26.com and enter the code: confession]

chapter 86

Natasha watched the video as the monster delivered his message.

Eyebrows lowered, eyes focused directly at the camera. Like so many of history's greatest monsters, he looks ordinary. Like the businessman who might sit next to you on a plane. The person you stop to ask for directions in a strange city. The kind-faced average guy in a bar who buys you a drink, and you think nothing of it, because we are trained from birth to trust those who appear ordinary, and fear those who are unusual or freakish.

"My name is Julian Blair, and I want to help you escape the maze."

At that moment, all became clear to Natasha.

Blair.

B-L-A-I-R

Hidden in the surname itself:

L-A-B-y-R-I-n-t-h

A family joke.

The final riddle.

Natasha shuddered at the realization. All this time, Damien was chasing the monster, and the monster *was his own brother.* A coin toss had decided his fate. One brother on the side of law and order, the other lost to the darkness. Why hadn't Damien told them any of this? Why was he so afraid to admit the truth? This could have helped them immeasurably in their hunt for Labyrinth. The knowledge would have changed everything.

Then she realized—it could still change everything.

Natasha plucked the phone from her hip and dialed.

Pennsylvania General did not have a forensics lab, of course. But they were perfectly equipped to analyze blood samples. A DNA match could take hours, if they were lucky. But Labyrinth was never that straightforward with his clues. There would be some other message in the blood.

First thing—Dark ordered a tox screen, telling the techs to take every precaution possible. Then Dark hunkered down in front of the microscope with his own sample. Maybe Labyrinth had mixed something else in the blood. Or maybe the real message was etched in the glass tube that held the blood, and the sample itself was meaningless. Something to distract them from the real menace.

See you in a while. . . .

As he sat at the lab table, Dark felt the seconds ticking away in his head. He hated these ticking clock games. He was a brooder. He was his best when he could sit in a cold, quiet room with the lights down and let the pieces of the case float around in his brain until they settled into place.

A lab tech tapped him on the shoulder. "Mr. Dark? You need to see this."

There was something wrong with the blood in the tube, it turned out. It was slightly irradiated. Which meant the "donor," dead or alive, had been exposed to radioactive material. Was this a reference to horrible nuclear accidents in Japan? Did Labyrinth have some kind of ecological message to deliver?

No. That felt wrong.

Think, fucking *think*.

The key was finding the donor. The identity would complete the story. But DNA matches took hours, sometimes up to half a day. There wasn't enough time left. . . .

And then Dark's phone buzzed—

Natasha.

"There's a new video," she said, "and Labyrinth just revealed his birth name. It's Julian Blair."

"Brothers . . . ," Dark said quietly, the pieces silently clicking into place. He couldn't help but think of their brief, strange conversation in Edinburgh. Labyrinth had been dropping hints even then. *Brothers under the skin. You and I, Steve Dark.*

"No proof of that, but they're about the same age. It makes sense, though. All of it. But I still don't know why Damien didn't tell us."

I know exactly why, Dark thought. Because if you've got a monster for a brother, the last thing you want to do is let the world know about it. The moment they know the same blood runs through your veins, your life will never be the same.

⸸

Alain Pantin watched the Labyrinth video from a green room at BBC World News. They'd flown him in to discuss the latest developments in America, and he knew in his gut that it would only be a matter of time before someone linked him to Trey Halbthin.

Trey Halbthin, the madman killer known as Labyrinth.

Part of him despaired that this was it, the end of his political career, the sole focus of his every waking hour for the past three years.

Created by, and ultimately done in by, a monster.

". . . the world's worst nightmare come to life . . ."

Pantin knew that he should be filled with dread, but much to his surprise realized that he wasn't. Not really.

For while Trey Halbthin may have been a monster—

". . . you still have the power to rise up. You can still take control . . ."

—he was absolutely *right* about his message. And it was a message that Pantin still very much believed in, despite the way in which it was delivered.

A voice spoke from the doorway behind him.

"Mr. Pantin, are you ready? Can I get you anything before we go on?"

Pantin looked at the pretty-eyed studio escort in the mirror, smiled at her sweetly, then said,

"I'm fine."

chapter 87

Dark called Riggins from an FBI sedan headed south on I-95 at truly unsafe speeds.

"Riggins, I need a plane."

"Steve? Is that you?"

Dark was surprised that his former boss's voice wasn't slurred. The day before Christmas Eve was traditionally a day to get shitfaced. Most federal employees were cut loose at noon; nonessential government business shut down. Riggins enjoyed this time of the year more than most. He tended to avoid his family and tried to drown out the holidays with as much vodka as possible. Usually in a motel room, just in case anyone tried to call to wish him Merry Christmas or some shit like that.

"I need a plane now."

"A plane to where?"

"I'll let you know when I figure it out. Can you get one, fueled and ready to go?"

With Damien Blair gone, so were the mighty resources of Global Alliance. There was no chain of command, no redundancies built into the team. That meant there was no money. No planes. No staff. No fancy motorcycle delivered to your doorstep in ninety minutes or less. *Nothing.* Without Damien, the remnants of the team—Dark, Natasha, and O'Brian—were on their own. So Dark called on the only resource he had left.

"Shit, Dark. Are you serious? Is this a hunch, or do you have something solid?"

"Labyrinth is in custody, but he has one attack left," Dark said. "I have most of the pieces, but I need a little while to figure it out. In the meantime, I need a plane fueled and ready to take me to pretty much anywhere in the world."

"You don't ask for favors often. But when you do . . ."

"Where are you?"

"At home. What kind of threat, Dark? What's going to happen?"

"The worst kind. The kind where thousands and thousands of people die."

Dark couldn't see Riggins, of course, but he could imagine him sitting up straight in whatever bar stool he happened to be squatting on. Tom Riggins was a fuckup in every area of his life except one: his job. Which was good, because he'd sacrificed everything else for that one thing.

"I think I can get a plane ready," Riggins said. "But I need one thing from you."

"What's that?"

"I need you to rejoin my team."

"Fuck, Riggins, are you serious? We got to do this now?"

"Give me that one last satisfaction before I'm through. That we can work together again. Just like we used to. When we were a team, we were unstoppable. You remember those days?"

Yeah, Dark remembered those days. All too well.

"You're too drunk," he said.

"I'll sober up by the time you figure out our location."

The minutes were slipping by. What choice did Dark have?

"Yeah. Fine."

And with those words, Steve Dark rejoined Special Circs. Even if the division itself was about to be dismantled, and its head was too far gone to save his own job, let alone anyone else's.

By the time Dark arrived at Philadelphia International, Riggins had made good on his word. Cashed in every last chip and borrowed a few more to arrange for a private jet loaded with enough fuel to take them halfway around the world.

The problem is—where? It could have been any place Labyrinth had visited in the past few months. But then Dark thought about Labyrinth's grudge against his brother.

I can move anything I want to anywhere in the world, Blair had once boasted. *No questions asked.*

Damien and Julian Blair were practiced with the same skills. They knew how to fund, acquire, and ship any object to pretty much anywhere in the world.

Like a dirty nuke, to Global Alliance HQ.

chapter 88

DARK

"So what are we really up against?" Riggins asked.

They were on their way to Global Alliance HQ in a government SUV—also arranged by Riggins back in the United States. France's General St. Pierre, who had coordinated with them on the Sqweegel case five years ago, felt enough gratitude to Riggins and Special Circs to loan them not only the vehicle and some weapons, but a small outfit from the Commandement des Opérations Spéciales to help secure Global Alliance HQ.

It was Riggins's peculiar genius that he could arrange for an assault in Paris, using French special forces, without going through the usual channels. Because there wasn't time to go through the usual channels—and the last thing he wanted was to spark an international panic.

Over the phone, interrupting the general's Christmas Eve feast, Riggins had framed it simply: following up on a Labyrinth loose end.

"Labyrinth has been captured, correct?" General St. Pierre had asked. "I've been keeping one ear on the radio."

"Yes, but he had a conspirator working inside Global Alliance."

"Which is why Global Alliance does not want to send their own team to secure their own facilities. I understand."

"Yeah," Riggins had said, unable to help himself. "They called in Special Circs to give them a hand."

Conveniently omitting the part about the possible nuclear weapon hidden in the catacombs under Paris.

But now the bullshitting was over, and Riggins wanted to know about the odds they were facing. For real.

"It's not going to be pretty," Dark said, then told him about Global Alliance HQ. Very few ways in and out. Guarded at all times by ex–special forces soldiers *handpicked by Hans Roeding.*

When he was dying, and Roeding spoke the words—

"Enter the maze."

—he was preparing them with a secret code.

They would be prepared to fend off any invaders.

The last time Dark was here at Global Alliance HQ, he was escorted by these private guards, many of them mercs and black ops professionals. They were trained to fight fierce—and dirty. They had no idea what they're protecting, and Dark suspected they didn't care. Their paychecks were *fat.* They could not be reasoned with—not once a command was given.

The only way past them was to blitz them.

Riggins divided the French special ops guys into strike teams, then handed Dark a radiation detector. "Here. In case we all *do* make it past those guards alive."

"How did you explain these to General St. Pierre?"

"Told him we suspected a Labyrinth agent may have poisoned the water down here."

Before they parted, Dark put a hand on his mentor's shoulder.

"Riggins," Dark said, "listen, just in case . . ."

"Hey, save it for after we kill the bad guys and save Paris, okay?"

"Okay," Dark said. But the words that were about to tumble out of his mouth weren't exactly an apology. He wasn't sure he could ever forgive Riggins for hiding the truth. Not that it mattered now, anyway—they could all be dead in a matter of minutes.

While Riggins led a team through the parking garage, Dark's team assaulted the other weak link—the backup entrance at a sewer junction. Of course, *led* was a misnomer—Dark stayed behind the half-dozen soldiers as they stormed down the fetid and gunk-caked pipe, moving so quickly it was difficult to keep up with them. Dark wore body armor but insisted on carrying a Glock 19, the weapon he was most familiar with. No sense carrying an automatic weapon unless you've spent weeks upon weeks with it.

A French special ops leader whispered something and gestured with two fingers, but Dark did not have a chance to understand because within a fraction of a second the entire pipe was full of gunfire.

The Global Alliance mercs had not waited for the invaders to fire the first shot. They opened up a fusillade of bullets from the first hint of trouble in the pipe. No doubt they'd already radioed their teams guarding the other entrances.

Dark crouched down, waiting to take his shot—no use blasting away in the dark and smoke and confusion. A special ops soldier fell to his right, his forehead blasted open. Fuck. Dark stepped forward, saw a blur at the far end of the pipe. He squeezed the trigger, and followed the blur the best he could.

The brutal engagement felt like an eternity to Dark, and it occurred to him that maybe this is what it felt like when you were about to die—the last seconds of your life, elongated to almost infinity.

Then there was a horrible, eardrum-spiking blast and hot relentless fire in his face and then he realized this was it—this *was* death.

chapter 89

DARK

The Glock was still in his hand.

That was the first thing Dark was aware of when he regained his senses:

The Glock was still in his hand.

And there was movement all around him.

Someone pressed fingers to the side of his throat. Something else pressed up against his temple.

The barrel of a gun.

Opening his eyes would mean instant death. Death was going to come in a second anyway, because in one second the merc crouching down next to him would feel the beat of the blood in his carotid artery and then he would pull the trigger, blasting through skull and brain and that would be the end.

So Dark kept his eyes shut and squeezed the trigger, the bullet smashing through the sewage and into the merc.

A gunshot popped LOUD right next to his head—the merc squeezing off one last shot and missing by the slimmest of margins.

When Dark finally opened his eyes and scrambled backward until he reached the edge of the pipe, he saw the devastation all around him, and realized what had happened. Someone—either the mercs, or the French special ops—had set off a grenade. That was the only thing that could explain the horrible twisted bodies around him, and why Dark could hear no sound outside of the thundering of his own heart. Dark wondered if Labyrinth would find that amusing. Threaten to puncture a man's eardrums, and karma pays you back.

Dark slowly rose from the bottom of the pipe and made his way forward. The face of his watch had been shattered, but if the time was still accurate, they had only three minutes left.

There was no sign of anyone else inside Global Alliance HQ. The mercs must have cut the power immediately and put the entire facility in lockdown mode. So here was Dark, mostly deaf and almost blind, looking for a container the size of a dirty nuke, somewhere down here. A weapon that could have been placed here God knows when—weeks? Months? Maybe even years ago? Julian Blair could have been spying on his own brother since the very beginning—since the moment he arranged for the use of this space.

Two and a half minutes now.

Dark unclipped the radiation detector from his belt and hit the power button. Nothing happened. He tried it again—nothing. Fucking no.

NO.

The radiation detector, which must have been damaged in the blast, was dead.

If Labyrinth could see Steve Dark now, he would surely be howling in delight. The one man who could stop him was now literally lost in the maze of his own making, blind and deaf and lacking the artificial sense that could save him, that could have saved them all. . . .

Two minutes now.

Fuck it.

Dark would spend his last seconds on earth searching anyway.

Riggins was on the floor of Damien Blair's office, sitting like a kindergartener, legs splayed. Dark saw the other radiation detector on the floor to Riggins's right, as well as a steel box between his legs. He'd done it. He'd found the damned thing. Hidden all this time in a secret compartment under Blair's own desk.

Brothers, to the last.

Riggins must have heard the movement and spun around with a gun in his hand. Sorrow washed over his face when he saw that it was Dark.

Now Dark could see the contents of the box—the most important being the digital timer, telling them there were only forty-seven seconds remaining.

Can you hear me? Riggins asked, gesturing to his own ears.

The words were muffled, but Dark nodded. Yeah, I can hear you.

Everybody else is dead, Riggins said. *They died so that I could get in here. But what good is that? I have no fucking idea how to stop this thing.*

Dark kneeled down next to his mentor and now saw how damaged he was. He'd taken at least one bullet, because blood was pooling around his legs. The smear on the floor told Dark that Riggins had literally crawled in here, fucking radiation detector in hand, hoping against hope to find the bomb.

And he had.

And there was absolutely nothing he could do to stop it.

Thirty-five seconds remaining.

You didn't by chance take a course in any of this stuff, did you?

Gallows humor from Riggins. Dark looked into the box and saw, beneath the tangle of wires, a wooden maze. The kind you'd use in a lab experiment to test mice and their memories. Nothing fancy—probably something that a grad student labored to build over a long weekend, gluing the barriers and painting the wooden slats a neutral color. The timepiece was in the middle, at the heart of the labyrinth.

Yeah, I didn't think so. I've been trying to work up the courage.

Nineteen seconds remaining.

Dark squeezed Riggins's shoulder. Riggins lifted his gun from his lap. In Dark's mind, he saw the gun continuing on a path straight to Riggins's temple. Oh God no. Don't do this. Not now, not like this—what the hell was the point?

Thirteen seconds remaining.

But instead, Riggins pointed the gun at the digital timer and squeezed the trigger.

chapter 90

DARK

On his way home from the airport, Dark stopped off at the Grove to buy a dress for Christmas.

The actual holiday was seven days in the past, but Dark knew he couldn't show up empty-handed.

The doll store at the Grove was three stories of pure unadulterated innocence—tiny cribs, bibs, accessories, and of course, outfits. The previous Christmas Dark had bought his daughter a doll on a whim. Little Sibby had loved it. Hugged it, refused to part with it the entire Christmas break. Since bringing Sibby back home to live with him, Dark had come back to the same store to buy more dolls, more accessories. He told himself that this was a way of telling Sibby that they'd have some kind of normal life. Buying things. Building a home for lost children. Only a madman would purchase so many things if he didn't intend on keeping them around . . . right?

Even though Dark had come here often, he felt strange every time he stepped through the front door. Especially now with a loaded Glock weighing down his jacket pocket. The store was meant to be a throwback to a more innocent time—a safe haven for little girls to be little girls. There were even tea parties and fashion shows held here.

Dark, though, was glad that innocent times could still exist.

Thankfully, Riggins's somewhat ill-conceived idea of taking his .45 to the timer and ignition system on the nuke worked. He shuddered at how close they had come. How close Labyrinth had been to destroying part of this world, to leaving Sibby without a father.

Though Labyrinth was no longer a threat, rioting and violence continued around the world. New Labyrinth copycat crimes sprung up on an almost daily basis in America, Europe, Asia, and Africa, targeting the same "pillars" he was so intent on taking down: medicine, law, education, politics, art, and so on. Even more disturbing, ordinary citizens were increasingly vocal about blaming their governments for failing to stop the outbreaks. Which in turn emboldened Labyrinth acolytes to commit more acts of protest and violence.

Labyrinth had started a fire, and left the rest of the world to sift through the ashes. Even the United States wasn't immune. Congressional hearings were kicking up, a lot of stones being unturned, and it sounded like nobody would be handing out slaps on the wrist anymore. Too many were watching, too many people were paying attention. And it was no longer just the threat of losing reelection. People were dying.

But the most vocal, of course, was Labyrinth's "Other."

Alain Pantin—the man who had been secretly mentored by Labyrinth himself under his guise of "Trey Halbthin." There was some shock in European political circles after the link made headlines. But Pantin came forward and explained that while he regretted the link to such a vile killer, his views and message were the same. Governments and corporate leaders needed to be held accountable for their actions. The revolution may have been inflamed by a diseased mind, but that did not negate the need for a revolution.

Pantin was ultimately untouchable, because he'd done nothing wrong. Dark and Natasha had dug deep but could find no evidence that linked Pantin to any of the attacks. Some commentators even argued that Pantin was just another of Labyrinth's victims—but continued to speak the truth even at great personal cost.

There was no personal cost, Dark realized. Pantin's approval ratings were climbing daily, and his voice heard in more and more corners of the globe.

That's what scared Dark the most. Labyrinth's message, his cause, was still alive, still spreading.

How can you fight that? Dark wondered.

As he strolled out of the store, Dark's mind turned to Natasha. She couldn't make it for the holidays, but she'd be here in L.A. in just a few days' time. She wanted to talk about the future of Global Alliance. Even with two members missing, it was still a force of good in the world.

Dark told her he'd have to think about that, then asked her if that was the only item on the agenda.

She told him,

"Well, let's just say you and I have a *lot* of catching up to do."

Later that night, New Year's Eve, Sibby threw an impromptu tea party. She poured a pretend cup for Riggins, who was on their living room couch, his arm in a sling.

"Cream or sugar, Mr. Riggins?" she asked.

"You think you could toss a little bourbon in there?"

Sibby's face knotted with confusion. "Bur-what?"

"Daddy will handle that part," Dark said, pulling himself out of his chair. His hearing had returned slowly, though it wasn't a hundred percent. Never would be, most likely. Dark took the bottle of Knob Creek from the counter, paused, then grabbed another tumbler. Might as well join him.

Riggins had come here straight from the hospital, no warning, no call. He simply knocked and planted himself on the couch. Dark didn't question it. He knew they had unfinished business.

But he didn't get to it—at least not right away. Not until Sibby had finished serving her tea, then kissing Dark and Riggins good night. Dark refilled their glasses. They drank bourbon until it was only a few minutes before midnight.

*

"I'm retiring," Riggins said finally.

Dark knew better than to feign surprise or confusion. Very few people lasted very long at Special Circs; Riggins's quarter-century tenure qualified as an outright miracle. He suspected that Riggins would have retired at least ten years ago if it hadn't been for the Sqweegel case—and the nightmarish effect it'd had on Dark.

Dark nodded.

"They're in serious need of fresh blood," Riggins said. "If you haven't noticed, the world's kind of going to hell. I have a feeling Special Circs is going to be busier than ever, and they're going to need someone good in that top spot."

"They'll find someone, I'm sure."

"I told them they should consider you."

"Me? You're kidding, right? I'm the furthest thing from fresh blood."

"Look," Riggins said, "I'm not going to sit here and blow you. Even though you have poured an obscene amount of fine bourbon down my throat. You and I both know you're the best manhunter going. You should be training agents, passing on the wisdom. And if anyone could get Constance to return to the fold, it's you."

"Could you honestly see me sitting behind your desk?"

"Hell yeah I could."

"Really? The brother of a Level 26 killer, running the very department trained to catch them?"

"Fuck you," Riggins said. "That doesn't matter, and you know it. You were meant to do this."

"I know. The question is whether Special Circs can really get the job done. Or is it too bound by bureaucracy and red tape?"

"We all need boundaries, Dark," Riggins said. "Speaking of which—Labyrinth. Think he'll ever come out of that coma?"

Dark turned to his mentor, to the man who made him what he was. Dark knew he would never go back to Special Circs. Global Alliance provided everything he needed to catch killers. He had already spoken with some of Damien Blair's benefactors and they seemed interested in continuing the fight. Dark could do what he needed to do, not what he was *allowed* to. And that made all the difference. If Dark was at Special Circs, Labyrinth would be in a cell somewhere, waiting to get off on a technicality. Dark was going to make sure that Labyrinth would no longer be a threat to anyone.

And so Dark looked at the closest thing to a father he had and—as sons are sometimes forced to do—he lied.

"I don't know."

Much later that night, after Riggins had taken a cab back to his hotel, and all was calm and still in the house, Dark received the call. He listened, then grunted a brief thanks.

He stood up.

Finally—it was time to *end it*.

[To enter the Labyrinth, please go to Level26.com and enter the code: revolution]

acknowledgments

Anthony E. Zuiker would like to thank: First and foremost my kids: Dawson, Evan, and Noah. You mean more to me than you could ever know. To the cast and crew of *Dark Revelations*, thanks for sending us out with a bang and helping us finish this series strong. To Matthew Weinberg, Orlin Dobreff, Jennifer Cooper, and David Boorstein, thanks for helping me see this trilogy through from start to finish. Once again, major thanks to Duane Swierczynski, bringing it home with our third book. Thanks for the continued support of Team Zuiker: Margaret Riley, Kevin Yorn, Dan Strone, Alex Kohner, Nick Gladden, Shari Smiley, and Jonalyn Morris.

Thanks to Brian Tart for taking a chance on a series like this; our fearless editor, Ben Sevier, for his continuing support; and everyone else at Dutton who helped make the digi-novel possible, including: Jessica Horvath, Melissa Miller, Stephanie Kelly, Erika Imranyi, Christine Ball, Lisa Johnson, Rachel Ekstrom, Carrie Swetonic, Kirby Rogerson, Susan Schwartz, Leigh Butler, Aline Akelis, Sabila Khan, Hal Fessenden, and Adina Weintraub.

And last, but not least, a very special thanks to Joshua Caldwell. We're proud to hand the directing torch over to him. I know he'll make us shine.

Duane Swierczynski would like to thank: My wife, Meredith, son, Parker, and daughter, Sarah. My partner in crime, Anthony E. Zuiker, for an intense and always-wild ride through Dark Country. The entire team at Dare to Pass—especially Josh, Matt, Orlin, and David—for their support and guidance and collective brainpower. The kind folks at Dutton—especially Ben Sevier and Stephanie Kelly—for bringing everything together. And finally, David Hale Smith (and the entire Inkwell team), for pretty much everything else.

dark revelations

STARRING

Daniel Buran as Steve Dark

Hal Ozsan as Labyrinth

ALSO STARRING

Dave Baez as Detective Perez

Tom Ohmer as Detective Largent

Marlon Gazali as Homeless Man

Andres Perez-Molina as Cruz

Voltaire Sterling as Dre

Garret Davis as Sergeant Smith

Tiffany Brouwer as Faye Elizabeth

Daniel Probert as David Loeb

Alan Brooks as Charles Murtha

Jesus Ruiz as Lisandro

Thomas Mikusz as Alain Pantin

Bella Dayne as Maria

Christopher Frontiero as Johnny Knack

Jared Ward as Shane Corbett

Nathalie Fay as Andrea

Haley Strode as Lisa

Jennifer Holland as Simone

about the authors

ANTHONY E. ZUIKER is the creator and executive producer of the most-watched television program in the world, *CSI: Crime Scene Investigation*, and a visionary business leader who speaks regularly about the future of entertainment. Zuiker currently lives in Los Angeles, California.

DUANE SWIERCZYNSKI is the author of several thrillers, including *Fun & Games*, and writes for Marvel and DC Comics. He lives in Philadelphia, Pennsylvania.